Keeping Secrets

WENDY CHARLTON

This paperback edition October 2020

ISBN: 9798692936943

In memory of my lovely Mom Laura.
In honour of those who live with dementia
every day: patients, carers, families and friends.
And most importantly, with love and thanks to Andrew.

CONTENTS

Keeping Secrets

PROLOGUE

Tbilisi, 10th November 1989

It was the best day of his life, but it would also be his last.

Shura Vlasta leant close to the radio set. He didn't want to miss any of the details. It was 4am. The BBC World Service had been broadcasting the astonishing news for several hours. The Berlin Wall had fallen!

"The stream of people has not stopped since this afternoon, and even now hundreds of East Germans are crossing into the free west for the first time. They are cheering, crying and punching the air. But there is also fear that it may close without warning if the authorities have a change of heart."

The reporter's impeccable English accent was coming live from Checkpoint Charlie. He was trying to interview people on the street. Most were jabbering away excitedly, while a few were just stunned that this was happening at all.

Even over the crackling signal, Shura could hear the cacophony of celebration interspersed with car horns. He absentmindedly ran his fingers through his dark curly hair. The damp of the basement invaded the khaki serge of his officer uniform, and he shivered.

The reporter continued. *"A huge crowd of friends and relatives has formed on the other side, waiting to see if their loved ones have made it across. They are hugging and kissing each other. The elation and joy is palpable."*

Sitting in Tbilisi, Georgia, perched on a tubular steel-frame stool, he listened intently to the illicit radio receiver as history unfolded. He felt transported, as if he were there in person. He sensed the iron grip of the Soviet Union begin to weaken.

He closed his eyes and let his imagination translate the commentary into vivid pictures. It was almost like watching a movie. These events were a sign.

Shura felt that the passion, and sometimes violence, with which the campaign for Georgian independence had been fought was justified. The prize was worth it, even if the cost was high. Some of his friends had been arrested and imprisoned. Some were 'lost' in the system. The few who had been released were shadows of their former selves.

Five years ago, as a young man of nineteen, he had been conscripted. After training he had been sent to Germany as part of the Soviet force patrolling border checkpoints. His service had shaped his view of the world. Even on good days the border stations were bleak places. The sun shone intermittently, but it failed to make them feel warmer. Roads on either side of the border were always quiet. Deserted, except for stationary tanks; great, iron sentinels warning of the force that was just an act of disobedience away.

On bad days the barbed wire fences were decorated with the drab streamers of torn clothing from victims who had tried to scale the wall. They were the seekers of freedom who just wanted to live their lives without oppression.

Every day he had served there he watched the few silent commuters move slowly through the barriers. No one spoke, and they avoided eye contact as they presented their papers to visit the other side. Soldiers with guns shouldered had chain-smoked and watched the morbid procession, ready to pick off those whose nerves failed them at the last minute. The pangs of guilt Shura felt were fainter now, but they were still there.

He'd thought his resistance work was a secret, and hadn't realised that he had come to the attention of MI6 until they approached him. They'd offered their help and support. He had found it far easier to become a spy than he ever thought possible.

As a junior officer he ran the document archive in the Vaziani Military base on the outskirts of Tbilisi. It was housed in a large, windowless bunker about the size of a tennis court, and was filled with green metal filing cabinets that were arranged in ranks that ran down both sides of the room. As a workplace it was functional; cold, impersonal and harshly lit by flickering strip-lights. In the centre aisle stood an ageing industrial photocopier, protected by a code that only Shura knew.

He was responsible for thousands of files containing military, financial and operational details that had a tangible value to enemies of the Russian state. His only regular visitor was Boris, a young army corporal with acne and halitosis who spent his days collecting and delivering dog-eared manila folders on a heavy-duty, metal trolley.

Grateful officers would make their way to Shura to copy a document or a map when their own less reliable machines malfunctioned, unaware of the little-known feature of his machine that enabled it to retain a copy of the last document it printed in its memory. He found it surprisingly easy to copy all sorts of 'secret' documents and smuggle them off the base in his lunch box.

Shura was popular with his fellow officers and staff. His helpful nature and willingness to do jobs that no one else wanted had earned him a lot of favours over time, none of which he had ever called in. Two years ago he had been promoted to Lieutenant for his diligence. Maybe that was why no one suspected him.

Of course, he could not have carried out his unofficial work without the support of his wife Milena, who knew he was working for the British. She shared his politics and his dislike of the Russian occupiers. She had always supported him, although the birth of their daughter Sykhaara six months ago had made her more reticent.

Shura understood her concerns, but he assuaged his

own conscience and turned a deaf ear to Milena's objections by believing he was doing the right thing for his family. He wanted their little girl to grow up in a different world. A world where she did not have to live under a cloud of fear and subjugation. He wanted her life to be better than his.

Their flat was located directly above the basement he was sitting in now. It was on the ground floor of a large apartment building in the Sololaki district. It had been the centre of Georgian artisan culture in the 1920's, and the buildings, with their striking Art Nouveau architecture, had once been magnificent. Shura admired the beauty of the decorative wrought iron balconies and stained-glass panelled doors that had survived the Soviet era, even though many were so neglected they were beyond repair.

His apartment was once home to the building concierge, and it gave him exclusive access to the thick-walled cellar. It had once stored the coal for the old furnace, but now it housed the radio receiver given to him by his British contact. He always felt a surge of anticipation when he switched it on to listen to what was happening in the rest of the world. He wondered if he was the only person in the city at that moment who knew that history was being made.

The cold licked at his face and crept through the layers of his uniform. He rubbed his blue-tinged hands together, warming his fingers with breath that was clearly visible in the frigid air.

He would have to leave for work soon. Today, he would take a short detour via the Metekhi Bridge to the drop-point. He was always very careful to make sure that no one saw him when he left the chalk mark that told his contact he had something for him.

His contact was codenamed 'Uncle', and Shura had been working with him for nearly a year now. He knew that real names were never used by agent handlers, but thought his handle was particularly apt. Uncle was every inch the stereotypical Englishman. Traditional in his dress, well-mannered but always aloof.

It seemed to Shura that the British had sympathy for the plight of the Georgians and were keen to help them regain their independence. As a realist, he also knew it was in their interest to see a weakened USSR. Shura suspected that Uncle could be ruthless behind that English stiff upper lip. That was simply the nature of the business they were engaged in.

It had taken several weeks of clandestine meetings before he had finally agreed to pass classified information to them. Where Shura provided them with information that identified Russian military resources or any weaknesses that could be exploited, he was serving a valuable cause, and they were willing to pay handsomely.

Shura wanted nothing himself, but the money they provided would help to support the fight for independence.

The British had even agreed to keep his payments in a bank account until he needed it. And as the events of the last few hours were finally bringing things to a head, Shura wanted to be ready to strike. In this communique to Uncle he had hurriedly added a request for some of his money.

He turned off the radio and placed it carefully into the hidden recess in the wall. He smiled at the irony as he covered the hiding place with an old oil painting of Stalin.

Shura pulled his heavy great coat over his serge uniform, wrapping it tightly around his lean body. He no longer noticed the smell of damp that clung to him. Sweeping unruly hair back from his handsome face yet again, he picked up his father's old hat. It was a traditional Ushanka, with fur-lined earflaps. It protected him against the November cold, and he preferred it to a modern crash helmet.

Milena appeared in the doorway at the top of the cellar steps. She held his lunch, wrapped in brown paper, and a bottle of warm black tea. She was small with raven-black shoulder-length hair that fell in thick waves. Her deep green eyes contained a sparkle that could either seduce you or shrivel you, depending on her mood.

He was unable to disguise his excitement. "The Berlin wall has fallen! The genie is finally out of the bottle!"

She smiled as she descended the steps. "The only bottle I am interested in is the one your daughter will demand the moment you close the door."

"I am serious, Milena, it is happening. This will weaken the Russian claim on us!"

He folded his arms around her petite frame and bent to kiss her. "This will turn the tide in our favour; they cannot deny us our birth right for much longer."

He looked into her beautiful eyes and felt the excitement and emotion of the last few hours stir inside him. He swallowed hard to regain control. "I will be back around six, we can celebrate then. How about some khinkali with vodka for supper?"

Milena smiled back. "I will see what I can do."

He kissed her again, and taking his lunch pack from her, he climbed the well-worn stone steps. Milena followed close behind as he made his way out to the heavy front door.

His battered Vyatka scooter stood in the hallway by the large double entrance doors. He checked there was no one else around before slipping a sheaf of documents under his lunch at the bottom of the canvas pannier. Opening the main door, he lifted his scooter down the steps and wheeled it to the end of the road.

Milena stood in the doorway watching him go. The street lighting was poor in this part of town, so he turned the scooter's headlamp on to help him avoid the worst of the potholes. He never started the machine directly outside his building in case it woke the baby.

He turned back and waved to Milena; then, pulling on his soft leather gloves, he donned the Ushanka, not bothering with the chin straps. He straddled the scooter and turned the key. His machine spluttered noisily into life. A feeling of optimism rose in his chest as he slipped the clutch, engaged first gear and set off for the bridge.

Shura didn't see the dark sedan parked a little way down the street. He didn't hear its idling engine, or see it pull away from the curb. The car's headlights were off as it took up a position some distance behind him. His mind was buzzing with other matters as he navigated the five kilometre route.

He wasn't concentrating on the journey, and his mind went into autopilot as he considered what actions the Russians might take next. Would they adopt a moderate line and follow in the East German 's footsteps? Would they relax restrictions on movement and embrace Glasnost? Or would they batten down the hatches and accelerate the arms race with the West? As these thoughts raced through his mind, the car continued to follow silently in his wake.

As he approached the bridge, his thoughts snapped back to the present. The headlights of a car had suddenly appeared in his side mirror, as if from nowhere. The roads were normally deserted at this time in the morning. The vehicle was overtaking him as he turned onto the bridge.

It drew level, then suddenly swerved hard into him. It collided with his scooter, flinging him high into the air. The bike careered away, and he hit the road, a crumpled heap in the gutter.

Sickening pain shot through Shura's shoulder and chest. He heard his collarbone break. His head cracked against the concrete kerb, and he lost consciousness for a few seconds. His Ushanka had offered far less protection than a crash helmet.

As he came round he felt blood flowing from a gash on his forehead. He was confused, and in pain. As he opened his eyes he saw a bright flash of light. He focused on the reversing lights. The car was backing up towards him.

Had it been just a terrible accident? Were they coming back to help him? The car stopped sharply about ten meters away, level with his scooter. The door opened and the driver got out. Staring towards Shura, he walked over to the crumpled machine. Its engine still spluttering, the man unstrapped Shura's pannier and carried to the trunk of the waiting car.

Another flash of the car's interior light illuminated the figure for a split second. It was long enough for Shura to recognise the man. He wondered if the bang on his head was making him see things. The driver got back into the car and wound the window down. Reaching out to adjust the wing mirror, he made sure he could see Shura lying in the road. Then, revving the engine, he put the car into reverse and accelerated towards him. The last thing that occurred to Shura was that a good Uncle would not have spoiled this special day with such vile betrayal.

1

London, 1st March 2018

Daniel Grant exited the elevator on the seventh floor of the Secret Intelligence Service, Thames House. From the outside, its classic profile was reminiscent of an art deco wedding cake, with cream and green geometric lines in fierce symmetry. The inside was all corporate sterility, with brushed stainless steel and frosted glass. He strode purposely across the hallway towards a door marked 'Director General'.

Grant was forty-eight, but everyone said he looked younger. He was an attractive man with a year-round tan; handsome, with watchful eyes. He carried the permanent hint of a smile around his mouth, and his muscular frame was well-disguised beneath an impeccably-tailored navy suit. There was a vitality about him and the way he moved; his poise and posture made him look ready for action.

The receptionist looked up from her computer as he entered the room. "Good morning, Commander Grant. It's good to see you again."

"It's just plain Mr Grant now, Anna-Marie," Grant said. "All of that was a lifetime ago."

"Yes, it's been quite a while, hasn't it?" she said, her mouth briefly registering a smile.

"Please take a seat, she's nearly ready for you. Would you like a drink?"

"No, I'm fine, thanks." A faded memory swam into Daniel's head. "How's that pup you had? I think you were trying to train him, last time we met."

The receptionist laughed. He's nearly two now. My trainer says Labradors are born half-trained and terriers die half-trained, and I know exactly what he means! My Jack Russell is a nightmare, he terrorizes most of the other dogs in the park."

Dan took a seat on one of the unyielding designer sofas opposite her desk, smiling in sympathy. A lifetime had passed since he had last seen her. He'd had a distinguished career as an agent. He'd survived many dangerous situations and come through it all relatively unscathed. All of that had changed after his last mission in the Middle East, however. The mission had gone sideways and although he had escaped with his life he'd received two bullet holes into the bargain. His recovery had taken a few months, after which he had been advised to take a desk job.

So, eighteen months ago, he had taken on a new

role for the service, far removed from foreign postings and espionage.

He watched as the PA resumed her keyboard tapping. Exclusive interior designers had been responsible for the decor in the recent refurbishment of the executive offices, and they must have selected the furniture specifically for its ability to put visitors at their greatest physical discomfort. Daniel felt an unreasonable annoyance at the rumoured £4 million they had spent. He was having to go into battle to fight for money to protect his project, whilst senior civil servants worked in the equivalent of a five-star hotel.

He forced himself to focus on the task at hand. He had prepared a presentation for this morning as requested, but the brief had been sketchy. He hoped he had pitched it right.

Daniel Grant ran Shady Fields, a care home with a difference. Its clientele consisted exclusively of former secret agents who were well versed in the dark arts of subterfuge, spying and counterterrorism.

A discreet buzzer sounded on Anna-Marie's desk and he tensed slightly. Still typing, she looked across at him and said, "She is ready for you now Mr. Grant, please go in."

He stood up and walked across the expensive carpet, his shoes sinking into the pile. He opened the door, pausing for a second to assess the room. His experienced eyes acknowledged the exits and potential threats. Old habits die hard.

The office was spacious but characterless, with a single piece of corporate art adorning the largest wall.

The room was decorated in neutral tones of grey and white. The huge windows looked out over Vauxhall Bridge and the Thames. In real estate terms, it was a multi-million-pound view. Her desk faced into the room, ensuring that view was not a distraction.

"Daniel, thanks for coming, take a seat. Would you like a coffee?" Celia Browning, the Director General of security services, waved towards a vacant seat set opposite her.

"No thanks, water will be fine." Dan replied as he sat down.

Celia was a slim sixty-year-old with stylishly cut, steel-grey hair, wearing a charcoal designer suit that simply exuded power. She had been totally supportive of the Shady Fields project; helping him secure the initial funding to get it off the ground and even locating the building that housed his residents. He had been given a free hand to run the facility. His ambition was to create a safe haven for ageing spies, and Celia had supported him every step of the way.

Two weeks ago however, she had suddenly announced that she would be retiring later this year. That was cause for concern for Daniel. Word on the street was that the new DG may not be as supportive.

Sitting in the room's remaining chair was Bernard Cummings, her deputy and the Department Director of MI5. He was also the man being tipped as her successor. He was tall, lean, balding and a flamboyant dresser. Today, he wore a black chalk-stripe three-piece suit, a handmade pale lilac shirt and a purple and pink silk tie with matching pocket square. If the overall effect he wanted was sartorial elegance, his Jermyn Street tailor had delivered it in spades.

Bernard stared fiercely at Dan, a withering warning shot across the bows before serious engagement was made. Dan stared back. Bernard had a reputation for being a seasoned player; privileged, materialistic and with more than a hint of arrogance. He had made it clear from the outset that he didn't rate Dan 's scheme. He had been critical and dismissive of it in equal measure.

Bernard was 'old-guard', the type who thought promotion was gifted for length of service rather than capability. He also had little time for agents who were passed their sell-by date. Worse, he really didn't care what happened to them after they had ceased to be useful.

Dan disliked Bernard intensely. It was clear to him that he spent more time politicking with power brokers than doing his job. But Dan was a realist, and since Bernard was higher up the food chain, he felt it would be better to have him on his side rather than working against him. He needed his support if they were going to survive.

"Good morning, Bernard, I didn't realise you would be joining us. To what do I owe the pleasure?"

Bernard gave him a cold stare. "No pleasure, I can assure you. I'll let Celia explain."

Celia shifted in her seat. "Under the new Chancellor, the treasury has changed the way it conducts departmental reviews. Every department is to undertake full evaluations of its activities and compare them to three core tests. They have to measure their performance against National policy to ensure they align with government strategy. They have to show that they represent efficient use of resources. And they need to consider if those activities could be outsourced to save money. Due to the financial pressures we're facing at the moment, we're starting with projects that sit outside our core remit. Shady Fields falls into that group."

"I see. And how will that work in practice, then?" Daniel did not like where this conversation seemed to be heading.

Bernard puffed out his chest a little. "I'm supporting Celia with this activity, so I've engaged an external consultancy company experienced in this type of work to conduct an independent review of your team, Daniel. Maguire's have had lots of experience working with government departments. They focus on ensuring value for money, and where that cannot be proved they help with outsourcing services to the private sector." Bernard was warming to his topic.

"With all due respect, Bernard, our residents have served their country with courage and personal sacrifice. Potentially, their reduced mental capacity puts them, and the service, at risk. There are significant dangers in outsourcing us."

Bernard Cummings adjusted his tie, and treated Daniel to his most supercilious smile.

"I really do understand where you are coming from, Daniel. Good grief, I've served with some of these people. I know the sensitivity and the value of the information our former colleagues may possess, but I really do wonder if the lengths we are going to could be viewed as…" he paused, searching for the right word,"…overkill? Some would argue that we should just take our chances and then solve any problem if and when it arises.

"The general public probably wouldn't believe their stories, anyway. They have dementia, for goodness' sake! People would just put it down to some batty old codger in the corner. They wouldn't take them seriously."

He steepled his fingers and looked at the ceiling. "It was so much easier when the enemy handled these problems for us. Cheaper and cleaner. After all, what's a garrotting between friends!"

Celia gave him a sharp look.

"I don't think gallows humour is appropriate in this setting, Bernard."

"No. Quite so, Celia. Sorry, just musing aloud."

Bernard's statement angered Dan. He had witnessed the effects of this terrible disease first-hand when he lost his parents. When he set Shady Fields up, he'd vowed that they would show more respect for the people in their care.

Celia glanced at her computer screen. "This needs to be completed before the end of April this year so that we can set realistic budget requirements. I have asked Bernard to pull together a project team to ensure it happens. Immediately after we have finished here, the group will meet downstairs to get the ball rolling."

Bernard was nodding in agreement, fingers steepled

and eyes closed. Daniel felt his dislike ramp up a notch.

"I want a preliminary report of initial findings by the end of March, with some recommendations. And while I understand the driver behind these reviews, I am also mindful of your residents, Daniel. I have briefed the consultants accordingly that this work needs to be done in a respectful manner, and with minimal disruption to daily operations. All security vetting has taken place, and the data access restrictions that normally apply to our contractors apply in this case, too."

She noted Daniel's expression. "Look, Daniel, none of this is ideal, but it comes from on high, so we need to make it happen. Bernard is leading on the evaluation project so please, play nice, boys." Her last comment was directed at Bernard.

Daniel walked back into the reception area. Anna-Marie, who was still typing, raised a quizzical eyebrow.

"Did everything go as you wanted, Mr Grant?"

"No, not really. I could do with a few tips from your trainer, I think. Email the next meeting date across, would you? I have to dash; the next meeting is downstairs, and started five minutes ago. Nice to see you again though, Anna-Marie."

Bernard caught up with him at the lift. Their journey down two floors could only be described as frosty. "It will be good to work together, Daniel. I don't think our paths have crossed operationally before. With Celia going, I want to get to know my key people better so I can restructure effectively when I need to."

Daniel nodded. "So you have been confirmed as her

successor then, Bernard?"

"Not officially, but it will just be a formality. That's how succession works. You do your time in the shadows and keep your nose clean. Then when your time comes, you step out into the light."

Right on cue, the lift doors opened.

2

The meeting room on the fifth floor had been spared the refurbishment, and was basic in comparison with Celia's office. No multi-million pound view, here. No view at all, in fact. It was a windowless meeting room that deprived occupiers of a sense of time and season. The light was artificial, the air was mechanically cleaned, and the temperature was remotely set. A large veneered boardroom table occupied most of the space, with standard-issue black fabric meeting chairs placed around all four sides of it. The chairs were designed to become uncomfortable if you sat on them for more than an hour. A very effective way of limiting the length of meetings.

Bernard walked over and sat in the vacant chair at the head of the table, leaving Daniel to sit half way down the length of the room, next to a large flat screen monitor that was mounted on the wall.

Sitting to Bernard's left was Mitchell Bennett, his deputy and the Domestic Operations Director. Daniel and Mitch went back a long way. In fact, if it had not been for Mitch, Dan may not be sitting here today. He smiled, and nodded a brief greeting.

Mitch had risen through the ranks, and was a well-respected operative. Self-sufficient, well-organised and a risk-taker, he was one of the youngest 'seniors' in the Service. At forty-one, he was a mix of physical presence and cleverness. One of the few, in fact, who had come into the service from a non-Oxbridge route. He also shared Dan 's dry sense of humour.

Daniel also recognised Jean Terry, Head of Finance for the service. She acknowledged him but remained silent.

The two other people in the meeting sat to Bernard's right. Bernard introduced them as Mike Shannon, a Program Consultant, and Sarbjit Ghiddar, Mike's project manager, both from Maguire's Management Consultants. Company men in corporate uniforms. Mike was overweight, with dark-blond hair and evidently a tendency to sweat, given he was doing so despite the cool temperature of the room. In contrast Sarb was young, slim, smartly dressed, and bespectacled. He looked like a stickler for detail, with his matching notebook and pen. Dan felt his prejudice towards corporate consultants begin to stir. He hated the way they told you what you already knew then charged an eye-watering sum for the privilege.

Bernard Cummings cleared his throat theatrically. A sardonic smile appeared on his face before he began to speak.

"Due to the financial pressures all government

departments are facing at the moment, the treasury has decided to commission evaluations of all projects that sit outside the core remit."

Dan almost winced at the management speak in the sentence.

Bernard continued, "Mike and Sarbjit will be working with your team, Daniel, to evaluate Shady Fields and decide whether it is providing value for money." Bernard lingered over the word 'evaluate' like a tiger stalking its prey.

"Mike will lead the review, and Sarbjit will work closely with your managers, gathering data to produce an interim report for our project board."

Dan was desperately pushing away the thought that he had been trained to kill a man with a blunt pencil. He focused his gaze on the two business consultants, but spoke to Bernard. "Efficient as ever, Bernard.

"It would have been helpful to have known about this before today's meeting. I could have prepared a more formal presentation. I presume that the details of what we need to provide have been emailed to me?"

Bernard nodded, "Perhaps it might be helpful for you to give Maguire's some background information anyway, to explain exactly what your little project is about."

Dan turned his attention to his iPad and selected the presentation he'd prepared for Celia. A couple of clicks later, and the large screen on the wall burst into life with an estate-agent quality colour photograph of Shady Fields. He realised that his opening gambit needed to be powerful so he took a deep breath and began.

"Since the end of the cold war, our special agents are rarely killed in the line of duty. And we lose fewer of them to heart attacks, perforated ulcers or strokes, because stress levels are not as high as they once were. In fact, many former agents now reach normal retirement age, and are drawing their pensions. Some of those pensioners are diagnosed with dementia, or Alzheimer's. To put it bluntly, this has given the service a serious problem. Brave men and women who have served their country, thwarted acts of terror, or carried out important missions, are losing their faculties. In some cases they are beginning to talk about their experiences, and the secrets they still hold. The problem with espionage is that agents who were active in the sixties, seventies and eighties still carry information that could affect national security today."

He quickly scanned the faces in the room, looking for reactions. Bernard and the consultants looked bored, and the room remained silent. He needed them to appreciate the severity of the risks involved, so he decided to up the ante.

"Perhaps I should introduce you to a couple of residents to demonstrate why Shady Fields is so necessary. 'Luckie' was an agent who spent nearly three decades operating in South Africa; he provided us with a lot of valuable intelligence over the years. In 1989, when the ANC had begun dismantling their guerrilla camps in Angola, he was instrumental in setting up the first meeting between President Botha and Nelson Mandela, who was still imprisoned on Robben Island at the time. We estimate that the end of apartheid would not have happened for another decade, had our agent not been involved."

He paused. Sarb, at least, was now paying careful attention.

Dan continued. "The detail of those negotiations is

still sensitive. The British government had to agree a number of advantageous trade and finance treaties in return for a managed political transition. Those incentives could be misconstrued by people seeking power, even today."

Dan took a sip of water from the plastic bottle in front of him; he wanted the implications of what he was about to say to really hit home.

"Sadly, Luckie is now exhibiting significant signs of dementia. We have a very real concern that if an investigative journalist showed interest in him because of who he claims to be, his work for the service could also be exposed. Information leaked could result in a significant economic and political crisis, even today. So Luckie needs a safe place where he can get the care and support he needs, and where we can maintain national security."

"Who does he claim to be?" Sarb had been taking notes, listening intently to Dan.

"Lord Lucan," replied Dan, satisfied with the open-mouthed reaction from Sarb.

"Dementia is a strange condition, Mr Ghiddar. Sufferers experience long periods of lucidity where they have full mental capacity, but when they have dementia episodes their judgement and perspective changes. They can experience hallucinations, delusions and changes in personality. Luckie only thinks he's Lord Lucan when his dementia is in full swing, but when it is, he insists on telling his story to anyone who will listen. And one thing could easily lead to another, particularly when you may have noticed that the tabloids run a 'we've found Lucan' story annually."

Dan let this statement hang in the air for a few seconds before continuing.

"Another of our residents is a man I will call 'Trilby'. He's in his late seventies, and as a younger man he became a very senior analyst, one of our most productive back room boffins. He has vascular dementia now, but in his day he was quite brilliant. He worked with security services in the seventies, developing surveillance technology. He set up one of the first cyber intelligence teams in the world. In 2001 he recruited and trained a young group of analysts and developers from Cambridge and MIT to create the first autonomous hacking programmes. A few years later, MI6 suffered a serious data breach after his tool was used against us. We lost three agents, and Trilby left the service by mutual agreement as a consequence. He felt solely responsible, and that took a toll on his mental health. He fell off our radar completely until a year ago, when he had a brief encounter with a reporter from the *Sunday Times*. He disclosed to her that he was writing a book about the real activities of the service. The press besieged him, and when I visited him, he was showing clear symptoms of confusion. He always carries a copy of his manuscript around with him, but to the best of our knowledge he's not yet allowed anyone to read it. It made good sense to place him in Shady Fields so that we could control his exposure. What he still remembers about who we had under surveillance twenty years ago, or the secrets we acquired from our operations around the world, could do serious damage to international relations if any of it got out. We are safer if we know where Trilby is and who he sees."

Dan paused, "Are there any questions?"

Mike, the lead consultant, rubbed his chin and flicked through the papers in front of him. "The running costs of your care home seem very high, almost £2 million a year. What's the return on investment?"

Dan took a breath, and eyed the ballpoint pen he was rolling between his fingers. "We refer to it as a residential home, and there is a full cost-to-benefit ratio on page four of our annual report. I am sure you can appreciate that in matters of national security, it's difficult to use a blunt instrument such as money as the main indicator of effectiveness. The bigger picture is more important because it's not just national security at stake, it's potentially global stability."

Jean sat up straight in her chair and looked directly at Dan.

"Blunt instrument or not Daniel, I am sure you appreciate that in the current economic climate all government departments have to make sure they deploy their resources in the most efficient way. I see that you have spare capacity in your staffing budget. Are there savings to be made there, perhaps?" She obviously expected a response.

"We have just appointed a new manager, Hilary Geddes, who joins us next week. She is a necessary and valuable addition to the team, but we could certainly look at other expenditure for savings." He thought that this was probably not what the accountant wanted to hear right now, and he could feel his own impatience growing, so he took a steadying breath.

Bernard was obviously keen to bring this initial meeting to a close. "I think it might be helpful if I summarise our position, to make sure we have a common understanding. Shady Fields was set up to prevent the disclosure of sensitive information that could compromise national security. After all, information is a tangible commodity in our world." Dan noted that everyone nodded in agreement.

Bernard continued "We knew the initial set up costs of Shady Fields would be high, but the treasury expects all Government departments to make significant operational savings this year, and we cannot exclude Shady Fields from our overall target. The financial forecast you've submitted in this year's budget allocation, Daniel, indicates an increase in operating costs, and Celia and I find that unacceptable. You have a month to demonstrate how you can break-even in the short-term and reduce your running costs by the end of the year."

Dan knew that his team had just been given a mountain to climb.

Mike now chipped in. "The Maguire's evaluation will give the Director General an independent view of Shady Fields as a viable solution, longer term." He looked across at Daniel. "We have been asked to present preliminary findings to this group in four weeks' time, with a draft report to Ms Browning to follow within 10 days of that date."

Bernard nodded, and the meeting was formally closed. People began to collect their papers and belongings together.

Mitch came across to Dan as he closed his iPad.

"Well that was a bit abrupt. I'm still wondering why we've bought in external consultants. We normally keep this sort of stuff in house."

Dan shrugged. "It's the way of the world at the moment, Mitch. Four weeks is nowhere near enough time for them to understand the nuances of what we do, so I have to draw the conclusion that this is just a tick-box exercise. Either way, my team will have an uphill struggle to get them to see the value of what we do to protect national security. They need to fully appreciate the implications of us not existing at all." His was already starting to compile a 'to-do' list in his head.

"Anyway, how are things with you? I haven't seen you in a while."

Mitch looked over at the door and watched the back of his boss disappear through the door onto his next meeting.

"There are some people in high places that would like to see you fail with this, Dan. We know how volatile international relations are at the moment, but some would say it's safer and quicker to take those most at risk out of the game permanently. It would definitely be cheaper."

Dan shot him a disapproving glance.

"Not my view, of course," Mitch said quickly. "I could be one of these poor buggers in a few years' time, and I would hope my service would count for more than that."

Dan nodded. "I need to get back. You should come over for a drink and meet a few of our residents, you may even recognise a couple of them. I keep a bottle of your favourite tipple in the filing cabinet, in case you need an incentive."

"I might just do that. I know Bernard is planning to visit in the next couple of weeks. He was telling me earlier that William Wright is at Shady Fields. I know they worked together early on in his career. Was he the 'Trilby' case study?"

Dan nodded again and Mitch exhaled and shook his head.

"How sad. He wrote the book on cyber

surveillance. It was compulsory reading when I did my training."

"Yes," said Dan. "Those two go back a long way. When I mentioned him to Bernard, he was keen to visit. I was a bit surprised, to be honest; I didn't think they got on. Bernard breathes rarefied air these days; I would have thought fraternising with someone who used to work for him would hold no attraction at all."

They shook hands, said goodbye and parted. Dan turned and headed towards the elevators. Mike Shannon had just pressed the call button. He was deep in conversation with Sarb, but he looked up as Dan approached.

"Good presentation, Mr Grant, but a tough crowd I fear."

Dan nodded in agreement, and studied Shannon's appearance. His suit was tired and a size too small, the cuffs were shiny, and the jacket had an odd shape to the shoulders where it had obviously been draped over the back of a chair every day. He also noted the unpolished shoes, the crumpled look to his shirt, and the cheap polyester tie that completed his man-about-town look.

"It's not that difficult to put a price on national security."

The consultant smirked. "But that's the whole point of a strategic review. Bernard has clear ideas about the efficiency savings that can be achieved, and we're working closely with him on that."

Shannon's use of Bernard's first name was not lost on Dan. He could feel his hackles rising at the jargon he was spouting. He was not sure why Bernard was so cynical about his work, but he did have a growing realisation of the fight he would have on his hands if he succeeded Celia. Dan hated the politics of his role. At least when you were in the field it was easier to spot friend from foe. Enemies usually stabbed you in the front. He desperately wished he had a blunt pencil in his pocket.

3

Tbilisi, September 1988

William Wright was pleased when he was posted to Tbilisi. His cover was as a trade attaché with the British Embassy. In reality, he was an information analyst supporting the MI6 Station Head. His boss, Bernard Cummings, had a reputation for being principled, ambitious and terribly English. In the two years they had worked together, William had formed a different opinion. He found the younger man to be cynical, and driven purely by self-interest.

Their mission was to run a small network of assets to gain as much intelligence as possible about the Russian military in the region.

His technical expertise was why Bernard had requested him for this assignment. The quality of their information had gained Bernard recognition at the highest levels in London, and had been mentioned in dispatches. It was William's know-how that had achieved that.

Bernard had been most encouraging when he arrived in Tbilisi. "I want you to continue your development work while you are here, William. You have free rein to make gadgets if they keep us one step ahead of the Russians."

William found it highly amusing that the 'Q' character from the spy novels was based on people like him. He had never been asked to develop a rocket launcher for an Aston Martin or even an exploding fountain pen. His specialty was in gadgets that had the potential to save lives. If you could take a photo in poor light from a hundred yards and still identify the people in it, the less risk you had to take of being captured during an operation. If you could record a conversation in a room and hear every word whilst sitting in an armchair fifty miles away, the longer an agent could stay in play. Bernard deployed the surveillance equipment that William developed and it had paid dividends. That was the secret of their success.

If London had been pleased with them so far, they were about to deliver a real coup.

A few weeks previously, William had been sitting in his favourite local cafe. The coffee was excellent – strong and rich, with no bitter edge. Earlier in the day there had been another demonstration complaining about food shortages and the Russian occupation of Georgia. The police were still rounding up the protestors.

As William drained the last of his coffee the cafe door opened and a young man came in. He was breathing heavily and his eyes were flitting from table to table. The waiter serving behind the counter looked up. It had been a quiet afternoon; apart from William 's coffee he had only served two shots of vodka to an old man sitting in the corner, and coffee to two office workers on their way home.

The man closed the cafe door and stared anxiously back onto the street. His eye caught movement outside and he began to retreat further into the cafe, glancing from left to right as if willing an escape route to present itself.

As William followed his gaze, he saw a couple of armed policemen walking down the street towards the cafe. They would reach the door in thirty seconds or less and William was in no doubt that they would arrest this man. He had to act fast. He called to the man to join him. He asked the barman to bring vodka and coffee for two, and in a swift movement he pushed the chair opposite him, away from the table with his foot, encouraging the man to sit down.

A look of confusion appeared on the man 's face for a split second, before being rapidly replaced with one of gratitude. He came over and sat down, slipping his jacket off and onto the back of the chair. The waiter delivered a small bottle of vodka, two shot glasses and two black coffees. He had just got back behind the counter when the door opened and one of the policemen stepped into the cafe.

William picked up one of the full shot glasses and encouraged the young man to do the same. "Gagimarjos!" (Cheers!), William said, and the man copied him. They both knocked the vodka back in a single swallow. With watery eyes, William immediately filled the glasses again.

The young man began to laugh. He entered into the

spirt of things and raised his glass. He repeated William's toast and knocked the second glass back in the same fashion. It went down the wrong way. The young man began to cough and splutter. The policeman looked over to see what the commotion was. William smiled and shook his head.

"Youngsters! They just can't take it" he said in perfect Georgian.

The policeman shrugged in acknowledgement and left the cafe.

The young man's name was Shura Vlasta. "They would have arrested me if they had realised I was at the demonstration. Thank you."

They stayed there for the rest of the afternoon. They drank more vodka, and put the world to rights in a way that only strangers can.

William instantly liked Shura. He was passionate, and idealistic. Slowly, William gained his trust, and when Shura left to go home to his young wife, William was certain he could be turned into a valuable asset. He worked on the military base in the archives, and right now he was very grateful to William.

As the senior operative, Bernard would need to recruit and run him as an agent. It was clear to William that Shura was in a valuable position. He could be a goldmine.

Six weeks later, William and Bernard were sitting in the same café at a corner table, waiting for Shura to arrive. It was unseasonably cold and wet outside. They had taken their heavy overcoats and hats off to dry, laying them on the bench seat at the side of their table by the radiator.

The waiter now recognised William as a good

customer. He smiled cheerily as he deposited a large bottle of vodka, shot glasses and three cups of rich black coffee at their table.

The door opened, triggering a small bell, and Shura entered. He shook himself as if trying to rid himself of the dampness outside. As he walked to the table he smiled at William, but eyed Bernard with more caution. William stood to greet him and took his coat, placing it on top of his own, before gesturing him to take the third seat at the table.

'Shura, you know 'Uncle'. He will be the one you work with directly." He turned to Bernard, who spoke quietly.

"Nice to meet you again, Shura. I am pleased you are going to help us. I feel sure your country would be grateful if it knew the risks you are taking in the name of independence. You are a hero in your own way."

Shura looked down at his feet. "I understand the risk I am taking, and I want your assurance that my family will be safe. My wife is pregnant, and I need to be sure none of this will affect her."

William was not surprised by Shura's statement. He had been observing the family and it was clear how much in love they were. A new baby would add a complication into the mix. It may make him more committed over time, but conversely he might feel that the risks were too great and decide to stop spying for them.

Bernard offered some reassurance. "'Stephen' here will continue to protect your family and make sure none of you come to any harm. Your wife is as important to us as you are. We will keep you safe, don't worry."

Shura seemed to relax. "The money should be kept

in a separate account, like we agreed. I want nothing personally, but it will come in useful when our fight for independence gains traction. I will contact you when I have something for you. I have bought a document today as a gesture of goodwill." He made the slightest gesture towards his coat pocket.

'Uncle' raised his hand. "Wait until you are ready to leave." Shura reached for his coffee instead.

"There is a mailbox on the western end of Metekhi Bridge. Drop whatever you have into the compartment under the box early in the morning on your way to work and we will arrange collection. It is shielded from view by the height of the bridge wall, so it will be safe. Do you have any questions?"

Shura shook his head. He reached for his vodka and tipped it into the remains of his coffee. He took another drink, which seemed to relax him a little more. His shoulders dropped, and he looked to the waiter and nodded. "Marek has worked here for years. He is a true Georgian. He is happy to offer us a safe meeting place should we need one in the future."

'Uncle' shifted in his seat. "I think we should keep face to face meetings for emergencies only. Regular contact would put you at unnecessary risk and I want to avoid that. Let's use him as a message service. 'Stephen' here is a regular, so if we need to get a message to you, or you to us, we can do that through Marek."

Shura seemed satisfied with this, and made to leave. William slipped his hand into the inside pocket of the overcoat as he lifted it. His fingers closed around a thin sheaf of papers, which he removed and seamlessly slid into his own coat pocket underneath. Shura slipped his coat on. He nodded to the waiter and took his leave.

William sat back down. "What do you think, then?"

Bernard stretched his long legs out under the table. "I think he is exactly the sort to make a good asset. He has a cause that he truly believes in. People like him are so much more valuable than the ones who are only in it for the money. They take chances that others would not. His job puts him right in the centre of military and political information. We don't know his security clearance at the moment, so we don't know if he's worth the investment. But I have to say, I am cautiously optimistic."

William reached across, taking out the papers he had taken from Shura's coat and opening them. He gasped. He was looking at an inventory report that detailed the military spend for the Russian military in the country. It was clear that although the amount was significant, the trend was downwards. They were struggling to afford their military presence.

William handed the report to Bernard, who quickly scanned the pages.

"Christ on a bike! I was right to have a good feeling about this. If this is typical of the level of intelligence he can provide I won't be stuck here for long."

A sly smile spread across his face, and reaching for his coat, he secured the papers in his own pocket.

"Now, William, we need to look after him. I want you to make sure he feels secure. For the next few weeks I want a surveillance operation on him and his wife. Keep it discreet. I just need to know if there is any hint of suspicion. We need to protect this asset and make sure he is productive for as long as possible. Can you handle that?"

William nodded. He had already begun. Shura's wife was a beautiful young woman. He could understand why they were so much in love. She was physically beautiful, but there was something else, a spirit and kindness about her. She was the sort of woman that attracted attention, and now that made her more vulnerable.

He decided at that moment that he would do whatever he could to keep them all safe.

4

Shady Fields, 8th March 2018

Linda Bridges loved her job, but days like this were a challenge. As the Operations Manager at Shady Fields the buck stopped with her for all operational issues, while Dan was responsible for the management of the business. Their weekly meeting had become a delicate balancing act.

Steve, one of the orderlies, rushed into the office, breaking her concentration.

"Clem is refusing his medication again and he's getting quite argumentative. He won't listen to anything we say. Can you help, boss?"

Linda put her down her pen and made a mental note to get a 'Do Not Disturb' sign on her door. "Come on, then."

As they walked along the corridor she could hear raised voices. She entered apartment 21."Now, Mr Attlee, what seems to be the problem today?"

'Mr Attlee' looked up with vague recognition in his eyes. "Ah, good. At last, someone in charge! They are trying to poison me, and the spiders here are enormous!"

"No, Mr Attlee. They are trying to poison the man in the room next door." She waited to see if there was any recognition of what she'd just said in his eyes. Seeing none, she pressed on. "I've called the exterminators, and they are on their way. They have special spider traps. Until then, I need you to take this medication." She offered a measuring cup with three white tablets in. "Your blood pressure is a little too high, and you have important work to do later today."

Mr Attlee looked nonplussed but reassured. He took the tablets and swallowed them with a glass of water to ease them down his dry throat.

Steve watched in admiration. "Thanks, boss. I don't know why he wouldn't do that for us."

Linda led the orderly from the room. "Arguing with him is pointless, Steve. When he thinks he's Clement Attlee you just have to humour him. Try using the distraction techniques you learned in your training. Reassurance and confidence are the keys to success."

"Right, will do. Thanks again." Steve hurried off, in response to a crash that originated further down the corridor.

Linda walked down the broad staircase and across the imposing entrance hall. Shady Fields was originally the ancestral home of the Walshinghams, built by Thomas Hopper in the nineteenth century. The estate consisted of a large manor house with accommodation spread across three floors, set in over 20,000 acres of woodlands. At the turn of the 20th century it had been gifted to the nation and put to use as a military hospital during the first world war. In the 1930's it was used as a temporary store for government archives. Then, when the second world war broke out, the BBC used it as its international listening station. The Corporation vacated the premises in 1999, and it remained unoccupied until the Secret Service was looking for a suitable location for Shady Fields.

An extensive building programme had turned the property into a residential complex containing communal rooms throughout the ground floor, five luxury suites, fifteen large apartments and twenty two smaller studio flats on the first floor, and a range of nursing facilities, staff accommodation and secure rooms on the top floor. It was an outstanding facility, able to support and care for former security service agents in safe, secure and comfortable surroundings.

On her way to the kitchen in the east wing she passed the garden room. Linda waved at one of the residents, Charlie Bingham, who was sitting in a wicker armchair looking out into the grounds.

She liked Charlie. He was from a different era. There was a chivalry about him that was rare nowadays. Over the past few months had told her his life stories. He had more than one, but that was dementia for you.

Linda wanted to check on him to find out what Dr Arnott (their medical Director and resident GP) had said when they had met this morning. She decided she would speak to him on the way back from the kitchen. She desperately needed a cup of tea. She hadn't stopped once since her shift started at 6am. It was now 10am. Where the hell did her time go?

Her meeting with Dan was scheduled for half an hour's time. Then there was the visit from the security services after lunch to think about. They were coming mob-handed, to get a look at the work they were doing here.

Linda knew they were under scrutiny with the evaluation report. She had met with the consultants and had taken an instant dislike to Mike Shannon. Her main point of contact was Sarb and he was a different kettle of fish. He had been at Shady Fields for a week and had actually done a lot to dispel her concerns about their work. He was intelligent, quick to grasp things, and had a respect for their residents which she felt was unusual for someone in his late-twenties.

During a meeting they had got into a lively discussion about the role of older people in different cultures, and she felt his perspective was refreshing.

"I have noticed that in some western cultures youth is fetishised and the elderly are treated with impatience and disrespect," he'd said.

"If they have dementia they are treated as a problem to be hidden away or confined. Any respect for their age, experience or sacrifice suddenly counts for nothing. In my culture, we value them as mentors for the next generation." Sarb had also displayed a considerable knowledge about the legalities of dementia care.

She still felt uncomfortable that they were being put under a microscope, but at least Sarb understood what they were trying to do here. What she didn't want was for Shady Fields to be seen as an opulent care home for people who didn't necessarily have the capacity to appreciate it.

She poured herself a large mug of tea and stirred in two heaped sugars. If she had been at home, there would also have also been a generous nip of Famous Grouse added. She sighed with regret; not while she was on duty.

The madness that was her daily routine would calm down a little when the new manager started work. It was then she remembered that Hilary Geddes was also coming in this afternoon. Dan had asked her to come in to sign her contract. He was going to ask her to start straight away.

Gratefully sipping her tea, she remembered that she was going to check on Charlie. She poured another mug for him and made her way to the garden room. He was still staring out of the window when she arrived.

Charlie Bingham was an enigma. He had a strange accent that was upper-class English with a hint of South African, but he lacked the stereotypical bluster and arrogance of many of those countrymen. At eighty-four years of age he was in good physical condition, and his ramrod straight back reflected a military bearing. He had a head of thick white hair, with a matching and tidily trimmed beard. His bushy eyebrows were, by contrast, disconcertingly dark. He dressed well in old but good-quality clothes, and now walked about with a wooden stick. Linda believed it was more of an affectation than for support. On the outside he looked in pretty good shape, but when you spoke with him for a little while, the dementia soon became evident.

He was quite proud of his reputation as a gambler and a heavy drinker in his early years, while his privileged upbringing and family connections had placed him in an ideal position to be recruited by MI6. He was a descendent of an aristocratic family who were deeply disappointed that he had found a job. Even serving as a diplomat was considered paid work.

When he spoke, he painted a picture of a long-gone era. Diplomats he worked with were men who would always remember a lady's birthday but never discuss her age. Cocktail parties and Embassy soirees were commonplace. Spying was frightfully civilised. Linda noted that his file was one of the most incomplete they had, and suspected that much of it had been redacted for national security reasons.

Charlie often talked of the jet set he'd socialised with in the 60's and 70's; name-dropping was an integral part of conversation with him. He recounted tales of parties with Brit Ekland and Peter Sellers. He spoke about late night dinners with racing drivers, horse trainers and even the occasional royal. It seemed that he had enjoyed a good deal of the high life.

He had mixed with the powerful and the well-connected until it all went horribly wrong. He never gave specific details, but it was clear that his fall from grace had been absolute. To avoid a family scandal he suddenly found himself on a different continent, building a new life. And the complete exile that had been forced on him had affected him deeply.

Charlie's condition was difficult to spot unless you knew what to look for. Most days he would seem perfectly cohesive, but then he would start to tell you fantastic tales of big-game hunting, of being imprisoned on Robben Island with Nelson Mandela, or of being framed for the murder of his wife, Veronica. In honesty, Linda couldn't tell the difference between fact and delusion.

He now sat, lost, deep in thought.

The memory problems Charlie was experiencing, the gaps in the day that he couldn't account for, and the disturbed sleep, were things that he had put down to his age. Now he knew for certain that dementia was to blame.

Linda wanted to offer him help and support if she could. "Good morning, Charlie, I've made you a nice cup of tea."

His head snapped to attention.

"Sorry, I didn't mean to make you jump, you looked miles away. How are you today?"

Charlie looked up at her with a deep melancholy in his eyes.

"Saw the doc this morning. Sorry to report the news isn't good."

Linda sat down in the armchair next to him,

"I had a feeling that might be the case. Is there anything I can do to help you? Have you got any questions?"

Charlie shook his head. "Not at the moment. The doc was pretty clear about what I can expect in the next twelve months, which was helpful. I need time to come to terms with it. I just feel so damned angry!" Charlie looked at her with genuine concern. "Will I have to leave when the dementia gets really bad?"

"Of course not, Charlie. We have all the facilities we need to care for you here, whatever your needs are. This is your home, and we are your family. You can stay here as long as you want or need."

She hoped she had reassured him for the time being, but she knew this would not be the last occasion she would have this conversation with him.

"Thanks," said Charlie, "that means a lot." Suddenly he looked smaller and more vulnerable.

They drank their tea in silence for a few minutes and as Linda stood up to leave he reached out and touched her arm.

"Linda, I need to arrange an appointment to see my solicitor. I need to get my affairs in order while I still can. It's Schuster and Stokes, of Lincolns Inn. I wonder, could you ring them and make an appointment for next week, please?"

"Of course I will, I'll call them today. Now I'm afraid I have to leave you; I have a meeting with Dan that I will be late for if I don't get a wriggle on."

She walked back into the large entrance hall and made her way back up the sweeping staircase to the first-floor landing. Crossing to a large oak door marked 'Office', she entered without knocking.

The room was large and spacious, with tall windows on one side that looked out over the car park to the trees beyond. The high ceiling was ornate, and decorated with plaster mouldings. A large marble fireplace was flanked by two wing-backed armchairs. Three modern desks were comfortably accommodated in the room, along with a formal meeting table that could easily seat eight people. Dan sat at his desk by the window, lost in a telephone conversation.

Linda decided to make the call for Charlie while it was fresh in her mind. Appointment made, she went to look for him. He was reading where she had left him earlier, deeply engrossed in *Dead Lucky: Lord Lucan, the final truth* by Duncan MacLaughlin.

"Is it a good read?" she asked.

Charlie looked up. "Not really, it's a bit far-fetched for my liking."

"I've just spoken to your solicitors, and you have an appointment for Wednesday 21st at 10am."

"Thanks Linda, I appreciate that. How am I getting there?"

"William has a meeting with his legal advisors who

are in the same building, so I thought we could all go together on the train if you like?"

"Great. Do you think we'll have time to take lunch at my old club? It 's not far from Schuster's office."

"I like the sound of that, Charlie, but first, let me check with William."

"Tell him it's my treat, he'll be far more agreeable then. I can book a table online for the first sitting at 12.30."

Linda turned to leave. "Sounds good, I'll let you know later. Are you going to join us for the whist drive this afternoon?"

Charlie seemed to come to life. "Definitely! I hope I get a decent partner this week. Last week I ended up with Rita, and whilst she is a very attractive woman, she has no head for cards. Couldn't remember a thing! Spent most of her time playing footsie under the table."

Dan was already seated at the meeting table when she got back to the office.

"Morning Linda, is everything ready for our visitors later?"

She nodded as she took her seat. Her iPad flashed into life and she began giving her usual update report. There were a number of residents who had come to them for short term respite care and one who was in the later stages of his condition receiving palliative care. This week there had been no deaths, escapes or other incidents to report. Dan seemed satisfied.

They talked over a couple of new applications they'd received. The most interesting was from the notorious *Dynamite Men,* who enjoyed legendary status in secret service circles and with whom Dan had worked on a number of missions. They were an ex-special forces team with a natural talent for blowing things up. One of them, Bill Tandy, had taken the art of explosives to new levels. Legend had it that he could blow the wings off a sleeping bumble bee without waking it up. The other, Ben Faulkner, was the muscle; a powerful athlete who simply refused to be beaten. No bridge, building or construction was too high or dangerous for him to wire.

Dan felt it was important that he put their case to Linda.

"I first worked with them in Afghanistan. The insurgents were planting UEDs at the roadside, causing lots of patrol casualties. Morale was low, but Bill and Ben – The Dynamite Men – were absolutely fearless. Within three days they had located and booby trapped a huge weapon cache. When it got tripped, at least twenty jihadi fighters were taken out by the explosion. It damaged the ISIS operation irreparably."

Dan examined the medical reports. Bill definitely met their entrance criteria as he had an Alzheimer's diagnosis, but Ben was fine, and he'd made the application as Bill's lasting power of attorney.

"The difficulty is that they come as a pair. We'd need to take them both." Dan shook his head, sadly. "Ben is doing what he has always done, looking out for his mate."

"But surely they are both wealthy from the sale of their business. Can't they make private arrangements?" Linda asked.

"It's the same old problem. Some of their operations were really sensitive, particularly their work in Northern Ireland. However, if they come here they'll be self-funded. And at this stage, that could prove very helpful. They want to take our two largest suites. That represents a significant income for us."

Dan pushed the file across for Linda to examine. He continued.

"At the end of the day, Linda, it's up to us to decide who comes here. Knowing something of their history and background, I strongly advise that we take both of them."

Linda nodded her agreement. "Fine. I'll send the acceptance letter later today."

Dan selected another file from a bundle on his desk.

"Now, let's talk about your support. You know we've appointed Hilary Geddes, and I think you'll like her. She has the right mix of common sense, intelligence and tenacity. I've invited her along to sign the final papers before she starts next week, and I want you to give her the guided tour."

Linda shrugged her agreement, which Dan thought seemed a little half-hearted.

"I think you may have already met her. Do you remember Ada Hale? The amusing older lady who stayed for six weeks last summer after her chemo treatment?"

Linda nodded immediately. "Of course I remember Ada, she was so funny; we got on like a house on fire."

"Well, Ada is Hilary's Aunt. She visited every week while Ada was here. She mentioned that she was looking for a new challenge, so I reached out to her about our job. It will be great to have her on the team, and she'll take some of the pressure off you."

"I vaguely remember her, I think." Linda smiled, but still didn't look convinced.

They turned their attention to the spreadsheets Dan had printed off, and looked at the figures. "We're holding our own, but we're still heavily dependent on the funding we get from the service. Ideally, I 'd like to see us breaking even without that. It would probably take us another year to get there, but we may not have that sort of time. We have to convince Bernard of our value. His continuing support will be crucial for our survival."

Linda sighed. She had met Bernard on a couple of occasions, but doubted that she had appeared on his radar. She was much too lowly in the scheme of things.

She launched into her prepared speech.

"I've identified sufficient savings for next year, but trying to break even by the end of this quarter will leave us with a cashflow problem for the rest of the year. We could do it, but it means shelving all of the development work we had planned. It will be tight; our residents aren't exactly run of the mill."

Dan closed the report and gave her his boyish grin. "Impressive, Linda. I was hoping you could work something out. Is there anything else?"

Linda shook her head, and their meeting was over for another week.

5

Shady Fields, 8th March 2018 (late afternoon)

Hilary drove through the gated entrance to Shady Fields a little after 5pm. A large surveillance camera was trained on the driver's side window. Rhododendrons lined the tarmac driveway, and despite the noise of her engine she could hear birdsong.

As she pulled around the bend, the house came into view. She had forgotten how beautiful it was. It looked considerably bigger than she remembered, too.

Hilary's Aunt Ada had worked as a civil servant during the war. She had never spoken about her work, but Hilary couldn't believe she had been a spy. Whatever she had done, it had qualified her to use this facility.

Hillary's current job in the Department of Health was to develop a care strategy for the elderly. As part of that project she had looked at the state of residential care in England. Her conclusions made pretty grim reading. Funding was woefully inadequate and standards varied dramatically, as did accommodation.

She had been shocked at what she'd found. At one end of the spectrum she discovered tired looking buildings centred around a communal lounge that usually smelled of boiled cabbage and stale urine. Those places often had a carousel of bored staff who looked about twelve. They seemed to spend their shifts staring at their mobile phones, ignoring those they were paid to support. At the other end were state of the art facilities run by large commercial organisations. These facilities were usually decorated like boutique hotels. They employed activities coordinators, provided a programme of entertainment, and had an in-house hairdresser. These places were expensive, available only to those with money. Shady Fields didn't fit into either category.

Hilary parked her Audi TT Convertible, retrieved her briefcase from the tiny boot, and followed the path to the main entrance. A flight of shallow stone steps led up to an imposing set of carved wooden doors. She pressed the intercom button, and almost immediately a bright voice said" Hello Ms Geddes, please come in. I'll meet you in reception."

A muted buzzer sounded. She pushed the door open to reveal a spacious reception hall. It was beautifully decorated in cream and pale gold. A dark oak reception desk sat to the left, and a huge gilt mirror filled the wall behind it. A crystal chandelier hung from the high ceiling in the centre of the hall, while an imposing staircase rose up in front of her to a landing where it split into two, taking people to the east and west wings of the house.

As she looked around she could see a dining room set out for silver service through an open set of doors to her left. To her right stood a number of panelled doors, one of which bore the legend 'Library'. Several people were chatting together as they moved through the hall.

A door in the far left corner of the room opened and a tall, stocky woman came towards her with a business-like stride.

"Hello, I'm Linda Bridges the Service Manager. Welcome to Shady Fields. I think we may have met briefly when you visited your Aunt?"

She thrust out a hand, and Hilary shook it. "Call me Hilary," she said. "It's good to be here."

A light vibration drew Linda's attention to the iPad she was carrying. "Can I ask you to take a seat for a few minutes? Dan is on a call at the moment. We're meeting as soon as he's free."

She gestured towards the Library, then turned smartly and headed back in the direction she had come from.

Hilary crossed the black and cream tiled floor and positioned herself on a large calfskin sofa. She wanted to observe the comings and goings. She heard a door close nearby, followed by the footsteps of someone descending the staircase. She immediately recognised Dan Grant as he came into view. He crossed the hall towards her, extending a tanned hand.

"Hello Hilary, thanks for coming in today. We're

keen to get you up and running."

She met his firm handshake and noted that his skin was dry and cool even though the temperature in the hall was comfortably warm.

Linda reappeared on cue. She walked across the hall and breezed through the door into the library, holding it open for them to follow.

Dark wooden bookshelves lined two sides of the room. At a glance, Hilary spotted leather-bound first editions as well as well-thumbed paperbacks. There were comfortable reading chairs with accompanying tables arranged around the room, on top of which stylish reading lamps created small pools of illumination.

In the middle of the far wall there was a carved stone fireplace decorated with fat cherubs, bunches of perfect grapes and a club fender seat. It was flanked by two matching buttoned chesterfield sofas in red leather. Separating them was an oak coffee table. Hilary could see the silhouette of distant trees through large french windows. She knew this room would become her favourite.

She sat on the firm leather cushion of the settee, taking in the smells of wood smoke and old books. It transported her back to evenings spent with her aunt in Derbyshire.

The table had already been set for their meeting. Linda offered Hilary a choice of drinks. "Coffee please; white, no sugar."

Linda poured strong coffee from an elegant china coffee pot and handed the matching cup and saucer over.

"How long have you been here, Linda?"

"I came when we opened, just over a year ago. I was Head of Nursing at a military hospital before. This is a different sort of challenge; no two days are the same."

Hilary took a sip of coffee.

"When my Aunt came in the summer she was full of praise for the staff and the support she got from everyone who looked after her."

"That's good to hear," Linda looked towards Dan. "We work hard to keep up our standards and Ada was a real pleasure. How is she?"

'She's doing fine. She sees her specialist next month but we're very hopeful."

Linda handed Dan his coffee and took her own from the table.

'We offer higher levels of service and quality to our residents. Many now have dementia but spent their careers serving their country. We ensure that their physical and mental needs are met, and their dignity and independence is protected. It's the least they deserve."

Her intensity left Hilary feeling a little uncomfortable. "Were any of the residents here licensed to kill?"

Linda was slightly taken aback. "That's a bit melodramatic. All of our residents have worked for the intelligence service or special forces, but not all have seen active service. Many of them have unique skill sets. Some of them, in the course of their service, may have engaged an enemy. I can assure you they pose no danger to our staff, though, and 007 is definitely not living here."

Hilary realised she had offended the woman. "I'm so sorry Linda, that was a clumsy way of putting it."

She smiled, and accepted the apology. "It isn't like it seems in spy novels. Agents will have done lots of sitting around waiting for something to happen. Gathering intelligence, observing very little activity for hours on end, can be very boring. James Bond is really no reflection of the job."

"We don't deal well as a society with Alzheimer's or dementia. If you were in your thirties and had the same symptoms you would be treated for serious mental illness. But if you're over sixty, you are labelled and essentially left to your own devices. Only when you become a burden on family or a risk to yourself or others is action taken."

Dan drained his cup and placed it back on the table. "Steady, Linda, she's on our side."

Linda brightened. "Sorry, I get a bit evangelical about what we do," she looked at Hilary. "I'm not always this direct."

Dan smiled. "Yes you are!"

Hilary fixed Linda with a knowing look. "I really do understand your passion. There is so little understanding of these conditions. Just the word 'dementia' frightens people, because they don't understand it. Many don't know how to deal with people who have it. I think it's the unpredictability they struggle with the most."

"Exactly! Our approach is somewhat controversial. We agree with them, we sometimes indulge their delusions, but we never question what they say. Some think it's odd or inappropriate, but our residents are happy and stress free. That makes their condition more stable and manageable.

"I'll give you the grand tour if you like, and you can meet some of them. They may sound a little strange or fantastical, so you'll just have to take them at face value."

Dan opened his file and checked the top sheet. "Your references are back. You come highly recommended by Sir John Silver at the DOH. We were really pleased when you said you'd join us." He checked the file again. "I appreciate you postponing your holiday to start next week. We really need your knowledge and skills now. The treasury review is going on at the moment, so it's all hands on deck. Linda will show you around, then if we meet back in the office in about an hour you can sign the final forms."

Draining her cup, Linda nodded at Hilary. "Follow me, and feel free to ask questions as we go." With that, she stood and headed for the door, Hilary hurrying to keep up with her.

The communal rooms on the ground floor of Shady Fields included a TV lounge, dining room, bar, library, activity and wellbeing rooms. Kitchen, laundry and cleaning services were situated at the far end of the building, with the main staff administration offices situated on the first floor with the apartments and suites.

Residents apartments were of a similar layout to each other, but individually decorated. They had a small vestibule, comfortable lounge, a kitchen-dining area, a bedroom and bathroom. Studio apartments were on a smaller footprint and didn't have the vestibule. The architects in charge of the redesign had cleverly installed two spacious lifts to service all floors using the stairwells in each wing. In addition there was an office, a small staff room and a quiet lounge in each wing of the house on each floor.

Linda guided Hilary around the building, chatting to staff and residents as they walked. She quickly discovered that when a resident's condition became more complex, their needs were met with advanced levels of care and security.

The top floor was reserved for residents who required more intensive support and, in some cases, up to twenty-four hour nursing care. It accommodated some residents that were virtually bed-ridden, and others who needed to housed be in secure facilities due to their challenging behaviour. The same impeccable standard of decor was evident throughout the building and residents seemed to want for nothing.

They made their way back down the staircase at the end of their tour. Hilary was obviously impressed.

"The facilities here are second to none, and the atmosphere is like a friendly hotel rather than a residential home. How do you manage that?"

"People living here are not incarcerated in an institution. This is their home, and even though we have extra security measures in place it should still look and feel like home. Our staff are trained to the highest standards, so that helps too."

Hilary nodded. "I understand, but isn't there a risk, given their history? Presumably some of them could be quite dangerous as their conditions worsen?"

Linda nodded.

"Yes, but that's why we are so careful. Each resident is regularly assessed, and any changes in their condition are fully documented. All our staff are trained in techniques to subdue and restrain. But that's a last resort. In the bad old days, people would be involuntarily drugged to keep them docile. It was no life at all, and certainly not any way to show respect for their dignity. Shocking practice!" She shook her head.

"You'll soon pick up the important things. Your training programme will cover the assessments, the risk level colour coding system and the corresponding actions."

They entered the main office where Dan was seated behind his desk, just finishing a telephone call. He looked up as they entered the room. "Guided tour complete, then?"

Linda nodded, then turned to Hilary.

"Welcome aboard. I'll leave you here if I may – I have a meeting in the activities room with Layla, one of our senior assistants. She's organising a world music concert and we have to go over the security arrangements."

"Thanks, Linda."

The manager turned to leave but Dan called her back.

"I nearly forgot – can you look in on William, please? He seemed particularly agitated this morning. It might just be the after-effects of his infection, but he seemed a little paranoid. Said something about people trying to steal his manuscript again."

"No problem, I was heading that way anyway." She

59

smiled at Hilary, nodded to Dan and left the room, the door closing behind her.

Hilary took a seat at the meeting table and waited for her new boss to finish making notes on a large yellow legal pad. She'd done her homework on Dan Grant using some of the contacts she'd developed in Whitehall. The feedback was extremely impressive. He was respected and admired in equal measure. Her Aunt also knew him, as they had once worked together briefly years ago. Apparently, she had liked him immediately and had been flattering about him both as a person and as a professional. Hilary had been surprised; Ada didn't speak about many people with such affection.

As she watched him work she observed a man of confidence and charisma. He was obviously a natural leader. She knew instinctively that taking this job was her best career decision to date. She wanted to make a difference, to feel her work really mattered, and today had confirmed that working here would give her that opportunity.

Dan stood and walked over to the coffee machine. "So, do you have any questions so far?" He refilled his cup.

"I think I might have some difficulty telling fact from fiction with some of our residents. But my question is: how will I be able to work out which is which?"

Dan was pleased that she was already referring to them as 'our' residents.

"You might not. Some of our residents have skill sets that include unarmed combat, firearms and explosives training, sabotage and theft. They are all highly skilled in the art of deception. It makes for interesting times. Have you met Rita yet?"

Hilary shook her head. "No I don't think so."

Dan smiled. "You'd definitely know if you had. She was a brilliant agent in her day. A master of disguise, a honey-trap and a highly-skilled thief. There wasn't a safe or safety deposit box that she couldn't crack.

"She's been with us nearly six months now, and every day she changes her appearance. Wigs, clothes, accents – we don't draw attention to it, because it's who she is. It makes her feel safe. With all our residents, it all boils down to what their perception of reality is."

He moved back to the meeting table and sat down.

"Residents' personal files contain basic background and histories. In some cases, details are redacted due to security clearance levels."

Hilary thought for a few seconds. "I am going to need some time to get to grips with it all, but I'm keen to learn."

Reaching across the table, Dan a selected a manila folder that had been lying there in readiness for this meeting. "Charles Bingham is another case in point."

"Yes, we met Charlie as we were doing the tour." She looked up, recalling the details. "Incredible diplomat and agent with some significant wins under his belt, but at times believes that he is Lord Lucan."

Dan nodded.

"There's a strong likelihood that given his background, he may have met Lucan at some point. They may even have moved in the same circles. My point is that some of their histories are incomplete, and even we don't have the whole picture. The point is not whether we believe him, but what he believes. Can you imagine how vulnerable he would be if the press believed he was Lucan? They would have a field day! An over-zealous reporter may believe there is something in his story and start digging. What else might they uncover? If his role as an intelligence agent was discovered we could be in serious trouble. We are in effect looking after him and helping to keep the nation's secrets, secret."

Hilary nodded in agreement.

"You mentioned 'William' earlier, when Linda was leaving. Who's he?"

"Ah, yes. William is much more straightforward, as it happens. He was our very own 'Q', specialising in computers and technology back before the internet was even invented. He's writing his memoirs, and he's convinced there are people out to steal his manuscript because of who he's named within it."

"So who does it name?" Hilary's interest was piqued.

"I have no idea. He's never let anyone read it. He knows that if he wants to have it published, it will have to be vetted by the service, and of course, he doesn't trust them at all."

Hilary looked puzzled. "But there have been any number of books written by former secret service agents, so who vets them?"

"Celia Browning, our Director General. She's vetted a number of memoirs and spy novels. As long as they don't reveal operational details that could breach the official secrets act or create problems for agents in the field, people are free to publish. Ian Fleming and Stella Rimington became very successful authors using their Intelligence experiences. In fact Stella's first novel was deemed very pedestrian in its level of detail by those in the Service. She said that if she'd written the truth no one would have believed her."

Dan flashed a smile and Hilary almost blushed. "As for William, we're actively helping him to get legal advice and to find a publisher who might be interested in his manuscript, but that doesn't stop his paranoia."

Hilary exhaled." Clearly I have a lot to learn. But I'm so pleased I decided to take the job, Dan."

Hilary scan-read and signed the document Dan presented to her, then said her goodbyes. As she walked away from the building, and for the first time in a decade, she felt excited about Monday morning. Her life was about to change; this job was going to be anything but boring.

6

Shady Fields Workshop, 16th March 2018

Shady Fields had an Activities Room with a full agenda of interesting and diverting events. A first class coordinator called Sarah ran things to engage wandering minds.

William Wright never engaged in such frivolities. Instead, and with Dan's support, he had commandeered a large outbuilding to the side of the main house and converted it into a fully-equipped workshop. He and fellow residents could immerse themselves in practical stuff, and technical puzzles. William loved working on his inventions.

A fine selection of hand and power tools were affixed to a wallboard, with each sitting neatly inside its own outline. Sturdy workbenches ran along both sides of the floor. Sets of plastic drawers were mounted above these benches, containing electrical components, small batteries, screws, clips, and a variety of fixings. All were neatly labelled. Elsewhere, rolls of coloured electrical wire and tape were neatly organised on Dexion racking.

In one corner, a stand-alone workstation stacked with a plethora of electronic equipment stood next to a bright red Snap-on Tool chest. It held every size of wrench, spanner, screwdriver and the mother of all socket sets. The whole set up was in effect a grown up play room equipped to a very high standard. It was William's favourite place.

During his career, he had made technology his servant. He manipulated strings of computer code like child's play. In fact, he much preferred code to people; no troublesome personalities to deal with, just pure logic. He was at his happiest when he was immersed in problem solving and inventing gadgets. It calmed him.

Today, he was standing at the workbench with Rita's small laptop open in front of him, mumbling softly under his breath. He was entering quick, deliberate key strokes, totally engrossed in his activity.

He didn't hear Hilary enter through the side door.

"Hello, William. I missed you this morning at breakfast. How are you today?"

William briefly looked over his shoulder and returned to what he was doing. "Rita asked me to look at her laptop, it's infected with a virus. I'm not surprised, given the websites she visits."

He tutted, typed a few more commands then let

out a satisfied "Gotcha!"

Hilary moved closer to see what he was doing. The screen showed a diagnostic program that was producing streams of text and numbers faster than she could follow.

"It's not the first time this has happened, either. I've been telling her to keep her anti-virus protection up to date for ages. If she'd done as I said this would never have happened. The threats from malicious software get more sophisticated every day. She should be using our secure network so everything gets filtered through a firewall, but she will insist on doing things her way."

Hilary watched as William closed down the programs until only a single window was left, displaying the results of his efforts. He seemed pleased with the outcome.

"It's good of you to help her. She was telling me yesterday how much she depends on her laptop, and judging by the number of deliveries she gets, Amazon would have to issue a profits warning if she couldn't get it working again."

"It's really no trouble at all. I was working on a little project of my own, and only too pleased to give her laptop a good clean-up. You can never be too careful."

He gathered up a small black box the size of a matchbox and a couple of leads from the bench next to him, pushing them into an open drawer before closing it.

Hilary changed the subject. "I spent the weekend keeping a technician supplied with coffee while he attempted to fix the CCTV system at my house. It hasn't been working properly for a while."

William looked up at her. "What system do you have?"

"It's a Schneider KNX. It is part of a ……."

William cut in"…remotely controlled management and surveillance system that gives you full control over programmable electronic systems at your home. It allows you to set alarm zones, control your heating, lighting and external security all from your mobile phone."

Hilary was surprised. "Yes, that 's right. Only the remote control bit isn't working at the moment."

William looked thoughtful for a brief second or two. "That system uses a third generation processor that my team developed. Did your man fix it?"

"No, he said has to order a replacement logic board and he will come back when he gets the part. I think he just likes my coffee."

"Have you got your phone with you?" William asked.

Hilary removed it from her pocket and offered it to him.

"Unlock it, and I'll have a look at it for you." He anticipated her response. "It 's no trouble at all."

She held her thumb over the biometric sensor and the phone screen lit up. She handed it to him.

William quickly scrolled through the screens looking for the control app. He opened it and went directly to the diagnostics screen. Hilary looked at the display, feeling slightly embarrassed. She didn't know there was a diagnostic setting.

After a few more taps and swipes on the screen, he looked at her and said "He's having you on, he doesn't need a part for the system. It's a configuration conflict. There's nothing wrong with the logic board. He probably hasn't got a clue what's wrong and is using the old engineer's fallback of 'if in doubt, swap it out'. I can fix it, if you like?"

"Can you?"

In less than a minute he handed her the phone back. "There you go, it's all working now. If you want to alter the settings, just press this icon."

Hilary looked at her phone and pressed an icon that resembled a house with an eye superimposed over it. An image of her front door immediately appeared on the screen. She scrolled through other camera views, executing a virtual tour around her empty house more than fifty miles away. "William, you are brilliant! How did you do that so quickly?"

"I could tell you, but then I'd have to kill you." William smiled again, turning back to the bench.

She was getting used to secret service humour. "Thanks, I'll cancel the engineer's visit. So what's this project you're working on today?"

William quickly slipped into 'boffin' mode. "I am working on a sub-miniature, voice-activated recording device.

"The problem with most smart systems is that you have to be very explicit when telling them what to do.

For example, 'Siri, play Rachmaninov's piano concerto number two' or 'Alexa, what is the French word for doorknob?' What I'm doing is using unlikely key words to trigger certain operations. Like using the word 'roundabout' to trigger an audio recording, or an unrelated word like 'roadworks' to stop it. It will allow field agents to make clandestine recordings without alerting the people they're with. Practically, it could be any word or combination of words that could activate the device. I'm still working out the wrinkles, but I'm getting there."

"That is very impressive, William. You should mention it to Dan next time you see him, he's a bit of a techie too, and I'm sure he'll be impressed."

William's hand reached out instinctively to the drawer next to him, and touched the handle. "Yes, I think I will. I haven't seen him for a few days, though; what's he up to?"

"Well, we're in the middle of this evaluation at the moment, and he's poring over our financial reports. Boring, but absolutely necessary if we're going to get the funding we need to operate Shady Fields properly."

William looked dismissive. "People don't understand what it means to feel safe. That's what this place is to most of us. A place where we can feel protected instead of feeling that we have to do the protecting. Spreadsheets can't show that."

Rita's laptop bleeped, and William responded with a couple of key strokes. "Well, I'd better get this back to her. When she gave it me this morning she was a

Russian princess with jet-black hair and sunglasses. I hope I can recognise her to give it back."

Hilary smiled. "There's a blonde haired Scandinavian scientist in a red jumper in the library who just might be your happy customer."

He shook his head as he picked up the laptop to leave. "It could be worse, she could be the Arabian assassin with the frightening collection of blades again, then we'd all be in trouble!"

7

Shady Fields, 16th March 2018

Bernard was keen to get the results of the evaluation report published as soon as possible. The window of opportunity to shut down Shady Fields was narrow. If Celia decided to continue support it would be for a five year period. That prospect worried him deeply. A lot of damage could be done in five years. He wanted to nip this ridiculous project it in the bud and chalk the whole year-long farce down as an expensive but failed experiment. Closing it down would be a far better outcome for him, all things considered.

He had forgone his official chauffeured Jaguar today. Instead, he was pushing his cherished green Morgan Roadster through the picturesque countryside towards Shady Fields at speeds well above the national limit. The car handled beautifully. It also complimented his personal flamboyance. It was one of the few things in life that he had any real passion for, other than his desire to head up the Secret Services.

He felt the feeling of annoyance rise again as he powered the Morgan along the winding Shady Fields driveway and the magnificent building came into view. This level of luxury was expensive and unwarranted. He would have found a much more cost-effective solution to the problem of old and gaga ex-agents, if his boss had given him the opportunity.

Celia had been persuaded to support the creation of Shady Fields by the strength of Dan 's arguments, and because, in her words, it would have "great potential as a security services resource."

Bernard didn't share her optimism, but he was pleased when Celia had accepted his offer of help to undertake the evaluation of Shady Fields. He had immediately commissioned Maguire's Management Consultancy to lead the work. They had a reputation for ruthless hatchet-jobs on publicly-funded projects. Also, the owner was Sir Henry Maguire, a Black Country champagne socialist who owed him several favours. Sir Henry was a self-made man from Wolverhampton, a property developer, entrepreneur and a grateful recipient of a Knighthood for services to business. He had got himself into hot water when he was discovered to be in possession of an overseas development bid weeks before it was due to be officially released.

Bernard had quietly pulled a few strings behind the scenes to make the accusations of industrial espionage quietly go away. That meant the old man was now in his debt, and definitely in his pocket.

Maguire's specific expertise was focused on exposing the vast amount of public funds wasted on government vanity projects. Fortunately for its owner, his own organisation had escaped scrutiny. The irony of the situation was lost on Sir Henry, but it made him an ideal partner for Bernard's plans. He would tell them what the outcome of the review needed to be, and good old Sir Henry would obligingly deliver the verdict on his behalf.

Bernard parked the car and walked up to the entrance. It really jarred that he had to wait to be admitted through the security intercom. A female voice answered, "Hello, can I help you?"

"Yes. Bernard Cummings to see Dan Grant."

The security lock buzzed as the latch clicked open and he entered. The hall was empty, except for an attractive woman who looked to be in her late fifties. She had shoulder-length auburn hair, and wore blue jeans tucked into calf-length boots, topped off with chunky azure cashmere sweater and navy blue silk scarf. She was arranging magazines on the hall table and looked up as he entered.

"Hello, can I help you?"

"I am here to see Mr. Grant. Is there a member of staff about?"

Rita blinked at him. "I'm waiting for the afternoon

train to London. Do you know if it's on time?"

Her accent was decidedly Mancunian. Something stirred briefly in his memory but he pushed it away. He was certain he didn't know anyone from Manchester.

Bernard sighed. "You will have a long wait then, my dear. This is not the train station and there is no train to London. There must be a member of staff somewhere?"

The woman looked confused and began to get anxious. "But I simply must get to London. He will be waiting for me. I have to file my report. Lives may depend on it!"

Bernard didn't have time for this. He turned and walked toward the staircase, but before he reached the first step the office door behind the reception desk opened and a woman emerged.

She smiled and walked towards him. "Hello Mr Cummings, I am Hilary Geddes, the new manager here. I have informed Dan that you're here, and he asked that you go directly up to his office. I presume you know where it is?"

Bernard didn't move. He had never met this woman before, and when Dan had mentioned his new appointment he had simply focused on her experience, not how attractive she was. He calculated that she was about five feet six inches tall, obviously slim and well-proportioned, and wearing a business suit that emphasised her shape rather than disguising it. Her natural ash blonde hair was shoulder length, she had clear blue eyes and sported just the hint of a smile on her full lips.

She turned and addressed the other woman. "HI Rita, are you ok?"

"No I am not! He says there is no train to London and that I'm not at the station." Her voice was uncertain. "I must get to HQ, my report is very important."

Hilary took charge of the situation. "Of course it's important, Rita. I've already emailed your report. If your boss has any questions, he can call you to discuss it on the phone."

Rita visibly relaxed.

"Instead of going to London you could stay here for afternoon tea instead. There are sandwiches, scones and homemade fruitcake. How does that sound?"

Rita relaxed a little and nodded. "I would like that." She looked at Bernard briefly, and headed off towards the day lounge.

Hilary turned to face Bernard, who had stood motionless watching the exchange.

"Was there anything else, Mr Cummings?"

He continued to look her over. "You handled that very well. I can see that you are experienced in dealing with people like that."

"If by 'like that' you mean 'someone with dementia' then yes, I have considerable experience. And her name is Rita."

"Yes, she already told me." Bernard began to climb the staircase towards Dan's first floor office when it occurred to him that Rita's accent had changed during her last exchange; it was now very definitely home counties. Then it hit him; he knew exactly who she was. He continued up the staircase, making a mental note that if he was going to be visiting this mad house again he should to get to know Hilary better. After all, she might be looking for a new position shortly, and she struck him as decidedly competent amongst several other things.

He knocked on the office door and entered without waiting.

Dan looked up. "Bernard! I wasn't expecting you until next week."

"Yes I know, but Celia is extremely busy with far more pressing issues at the moment so I offered to get things moving with the report."

Dan was about to reply, but Bernard continued. "Look, I fully understand what you do here Dan, but we all have to pull our belts in these days."

"So how will it work? What do your consultants need in order to complete their report?" Dan waited for Bernard to provide some details.

"Well of course the financial and operational data will be collated by the consultants. I think it's important to include some feedback from the residents as well, though, and Celia thought I might be best the person to do that. Saves any further problems with additional clearances and suchlike."

"I understand that, but a member of staff will need to be present at each of the interviews. These are potentially vulnerable people and we take our duty of care seriously."

Bernard was satisfied with the fact that he had obviously irritated Dan. It would do no harm to emphasise the power relationship here, and he was becoming increasingly sure he would get the evidence he needed to shut this place down.

He passed a type-written sheet from his inside jacket pocket across to Dan. "These are the people I thought it might be useful to talk to. I've included old Charlie Bingham and William Wright because they already know me, and there are a couple of others on there too. I don't expect it will take too long; I should think about thirty minutes per interview maximum."

Dan scanned the list and nodded. "I'd like a copy of the questions you want to ask."

Bernard shook his head. "Well that's not going to happen. We wouldn't want your patients to practice their answers now, would we?"

"I hope you are not suggesting for a second that we would coach our *residents*. I just thought that you would be asking everyone the same questions to get some consistency for the study."

Bernard could sense the direction Dan was taking, and changed his focus.

"I would rather it were more informal, to ensure they are relaxed and able to answer honestly. I will cover the obvious things: their likes and dislikes about living here, food, services, you know the sort of thing. So when can we get started? Are any of them here now?"

Dan recognised when he was being railroaded. "I 'm sorry, Bernard, but that's not how this is going to work. First, we have to ask them if they want to participate, and then they need to understand what's involved. You can't just thrust it on them. I'll ask them over the next few days and arrange something for one day next week."

Bernard was visibly displaying his irritation, but Dan continued. "That's the best I can do I 'm afraid."

"If this is gameplay to delay the inevitable Dan, it won 't work. The interviews will take place on Monday. Have them ready by then." Bernard turned on his heels and left the office.

Dan couldn't work out why Bernard was taking such a hands-on approach. He normally left the real work to his staff. There was definitely a hidden agenda at play, but Dan wasn't sure what it was, yet.

Bernard went back down the stairs, checking the hall on the way. The train had clearly left the station, as Rita was nowhere to be seen as he left the building. How did anyone work in this mad house? He returned to his car, still inwardly fuming at the interference Dan was causing with his interviews.

As he opened the door he noticed an elderly, but spritely figure walking along a path from the gardens. It was William. Time had been good to him. Physically, he was upright and walked with regular, strong steps. He was wearing a beige canvas drover hat and a waxed green Barbour overcoat that looked as old as he did. But as he came closer, Bernard saw that his face showed significant signs of ageing. His pinched features emphasised his rheumy eyes, while his long, pointed nose was discoloured with a network of broken veins.

Delighted by his sudden change in fortune, Bernard realised that he couldn't pass up an opportunity like this. And Dan need never know.

He walked to the edge of the car park to intercept William, and called his name. William looked up, and scowled.

"Oh, it's you. I'd like to say it's a pleasure, but I won't, as it isn't."

Bernard ignored the rebuff. "My dear William, how the devil are you, old bean? It's been a long time."

"Not long enough!" William snapped.

"Listen, I'm glad I caught you. You won't know this yet, but there's a treasury review of Shady Fields going on, management cost cutting and all that. I've persuaded them to include comments from people living here to ensure the report is balanced. I wanted to give you all a voice, and I thought you'd be a particularly good person to talk to. You were always logical and objective. Just the sort of viewpoint needed. What do you say?"

"I wouldn't piss on you if you were on fire!"

Bernard gave a distasteful look.

"I'm not asking for my sake, William. Dan and the team will be under immense scrutiny in a report like this. I know what a great job they're doing and I wouldn't want to see anything untoward happen to

Shady Pines.

"I just thought you would want to make sure those Whitehall mandarins reading the report know how much this place is needed. However, I can fully understand if your mind is made up."

Bernard turned to walk away.

"It's Shady Fields, you arsehole, and if it's for Dan then that's different. What do you want from me?"

Bernard suppressed a smile. "It won't take long. Perhaps we could go down to the village pub and chat over a drink. Now, if you have the time. Just a few questions, and I'll have you back in time for tea. What do you say?"

"All right then. I'll just let Layla know where I'm going."

Bernard hesitated, "Is she one of the staff?"

"Yes, she's one of the attendants. Won't be a sec."

Bernard raised the Morgan's folding roof and secured it into position. He didn't want Dan or anyone else to see him leave with William on board. This was one interview he didn't want recorded. He got into his car and started the engine.

William came back a few minutes later, having ditched the Barbour in favour of a smart tweed sports jacket and Trilby hat. "I couldn't find Layla so I left a message with Rita. I don't want anyone to worry."

Bernard breathed a sigh of relief. The likelihood of Rita remembering anything of any importance was slim. He headed down the drive, gunning the accelerator and pushing William back into his seat with the force of the acceleration.

"Steady on, there are old people around here. You wouldn't want to hit someone now, would you?"

"No, you're absolutely right, William." He eased off the gas, and within 10 minutes they were pulling into the pub car park.

He had passed the Bulls' Head on the way here this morning. It looked like a typical quiet country pub. Painted black and white, it was set back from the main street and had the obligatory painted picture of a Bull hanging from a wrought iron signpost. He guessed that inside would be solid and original, not the faux beams and horse brasses that brewery's instant history departments adorned pubs with these days.

He was right. The main bar had a well-worn charm. There was a large inglenook fireplace with a real wood fire crackling in the hearth at one end, and a dart board at the other. Highly-polished tables and chairs were grouped around the room, while an upholstered bench seat ran around the perimeter of the bar area.

The landlord was throwing darts aimlessly at the board and turned as the two men entered. Like all of those in his profession, he gave them the customary once over. At this time of day the bar was empty, except for a farm machinery salesman nursing a pint and a sandwich at the bar. He was busy planning his afternoon calls on a tablet that bore his company's logo.

William walked past their fellow punter to a table by the fireplace, leaving Bernard to go to the bar. He called out, "A single malt, and make mine a double."

The landlord perked up a little. He walked behind a counter decorated with tall beer taps proclaiming their CAMRA credentials. "What can I get you, sir?"

Bernard looked at the choice of cask ales. He preferred a glass of wine to beer nowadays, but settled on a single malt, too. Without ice, obviously. He paid, then carried the drinks over to William.

"Well isn't this nice? Just like old times."

He smiled at William, who grunted in response and took a sip of his scotch.

"It used to be okay, until they built the new roundabout as you come into the village. Now it's all big lorries thundering through the lanes. It spoils a quiet drink." He shook his head sadly.

"How serious is this review? I mean, could it be trouble for us?" William looked genuinely concerned.

"Dan is a good man, you know, and Shady Fields provides us with a home. In some cases, it's the only proper home some of us have had."

Bernard nodded, gravely. "I'm not going to lie to you, William, it could be very serious. The treasury have ordered significant cut backs right across the service. Obviously they won't be pulling funding from overseas operations, and they're unlikely to touch MI5, either, so they're looking at other ways of saving money. I just want to make sure Shady Fields gets a fair crack of the whip."

William looked sceptical.

"It's unlike you to think about other people,

Bernard." He paused, and took another sip of his scotch. "So, what do you want to know?"

Bernard relaxed back into his seat. "There's no hurry. I wanted to catch up with you, see how you're doing. It must be twenty years since we worked together. Are you well? You look good."

William's anger rose. "You have a worse memory than I do. We last saw each other at the tribunal in June 2006.

"That was when you stitched me up and made me the scapegoat for Greenday. I only had a couple of years left. A few miserable months before I could retire on a full pension, but you saw to it that it never happened."

Bernard opened his mouth to speak, but William continued.

"Did you know that enforced retirement kills more people than hard work ever did. I never took you for a spiteful man, Bernard, until then. It was one thing to pile it all at my door but to recommend a downgrade that robbed me of half my final salary was nasty."

Bernard didn't answer immediately; he should be cautious.

"You, above all people, know how these things work, William. The department had to be seen to be holding people to account. Agents died, for God's sake! It wasn't personal, but someone needed to go."

William looked him full in the face. "Not fucking personal! We both know it was payback for Tbilisi. I knew the whole story, and you wanted me out of the way. The stupid thing was, I was never a threat. I didn't question how it ended. Orders are orders. I never told anyone at the time. And I had no intention of ever telling anyone, at least not until that journalist came to see me."

William shuffled his feet and rested his glass on the cardboard beermat, staring down at the floor.

"She sold me down the river, too! Asking questions and suggesting she wanted to get to the heart of the matter, when she just wanted an exclusive story." He paused and looked up at Bernard again.

"You will leave the service never having to worry about making ends meet. But what you did made life really hard for me. My savings are gone, and I'm living hand to mouth now. If it wasn't for Dan and Shady Fields I don't know what I would have done."

Bernard wondered how long this stream of self-pity was going to last. William continued.

"Something good did come out of last year, though. I started going over things in my head. I even went through my old papers. What if it wasn't as clear cut as I'd originally thought? Where did those orders to terminate the asset really come from? Did they ever really exist? And what happened to Shura's money?"

William had Bernard's full attention now.

"That's what gave me the idea of writing my memoirs. The manuscript is almost finished, and when I publish, I've been told I could make a pretty penny out of it. It seems that people love espionage and cold war stories. And as long as I don't breech the Official

Secrets Act I'll be able to put it all out there; how badly I was treated, why, and by whom.

"I was never a threat in 2006, but I might be one now."

Bernard shifted uncomfortably in his seat. "What exactly do you mean by that?"

A smile crept across William 's face. "Well, if I want to publish in the UK I have to jump through loads of hoops, but if I use an overseas publisher that problem suddenly goes away. Others have done it before. Peters published in Australia and the Government nearly shat themselves when they realised they couldn't stop him blowing the whistle on their dirty laundry." William chuckled at his mix of metaphors.

Bernard's chest suddenly tightened. William was in full flow now, his eyes sparkling with malice.

"Do you know what I think, Bernard? I think karma's a bitch! I think you need to make sure that this review shows us all in a glowing light and guarantees a safe future for Shady Fields.

"Memoirs can cause all sorts of scandal. The public may not be all that bothered about stuff that happened thirty years ago, but the establishment is sensitive about who it gives its gongs to. Knighthoods don 't go to people whose closets contain skeletons. It might even affect your final salary, Bernard, or worst of all, your promotion prospects!"

Bernard's jaw tightened as he clenched his teeth. He was being blackmailed by a contemptible little man who'd been nothing but one of the backroom boys decades ago! It was too ridiculous for words, and yet Bernard was angrier than he had felt in a long time.

William downed the last of his whisky. "If you have any more questions I'll gladly answer them next time you're here but I want to go back home now. Are you ready?"

Bernard left the rest of his drink on the table; he'd lost his taste for it.

They were silent on the drive back, and as they approached the perimeter gates it began to drizzle. Bernard stopped the car short of the barriers and looked straight ahead.

"Well, William, that was nice, we must do it again soon. I have to get back to London now and I want to miss the rush-hour traffic, so I'll just drop you here."

"It's a long walk back to the house from the road." said William.

'Shame you changed your coat, then."

William got out of the car and held the door open. "Good luck missing the traffic. The roadworks are a nightmare at the moment!"

He slammed the door shut and watched as Bernard floor the throttle, spinning the rear wheels as he pulled away.

As he drove off, Bernard looked in his rear view mirror and watched the old man pull his collar up against the cold to start the long walk up the drive. It began to rain more heavily. He would be soaked by the time he got back to the house. Bernard smiled.

William had been right about one thing, though.

Perhaps he was a threat now, in a way he'd never been before. What was really rattling him, though, was how close William had got to the truth without even realising it. Celia 's job was still open, and Bernard could not allow any scandal or even a question mark about his past to muddy those waters. That job was his by right, and no senile old man was going to threaten it.

He decided that he would make a phone call when he got back.

In his line of business it was easy to develop contacts with the wrong sort of people. Deni Dokka was the wrong sort of people. He wasn't that bright, but he was cheap, and he was brutal. He would get the job done, and there would be nothing to point back to Bernard.

8

Tbilisi, 9th November 1989, 9pm

'Uncle' studied the pair of painted icons lying on his dining room table. Their beauty was truly astounding. They'd been painted in the mid-17th century by the Russian artist Yuri Nikitin. The wooden panels were approximately twelve inches by ten inches and depicted brightly coloured religious figures in flowing robes. Both featured decorated doors that protected the striking images. On their backs, each icon bore a faded Cyrillic script label with a miniature metal seal set into the wood. That gave them unquestionable provenance. Pieces like this were incredibly rare and very valuable.

The Madonna and Child icon had a delicate jewel and pearl encrusted border. with gold hinges and a fine gold lock on its doors. The second was a simpler painting of John the Baptist, with a gold leaf border and gilded clasp on the doors. They were clearly worth the asking price and then some.

'Uncle' knew that in any struggling economy, there were many ways for enterprising individuals to increase their fortunes. He also knew that the minor Russian diplomat selling these treasures had a pipeline of stolen artefacts ready to trade.

Before he left London he met his old school chum Arlo Billingsworth for drinks. They celebrated his posting to Georgia, and Arlo's promotion as Sotheby's Russian specialist. Never one to miss an opportunity, Arlo had told him what to look out for while he was posted and how he could find grateful buyers for any acquisitions. These icons would be perfect. The price was good and his profit would be substantial. It was definitely worth the risk, and it wasn't even his money.

Vlasta's fighting fund was just sitting there doing nothing. 'Uncle' had access to it so there was no harm in 'borrowing' from it to make these purchases. His service salary was adequate, but since he'd been posted overseas he had acquired and cultivated some expensive tastes, and found that this kind of off the record enterprise supplemented his income handsomely.

He doubted that Vlasta had any idea how much was in the account.

The icons could be sent back to London in the diplomatic bag, ready for Arlo to collect from him when he returned. The money would be transferred back into the account within four weeks. No one would be any the wiser.

'Uncle' shook hands with the dealer and counted out the cash he had withdrawn earlier that morning. The diplomat seemed very pleased with the outcome. He put the money in his inside coat pocket and left. 'Uncle' returned the icons to their wrappings, and phoned for a taxi to take him to the British Embassy.

"Good evening, Sir. Late night?" the uniformed guard at the Embassy security check point asked.

"Yes, 'fraid so. I have to get these items logged into the registry and the paperwork will take forever."

The security guard gave a sympathetic nod and entered Bernard's name onto the visitor log, "Can I have your signature please, sir?" The guard turned the registration book round for Bernard to sign.

Bernard obliged with an illegible scrawl

"Thank you. Have a good evening, sir."

"Will do, thanks." Bernard picked up the package and moved swiftly towards the lifts.

Instead of taking the lift to the third floor, he pressed the button that took him down to the post room in the basement. He was sure it would be deserted at this time of night so he would be able to work without interruption.

Arlo had given him specific instructions about how to protect the items in transit, and he wrapped the wooden panels accordingly. He chose a suitable packing case from the post-room store, even adding an extra layer of protective wadding before tacking down the lid. Job done!

William was a stickler for detail so he would get him to do the paperwork. That way there would be no direct paper trail back to Bernard if there was a problem.

A noise startled him. He froze. He could feel his pulse increase. His heart began to race. The place should have been deserted at this time in the evening. He held his breath and heard the sound of keys jangling. He reached across the table, turning off the light. He was now in complete darkness. The footsteps came closer.

A key turned in the lock of the room next door. He heard a bucket and mop clank as the unseen janitor left the store room and relocked the door. He didn't breathe again until he could no longer hear footsteps on the concrete staircase. That was close.

He picked up the crate and opened the door. He checked the corridor; it was deserted. He closed the door behind him, turned left, and headed towards the back of the building. A service staircase at the end of the corridor gave him direct access to the office he shared with William. He mounted the stairs two at a time and was quite breathless when he reached the fire door on the third floor. He made a mental note to take more exercise.

He moved along the passageway and then into the office, his heart still pounding. The room was barely large enough to accommodate both desks, let alone the metal cabinet and the bank of office machinery. The only advantage was that it was always warm in the winter.

He put the sealed crate by the side of William's desk, and the written instructions of what to do with it in his top draw. They would be the first things William saw when he got into work the following morning.

A telex machine in one corner of the room was working relentlessly. It was highly unusual for there to be so much activity at this time of night. He was intrigued about what might be coming in on their secure line. He walked over, picked up the printout, and began to read.

Surely this couldn't be right? Reuters was reporting that the Berlin Wall had fallen. He had to read it twice to make sure his eyes weren't playing tricks on him.

He instinctively knew that if East Germany had lost control of its border, other Russian states could quickly follow. Georgia was one of them.

He added the telex message to a folder marked URGENT on his desk, and made his way down to the ground floor reception. The lift doors opened, and he heard excited conversations about the news. There were already a number of people milling about, with more coming through the entrance. Key staff had obviously been called back to work. That was indeed a stroke of luck. Now, no one would think that his presence here at this time of night was unusual. It was also unlikely that the security guards would have any particular reason to remember him.

He exited the building.

He needed a plan. His official car was back at his apartment nearby. There was a shortcut through the public park at the rear of the Embassy building. It would take minutes on foot, and the cold evening air would probably help him to focus.

As he walked, Bernard concluded that an event this significant would completely change the balance of power between the East and the West. New and dangerous ideas about inviting foreign investment into the Soviet Union were gaining traction. This could even mean an end to the cold war!

Bernard lived in an apartment block designated for foreign nationals and one of its few benefits was that it was equipped with central heating. He felt the bitter chill through his coat and gloves and was grateful when he entered the vestibule.

The ever-present concierge was sitting at his small desk, listening to a boxing match. So deeply engrossed was he on the crackling commentary, that he failed to register Bernard's arrival. Bernard made his way along the corridor, and opened the gated elevator doors. He punched the button for his floor, and the elevator clanked as it ascended. He stepped out on the second floor, closing the gates behind him, and crossed the landing to his front door.

He inspected the tell-tale indicators he had left to warn him of any unauthorised entry. Satisfied that everything was in order, he went into his apartment and closed the door behind him. In line with protocol, he slid the two heavy bolts into place and secured the dead lock. Only then did he remove his hat and gloves, and hang his overcoat in the hall closet.

He looked at his reflection in the hall mirror and noted how tired he was looking. Life here was taking its toll. He needed a drink. He went into the kitchen and poured a generous measure of vodka into a tumbler.

He had developed a taste for the premium Russian vodka that came from the state-run Shida Ex shop, which offered a wide range of difficult to obtain Western goods. Coca-Cola, Chocolate, Wrangler jeans, Swiss watches, American cigarettes, Japanese electronic devices and colour TV sets were all available. You had to pay with American dollars or English pounds, but at least this alcohol was safe to drink, unlike the bootleg stuff.

He flopped into his armchair, and switched on the radio. The world's media services were now reporting live from the Berlin Wall, speculating on what would happen next. The world was changing in ways that would disrupt his comfort and definitely damage his finances. He was not a happy man.

The more he listened, the more convinced he became that the power balance would shift. He may even be forced to become the junior partner in this arrangement if his Whitehall masters had anything to do with it. His lucrative income would be in jeopardy. He needed to engineer a solution. After another hour of listening to the news reports and he had a plan.

He would take the latest information that Vlasta was due to exchange, and make it his last, arranging a terrible accident for the agent. If there had been more time he could have persuaded the Russians to do it for him by leaking details of his activities to them. But it needed to happen immediately, so he would have to do it himself.

He'd have to request an immediate transfer for William, too. He had become far too attached to the family, anyway. From some of the minor details he had mentioned, Bernard suspected that he was in direct contact with the wife, and that was strictly against the rules. William was never cut out to be a field agent, anyway. It would be much better for him if he was moved to a desk job in London. And of course, he would also be well out of harm's way if and when the fallout happened. He downed the remaining vodka in his glass, and drifted off into a fitful sleep in the chair.

Bernard was woken by the alarm on his wristwatch. He had just enough time to freshen up before he left. The street lighting was poor and intermittent. As it was only 4.30am he felt confident there would be no one out on the streets. He slid into his Embassy car, started the engine and turned the heater controls to maximum.

As he drove across the river the temperature in the car warmed up. Ten minutes later, he turned his headlights off and coasted into Vlasta's street, stopping about two-hundred yards away from his apartment block. He arrived just as his asset was wheeling his battered old scooter down the steps of his building.

This operation would be straightforward. A surgical strike. Quick, clean and untraceable.

He noticed Vlasta's wife standing at the top of the steps. She waved him goodbye before closing the heavy door to keep out the biting cold.

Bernard thought how fortunate it was that she was so attractive. She wouldn't remain a widow for long.

9

Shady Fields, 17th March 2018

William was having a bad day. He just couldn't seem to focus. He could normally tell by the way people looked at him whether he was making sense to them. The trouble was that everything he said was absolutely real to him. Sometimes he relived things that had happened to him in the past. They felt real, like he was experiencing them for the first time. Sometimes he saw things that he knew others, by their reactions, could not see. Occasionally he didn't recognise where he was, or even who he was.

He had got caught out in the rain yesterday afternoon, and the chills had kept him awake half the night. He'd had terrible dreams about people from his past. He couldn't remember them exactly, just the feeling of fear and loss they left him with. He felt feverish, and knew there was something he should remember, but it wouldn't come to him. Instead, fuzziness filled his head and he could not concentrate. He experienced anxiety and distress on days like today.

As a scientist first and foremost, he prized his abilities for critical analysis and logical thinking. He knew the frequency of these episodes had reduced since he came to Shady Fields. It was so peaceful here. It normally gave him an opportunity to write, but today that quiet mind evaded him. Remembering was the easy part. Getting the incidents down in the right chronological order was difficult.

William had won a scholarship to Cambridge. His lecturers quickly labelled him 'a brilliant mind.' He excelled at his studies but was socially awkward, and found it difficult to make friends. He had worked for Marconi after he graduated, developing radio technology to improve Britain's listening capabilities. He'd liked that job. People left him alone to do his own thing, and he was able to make considerable breakthroughs in communication technology. That had bought him to the attention of MI6, and he was flattered when they recruited him as a scientific officer in the early '70s, where he worked on technology that revolutionised spy craft. His bugs and listening devices looked like buttons, lightbulbs and pens. He had genuinely written the book on cyber security, and was top in his specialist field.

Although he had not worked for the service for more than a decade he still enjoyed inventing things. His latest gadget had worked really well when he trialled it at yesterday's meeting with Bernard. The recording was as clear as a bell.

Bernard had always treated him in a dismissive way. He told him often enough that he was "unsuited for active operations," but he was wrong. Without his work, many more agents would have been captured or killed.

When they had been stationed in Tbilisi he had witnessed betrayal of the first order.

He felt responsible; after all, he was the person who'd convinced Shura to spy for MI6. Bernard had insisted that he engaged in surveillance of the family once they'd engaged his services. Milena Vlasta was a real beauty. She was a willowy, graceful young woman, with flashing eyes and a ready laugh. He watched them together, but he watched her in particular, mesmerised. He watched her throughout her pregnancy, and when the baby was born he watched her with the child. Motherhood suited her.

He didn't understand it at the time, but William had felt a powerful need to protect and look out for them all. Shura had been involved in a dangerous game, which would have meant certain death if the Russians had discovered what he was doing.

But of course, it wasn't the Russians he'd needed to look out for. William remembered the day Shura was killed and it still ate away at him. Could he have prevented it?

He had actually heard Gunther Schabowski give his

famous radio interview that night. He'd met him at a trade delegation a few months before: a thin, balding little man, with sharp eyes that betrayed a shrewdness that William found impressive. As a reformer he had helped to get rid of some of the corrupt characters in the old East German Politburo. He had spoken to William of the regime's new approach, and its content was in the speech he gave on radio that fateful day.

Schabowski was giving a standard briefing to the press when he suddenly paused, shuffling his papers, before issuing the immortal statement:

"This will be interesting for you. Today it was decided to make it possible for all citizens to leave the country through the official border crossing-points. All citizens of the German Democratic Republic can now be issued with visas for the purposes of travel or visiting relatives in the West. This order is to take effect unverzuglich" (immediately).

William remembered the confusion. One correspondent had asked, "What exactly does *unverzuglich* mean, in this context?"

Mr Schabowski had replied, seemingly without really thinking. "Well, it just means straight away."

William knew this was not a mistake on Gunther's part. It was a daring move to provide a catalyst for change. He thought it was one of the bravest things he had ever heard, even though history would record it as an error. The authorities had intended it to be a slow, bureaucratic process, carefully regulated.

Gunther had given an entirely different impression. According to him, the Berlin Wall hadn't really fallen – it had simply ceased to matter. The world had become a different place overnight. Gunther Schabowski had outmanoeuvred the whole of the East German politburo, and it still made William chuckle.

On the morning of Shura's last drop, William had been hidden in the bus shelter on the other side of the bridge. He wasn't sure why he had gone. He didn't believe in gut instinct, but something had compelled him to be there on that bridge. He had watched the car plough into Shura's scooter. He had watched as the shadowy figure retrieved the papers. He had watched when the driver drove over him as he lay on the floor, injured. He had watched Shura Vlasta die.

William had waited until he was sure the coast was clear to run over to Shura, but he knew he was already dead. Nevertheless, his training had not prepared him for the shock. His whole body had begun to shake.

He had been sceptical whether the photos he'd taken that morning would show anything, but he processed them, anyway. It had been dark. He was at least fifty meters away, but he hadn't stopped to think, his finger working the shutter automatically. He'd felt sickened. He knew this man and his family. But he couldn't talk to his boss, and he didn't know who he could trust at the Embassy. His main thought had been could he help Milena and the baby.

William woke with a start. He must have fallen asleep, or had he just been daydreaming? What day was it? What time was it? Where was he?

He looked around his room. Bit by bit, his anxiety lessened as his recognition grew. He saw a copy of his favourite painting, 'The philosopher and his pupils' by

Van Der Vliet, hanging on his wall. It had been a retirement gift from his team.

His wallet lay on the table next to his old typewriter. He felt himself relax a little. He looked at his digital clock, it read 16.00, so he knew it was the afternoon. He stood and steadied himself before he walked across the room and sat down by the window. There was already a sheet of paper in the ancient machine with a chapter heading: Tbilisi. He began to type. A soft knock at the door made him look up. "Come in," he called.

Layla Strong walked into the room and smiled at William. She was petite at just five feet, with very short dark hair and bright green eyes. She reminded William of the Harry Theaker pixies that illustrated his childhood storybooks.

"Hello, William. I thought I would come and ask if you wanted to join everyone downstairs for tea? The whist drive is this afternoon and I know you play a mean hand of cards."

William grumbled "It was called bridge in my day and there were no knockout rounds, either."

Layla continued, unabashed. "I don't know how to play. We had board games when I was at home with my mother but not cards; she didn't approve of gambling.

"If you don't want to play cards, then at least come for the tea. Chef's been experimenting, and there's a gluten free pecan pie, or coffee and walnut cake."

She smiled again as he took a breath to reply, and continued. "I know, in your day there was no such thing as gluten free."

William laughed, in spite of himself. He really liked Layla. She always had a smile on her face, and nothing seemed to lower her mood.

"Okay, I'll come down a bit later. But I want to finish this chapter first. I've been thinking a lot about it recently and I want to capture the events while they're fresh in my mind."

"Can I read it?"

William looked as if she had made an improper advance. "Certainly not! Maybe when it 's finished, but not yet."

"Okay," said Layla, "I'll save you some cake."

As she turned to leave, a strange feeling of familiarity came over William. The shine of her dark hair, her profile, and the soft accent in her voice reminded him of something in his past. He just couldn't remember what it was.

10

Trip to London, 21st March 2018

Wednesday morning turned out to be thoroughly miserable. Charlie, Linda and William gathered in the entrance hall, watching the relentless drizzle. Charlie pulled his raincoat on.

"This is the sort of rain that soaks you right through. William, I'd wear a raincoat if you don't want to be cold and damp for the rest of the day."

Much to Charlie's regret he did as he was told, and fetched his old Barbour jacket.

They took a taxi to the station, arriving on the platform just as the London train pulled in. Although they had reserved seats, it was still a struggle to move through the morning commuter crush to find them. Their journey was not a quiet one either, with mobile phones ringing out at frequent intervals. William and Charlie chatted quietly, trying to work out when the world became this hectic.

Opposite them, the seat next to Linda had been taken by a nondescript young woman in her early twenties carrying a large rucksack. She unceremoniously dumped it on the table and proceeded to dive into it, like a fisherman looking for pearls.

The two old men were mesmerised as they watched the cosmetic ballet that followed. After cleansing and moisturising her skin, the woman applied at least three shades of foundation cream, which she blended together with a wide flat sponge, giving her at least the appearance of a faultless complexion. Next, she combed and coloured her eyebrows, then added four neutral colours of eyeshadow to her eyelids. The resulting effect was the sort of smokey eye effect popular in TV commercials. Next, she applied copious quantities of mascara. A line around her lips accentuated a plump pout, and that was filled in with a pale earthy colour, topped off with a gloss coat. She used a pump spray to liven up her short, curly hair. The overall look was finished off with a watch to her right wrist, and a stack of bangles and rings to her left wrist and digits.

The transformation complete, an entirely different person sat there now. A more confident and sophisticated woman, who looked at least six or seven years older. There was an air of haughtiness about her.

She reached into her bag again, pulling out a mobile phone and a set of tiny white earbuds. Then, having inserted the headphones into her ears, she gathered her belongings together, and moved off down the train in the direction of the buffet car. Charlie leaned across to Linda and said, conspiratorially, "I wondered what took Rita so long every morning. Now I know."

Both men were fascinated that something their generation would consider to be the intimate act of putting on makeup should be done so publicly without a care for who might be watching.

Linda smiled at them, thinking how nice it was to be able to accompany them both to London today, leaving Hilary in charge at the home. Although she'd only been with them for a little over a week, their new manager was already making a difference. She was personable, and took every opportunity to get to know staff and residents. From day one, Linda had observed that she was a quick study. Her previous experience was clear to see, as she made decisions swiftly, meaning that things were already getting done. In just a few short days, Linda's initial misgivings had been dispelled. She genuinely felt able to enjoy today without worrying about what was happening back at Shady Fields.

The train pulled into Paddington Station and they waited for most of the commuters to exit the carriage before they moved. The three of them headed down the train towards the door, where a guard and a team of cleaners were waiting to board.

Stepping down onto the platform they were pleased to discover that they were next to the barriers. There were just a few people milling around. A young woman called out to a small boy wearing a pirate hat and wildly swinging a plastic cutlass; he stopped suddenly at his mother's instruction and came towards her meekly, almost as if he were walking the plank. Two business men with obligatory wheeled briefcases were standing nearby, both deep in conversation on their mobile phones. On a metal bench seat, a thickset, bearded man in jeans and a casual jacket sat staring at the sports page of The Sun.

Linda presented their tickets to a guard at the barrier and he nodded them through, out onto the main concourse. She then bought three Oyster day-cards from a ticket machine, and looked for direction to the tube station. It seemed that getting on and off the platforms had taken longer than the journey to London itself.

They arrived at Holborn Station, riding up a very long escalator to street level. Linda considered what might happen if these escalators broke down. She figured that she would find climbing the stairs a challenge, and she was reasonably fit. It must be a nightmare for the elderly, or young mothers with exuberant pirates in tow. Arriving at the top, the three companions did the funny little hop that people not accustomed to using them always make, and followed the signs to the station exit.

Their destination was just a short walk along Gate

Street in Lincolns Inn, and they found the office building easily. It was modern but uninspiring, with a large glass and stainless steel atrium, a wide reception desk, and a list of occupants displayed on the wall between the lifts. A quick look at the board revealed that Schuster and Stokes, Solicitors in family law & Commissioners for Oaths, were on the third floor. Newman Associates Intellectual Property and Copyright lawyers, the firm William would be seeing, were on the tenth floor. The lift doors opened and they all got in.

"I'm not sure how long this will take," said Charlie." I've booked a table for lunch at 12.30pm, and it's not far from here."

"We shouldn't be too long so we'll wait for you downstairs," said William. "You did say lunch was your treat, didn't you Charlie?"

"Yes, I haven't forgotten."

They both smiled. The lift gave a small jolt and the doors opened on the third floor. Charlie stepped out into a light, modern, open reception area. A smiling receptionist greeted him.

"Please follow me, Mr Bingham. Mr Schuster is expecting you."

Charlie had made notes about his will, and had a couple of queries. He knew the time was coming when he would not be able to make his own decisions so wanted to let his views be known now, before it was too late.

Mr Schuster's office was large and comfortable, and

he stood to greet Charlie behind his ornate wooden desk. The solicitor, who was in his early sixties, always dealt with Charlie personally. The Bingham's were one of the firm's oldest and wealthiest clients. As such he felt that 'Mr Charles' deserved the personal touch. They exchanged pleasantries, and as Charlie sank into a comfortable leather chair set out just for him, Schuster removed a folded copy of his last will and testament from a folder in front of him, scanning it briefly.

"So, how can we be of assistance to you today, Mr Charles?"

Charlie recounted the details of his recent diagnosis to Schuster. "I need to make a few changes to my will, and I need to create a Lasting Power of Attorney for financial and health matters" he said, quoting from his notes. The solicitor pressed an intercom button and requested that the relevant forms be bought through.

"Will your children take the power of attorney for you Mr Charles?"

Charlie looked directly at him. He had always thought it odd that he was addressed as Mr Charles. His father had been Lord Bingham, but his late brother's son Edward now held that title.

"No," he said, emphatically. "I haven't seen either of them for more than twenty years, so I hardly think it would be appropriate. I have chosen Daniel Grant to be my representative. I have known him for a long time and I trust him implicitly to act in my best interests. Unfortunately, his commitments meant that he was unable to make the meeting this morning, so I would ask you to bring the documentation to me to get it signed and witnessed."

Schuster made notes as Charlie answered his numerous questions, finally putting down his pen nearly an hour later. He looked at Charlie with an air of confidence.

"We'll draw up the documents, then once they're signed we'll register them to make it legal. I'll also bring the codicil for your will at the same time. That will also require a witnessed signature." He collected the papers together on the desk. "Is there anything else we can help you with today, Mr Charles?"

"No, I'm happy that everything is as I want it."

Schuster stood up. "Do you have anything else planned for the rest of the day? I don't imagine you get up to town much these days."

Charlie winced briefly as he stood up and accepted the proffered handshake. His joints were stiff today.

"Yes I do, actually. I'm here with a couple of friends so we're having lunch at my club. I haven't been there for a while, so it's a bit of a treat. I heard that the new management there are trying to give it a veneer of respectability; I expect it won't be a patch on the old days, but it'll be nice to see the old place again." Schuster escorted Charlie to the elevator, wished him well, and thanked him for his continued patronage.

Dan had found the contact at Newman Associates for William after a few brief enquiries. He felt it was important that William should understand the implications of publishing a memoir.

He hadn't read any of the manuscript – no one had. William had not been explicit about what he had included so far, but a short conversation with him had gleaned two things: it covered the whole of his career, and he was using it to set the record straight, righting old wrongs. He intended to name key people who had profited from their mistakes, in the belief that it was in the public interest to out them. If he was successful in getting the book published there would be very serious consequences for those involved.

Mr Erskine was the company's specialist on disclosure and data protection in publishing. William and Linda faced him across his desk now, each of them enjoying a cup of strong filter coffee. Linda passed William his manuscript from her spacious messenger bag.

The walls of Erskine's office were adorned with framed book covers advertising some of the more sensational reads the company had brought to market. It was indeed an impressive selection, with titles by Cherie Blair, Peter Mandelson, Roy Keane and Andrew Morton being amongst those that Linda recognised. William would be in lofty company if he worked with this man.

Mr Erskine addressed William directly.

"Dan has already given me a brief outline of what you want to do, William. I believe you have a few questions for me, is that correct?"

"Yes. In a nutshell, I need to know how to get my book published without being stopped by MI5. Others have tried to publish and been censored 'in the interests of National Security'. Well, I have important things that need to be said in the public interest. And I want to know what I have to do to make that happen."

Mr. Erskine rotated his executive swivel chair, and pointed to a couple of the pictures on the wall.

"These two authors experienced resistance from the security services. We were able to clarify exactly what they could disclose, and how to do that without a lengthy court case. I'm confident we can do the same for you, William." He pointed at the manuscript. "Have you bought that copy for me to read?"

William picked up the wad of tightly bound paper and held it close to his chest, shaking his head from side to side.

"It's not ready yet. I haven't finished it, and I don't want it read until it's complete."

"I can understand that you're worried about your thunder being stolen, William, but I have to read it so that I can see what we are dealing with, and how best to proceed."

William hugged the manuscript even more tightly, a slight panic creeping into his voice.

"This is the only copy. It isn't on a computer. I know how vulnerable it would be if it were."

Mr Erskine considered William for a while.

"William, at some point we *will* need an electronic copy to work with. We can produce a proofed manuscript for you, and our publishing lawyers can navigate any legal issues your book may raise. We can handle any disputes and challenges and if it's commercially attractive, our industry expertise can also advise on the potential for TV and film rights. Publications like yours are experiencing a surge in interest right now. You could be sitting on a huge success, but I can only properly assess its potential by reading it."

Linda, who had been silent up to now, touched William's arm to offer him some reassurance.

"Mr Erskine will need to read it to be able to give you the right legal advice. You have to finish it first, then decide how you want him to proceed. Let's take some time to think about what you want to do."

She turned to Mr Erskine. "With your contacts in the industry, will you be able to help William find a specialist publisher?"

Mr Erskine looked reluctant. "We can't get him a publishing deal, that's not what we do. I do have a lot of contacts, though, and I'll make a few enquiries to test the level of interest."

Turning to William again, he said "How much more do you have to do before you can give me a completed draft?"

William considered the question. Time didn't have the same meaning to him that it used to. Sometimes he had difficulty calculating it. He felt pressured to say something, though.

"Oh, a couple of weeks I expect," he spluttered.

"Fine, that gives me something to work with. So shall we talk again in a month and review where we are then? In the meantime, consider it an act of good faith on our part that we will produce the electronic version for you when the draft is complete, and make it ready to send to prospective publishers or agents. But please remember that when we meet again, William, I will need that manuscript to get the ball rolling. Is that acceptable?"

"Yes, yes, that will be fine," William said, as he handed the cherished manuscript back to Linda for safekeeping. Linda noticed that Erskine didn't really look convinced.

They said goodbye, and headed back towards the lifts.

Charlie was eagerly waiting for them in the lobby. "I 'd almost given up on you. Come on, I 'm famished. Let 's eat."

The rain had stopped and the weak sunshine was trying to dry the pavements. It was too far for them to walk to the club, so they made their way back to the tube station. They needed to get the Central Line to Bond Street. Charlie struck out in military fashion.

"The club's in Berkley Square, so a short walk will sharpen our appetites."

It was 11.45am, and not too busy for a Wednesday morning.

11

Holborn Station, 21st March 2018

As they made their way into Holborn Tube Station they passed a news stand where a bearded man was thumbing a copy of the London Evening Standard. They chatted about what they wanted to eat as they passed through the entrance and onto the steep escalator down to the platforms.

William stood in front, while Charlie had set off walking down the steps. Linda stood behind Charlie, to the right. She sensed someone close behind her, and moved to her left to stand behind William when a terrific force suddenly propelled her forwards. She tumbled head first past him, slamming into Charlie, who lost his balance and stumbled. She continued hurtling downwards, landing at the bottom with a sickening thump in a jumble of arms and legs.

People seemed to rush from all directions to help her. A quick-thinking guard had seen her fall and pressed the emergency stop button. He was on his radio now, calling for immediate assistance. He had seen accidents like this before, and knew it was serious.

A crowd gathered around Linda, who lay completely still. Her skin was already beginning to show a ghastly grey pallor. Charlie went into automatic pilot, and began ordering onlookers to stand well back, to give her room. The guard was kneeling beside her checking for a pulse, and to see if she was still breathing.

William caught up with them, sinking to his knees by her side and clutching her hand. The guard looked up.

"She's breathing, but I don't want to move her. The emergency services are on their way."

Within moments, they heard sirens in the distance. In just a few minutes more, the paramedics had arrived. Transport police were on the scene now as well, and they began to take control.

William stood to the side as a young paramedic in green overalls assessed the situation. Her partner connected a monitor to check her heart rate. The police officers moved people along. They had to stop a couple of people filming the scene on their mobile phones. One of the officers appealed for information from the bystanders, and Charlie tried to provide as much detail as he could.

A second ambulance crew arrived and went into what was obviously a well-rehearsed routine. They knew how to move a patient up to street level without causing further injury.

Linda was still unconscious. A stretcher and a neck collar were produced as if from nowhere and skilled hands immobilised her head. William spotted a smear of blood on the latex glove of the paramedic as he slid her onto the stretcher. A member of the crowd had identified himself as a Doctor and offered to help the paramedics. He fitted a cannula and taped the back of her hand. She remained completely still. Her eyes were still closed, and her pallor was ashen. It was clear they needed to get her into the ambulance as quickly as possible.

As William and Charlie sat in the back of the ambulance staring at Linda they could hear the driver talking urgently to the dispatch. He was relaying information to the trauma team at the nearest Accident and Emergency unit. With blue lights flashing and sirens shrieking, they hurtled into the traffic and made their way through the now congested London streets.

Both men stared at the paramedic taking Linda's vital signs. She was obviously used to the rocking motion of travelling at speed. Linda stirred briefly, and her eyes flickered open.

William lent forward and softly called her name. The female paramedic flashed a light to test for pupil dilation, and tried to get a response.

"Linda, can you hear me?"

It looked like she might be coming around.

"Hi Linda, I'm Emma. You've had a nasty fall. I need you to remain perfectly still until we can get you to the hospital. Can you do that for me?"

Linda's eyelids fluttered again, but then closed. The paramedic tried again.

"Linda, you've had a fall and we're taking you to the hospital."

This time she responded. Her eyelids opened a little way, and she tried to mumble something. The paramedic leaned forward to catch the words, but the noise of the sirens drowned them out.

"Your friends are here with you. Try and stay with me, Linda."

Her eyes closed again. All the men could do was watch as the paramedic continued to work. She monitored her blood pressure, heart rate and oxygen levels, the results automatically recorded by the numerous wires that connected to a machine above her.

The ambulance came to a standstill, and almost immediately the back doors were flung open. Green uniforms once again took charge, and manoeuvred the trolley, bearing its damaged cargo off the ambulance, and into the hospital.

They rushed through double swing doors and into a triage cubical staffed with waiting doctors and nurses. They worked together to transfer her from the ambulance trolley onto a hospital examination table, shouting instructions, status reports and requests to each other as they went.

The medics had been informed of her condition by the telemetry system, which was standard equipment in trauma units. William and Charlie looked on. The confusion and noise was disturbing to them, but staff seemed perfectly comfortable with it.

One of the nurses noted that Linda was coming around again. She began looking for a response.

"Can you tell me your name?"

"Linda," she whispered.

"Do you know what day it is, Linda?"

"Wednesday," the same small voice said.

William and Charlie allowed themselves to be guided into the waiting area. She had been speaking, so she must be ok.

As requested, Charlie spoke to the receptionist to complete as much of the paperwork as he could. William waited silently, praying that she would be OK. He suddenly realised that no one else knew what had happened. He dug into Linda's bag and found her phone. He tutted as he noticed her lack of security. No password at all! He scrolled through her quick dial directory and pressed the number for Dan.

The whole thing had taken just over an hour from the accident happening to arriving in A&E. He felt himself relax a little, at least now she was safe and in the right hands. All they could do was wait.

Another forty minutes passed and two empty paper coffee cups sat on the table between them as the two men waited silently for news. Then, the double doors to the trauma unit swung open, and a doctor came out. He called for Charlie by name.

"Are you her next of kin?"

"No," said Charlie. "She's the manager of the retirement home where we live. We came up to London for the day. We both had appointments in the city, so she came with us."

"I see. Have you informed her next of kin?"

William spoke. "I've spoken to her Manager; he's on his way here. He'll have more information about her family. I 'm sorry I can 't be of more help..." he tailed off.

The doctor looked troubled.

"We need to do a scan to see what's going on. She may need an operation, so as soon as Mr...?"

"Grant," said William. "Dan Grant."

"As soon as Mr Grant arrives, please ask him to go to reception right away. She's going for a scan now. We'll let you know what's happening as soon as we know more."

Another hour went by. They heard the electronic whoosh of the entrance doors open and Dan came rushing in, urgently looking for familiar faces.

"I was on the train when you called. What happened?"

"She fell down an escalator when we were going for lunch, and they bought her here. She's had a scan, but that's all we know. You need to go to the admissions desk right away."

Dan crossed the room and spoke quietly to the

receptionist. The same doctor they had seen earlier came out, and the two men spoke in hushed tones before the doctor returned to his patient. Dan turned towards the waiting pair. They knew by his look that something was wrong.

"They've done a scan and found a fracture in her skull. She also has a blood clot on her brain. They're prepping her for surgery right now. It's very serious – she's in a critical condition."

"But she was awake in the ambulance, and was talking to the nurses when we got here. She's going to be ok isn't she, Dan?" Charlie looked very worried.

"They won't know the extent of the problem until they operate, which is why they needed to know who her next of kin is. I've called her sister, and she's on her way."

Dan looked at William. He looked very pale and was hugging Linda's bag tightly to his chest.

"How are you doing, William?"

"We were on our way to lunch. She fell down the stairs right past me. It all happened so fast."

Dan looked at them both. "Have either of you eaten anything since breakfast?"

Charlie shook his head. "We hardly had time for breakfast, we had a train to catch. I was treating everyone to lunch at my club, but we never got there." His hands began to tremble.

Dan took charge. "Look, there's a café just over there. Why don't you two go and get something to eat. I'll stay here to wait for Linda's sister, and if there's any news I'll come and find you."

The two men got up and headed for the cafeteria. As they walked away, Dan thought they'd aged ten years. They had lived lives of risk and experienced their fair share of danger, but this had taken the wind completely out of their sails. They seemed defeated. Dan knew how much everyone cared for Linda, and the thought of her being seriously injured had shaken them to the core.

He took a seat, and began to mull over what William had said on the phone. He didn't sound paranoid when he had spoken, but he had been absolutely clear that this was no accident.

12

Shady Fields, 22nd March 2018

Hilary had only known Linda for a brief time, but she liked her. They had got on really well, and had begun to enjoy working together. As people came down for breakfast she had spent time trying to reassure them that the operations manager would be fine. Unfortunately, she didn't seem to be convincing anyone. Least of all, herself.

There had been little communication from the hospital overnight, other than to deliver the news that they had operated. The operation had been successful, but to give the swelling a chance to reduce, they had put her into an induced coma. Linda was seriously ill.

The three men had not got back until midnight, and had gone straight to bed. Hilary had seen Charlie when she had taken a breakfast tray up to him in his room, and he was clearly devastated. The reality had finally sunk in, and he was pacing back and forth, waiting for news.

By contrast, William had risen early, and was now out walking in the grounds, trying to clear his head.

Dan had just finished a call when Hilary came through the door. She was carrying a tray of hot black coffee and toast. He hadn't slept much by the look of him, and had worry lines etched into his face. The glint in his eye wasn't there, and a paleness was evident, even under his regular tan.

"Morning, Dan. Was that the hospital?" she asked him.

Dan looked up. "Yes, and it's not good I'm afraid. She's still unconscious. There was extensive damage, and they won't know whether things are getting any better for a couple of days. Her sister and brother in law are at the hospital with her."

Hilary crossed the room and put the tray in front of him.

"That's very thoughtful of you, Hilary; I'm really not hungry to be honest, although the coffee is most welcome."

She sat opposite him and took a sip from her cup. "So, what actually happened?"

"As far as I can tell they were on the way to Charlie's club for lunch. She fell down the escalator at the Tube Station, virtually all the way from top to bottom. Charlie and William saw the whole thing, and it knocked them for six. They're both close to Linda, so it was a terrible shock."

"If there is anything I can do, just ask."

Dan absentmindedly bit into a slice of buttered toast.

"I'm sorry to add to your load, Dan, but I have just taken a call from HQ. They informed me that Bernard's coming down this morning – he should be here about 11."

Pre-empting Dan 's question, she added "He didn't say what it was about."

"Damn, that 's all I need. The consultants are here this afternoon to work on the report. No doubt he'll want to oversee the last of the interviews with the residents."

The telephone rang on Hilary 's desk and she walked across to answer it. As she listened, she shot Dan a look of concern.

"Okay Layla, thanks. I'll be down straight away."

She replaced the handset." Layla said there are two police officers downstairs who want to speak with you about the accident.

"You'll probably want some privacy. Shall I bring them up, or do you want to meet them in the library?"

"Thanks, Hilary, but I think we should meet up here. I don 't want the other residents overhearing anything. Will you show them up, please?"

Hilary made her way down the staircase and into the entrance hall where two men in plain clothes waited patiently. The sight of them made her feel uneasy. She'd been expecting uniformed officers from the transport police.

"Good morning, gentlemen, I'm Hilary Geddes, manager here. Can I see some ID, please?"

Both officers offered their warrant cards for Hilary look at. "I'm Detective Inspector Dhillion and this Detective Constable Allen. We need to speak with Mr Daniel Grant, please."

"Of course." She led them up the staircase to the office and entered, announcing the officers in order of rank. Once the introductions had been made she left, closing the door behind her.

Dan gestured towards the two seats opposite him. "Please sit, gentlemen. How can I help?"

Constable Allen took out his note pad and pen, ready to make notes. The inspector spoke first.

"Mr, Grant, we were contacted at 6.30pm yesterday by London Transport Police about an incident at Holborn Tube Station involving one of your staff, Linda Bridges."

Dan nodded, and the Inspector continued. "They've reviewed CCTV footage of the incident, and that suggests an assault may have taken place."

Quickly consulting his notebook, the Inspector continued. "We need to question William Wright and Charles Bingham about what happened. I believe they were both with Ms Bridges at the time."

Dan studied the policemen. The inspector had a street-weary, cynical look, with a well-worn trench coat adding to the Sam Spade impression he was clearly cultivating. By contrast, his sidekick DC Allen was young and smart. He wore a slim fitting, well-cut suit, and fashionable polished shoes. He also possessed an enthusiastic attitude, which the job hadn't managed to harden yet.

"Yes, Inspector, they were both with Linda yesterday. As you may know, we are a residential home for people with dementia. Both gentlemen had appointments in London but we thought they should be escorted, so Linda agreed to go with them. I understand it happened as they were on their way to lunch.

"I'll need to check where they are at the moment. I know Charlie was in his room, but I'm not sure about William, I haven't seen him yet."

"We need to speak to them both as a matter of urgency, sir." The inspector adjusted his coat to give himself a little more freedom.

"I would like to be present when you question them please, Inspector. Dementia is an unpredictable condition, and a traumatic incident or a change in routine can trigger an unpredictable episode. I need to be sure that they are both okay."

The inspector looked briefly at DC Allen and replied "Yes, that will be fine."

Hilary had pre-empted the Inspector's request and had already tasked Layla with finding them both and bringing them to the office. The group gathered in the general office, seated around the large meeting table. The two police officers sat side by side, with William, Charlie and Dan opposite them.

The two residents described the events of the morning: the journey into London, their departure from Paddington station, and their entry to the tube. They then provided a brief outline of their meetings and their lunch plans. Inspector Dhillon was surprisingly considerate. He allowed both men to describe the events in their own words, and at their own pace. Charlie was a little more animated than William, who simply kept to the facts.

DC Allen scribbled away without speaking. Inspector Dhillon shifted in his seat.

"So now we come to the incident itself. I'd like you both to tell me, as fully as you can, exactly what you saw, and anything that you might remember now which you didn't think important at the time. Why don't you go first, Charlie?"

Charlie looked down at the floor. "We passed the newspaper seller at the entrance to Holborn station and went inside to catch the tube. I hate those escalators and the one there is particularly steep. I got on it first, William was just behind me, and Linda was behind him.

"I began to walk down the steps. Then, out of nowhere, Linda collided with me. She caught my legs and I almost lost my balance. I managed to steady myself, and saw that she was still tumbling down ahead of me, screaming as she went. She just kept turning over and over. She ended up at the bottom of the escalator, and she wasn't moving."

Charlie took a breath. Clearly reliving it was quite

traumatic for him.

"Someone must have stopped it, because I felt a jolt and realised I was still walking down the steps to get to her. She still wasn't moving.

"It all got very noisy at that point. The guard came running over and there were plenty of people who rushed to see if they could help. I knew she needed space, so I told people to keep back. I think there may have been a young girl who called the ambulance – she was using her mobile phone –although it could have been the guard, I'm not sure. He was on his radio, then we waited for help to arrive.

"The medics got her onto a stretcher and into the ambulance in no time at all, and we went with her to the hospital."

The inspector gave a slight nod. "That's great, Charlie, thanks – you're being a great help. Did you see anything you would consider to be unusual, or anyone that was acting suspiciously, either outside the station or inside, or maybe even after the accident?"

Charlie reeled at the information overload, and Dan took over.

"Just ask one question at a time. It might not feel so overwhelming."

The inspector nodded, and started again. "Of course, I'm sorry Charlie. Was there anything that struck you as odd or out of place?"

Charlie looked up from the floor, making eye contact with Dan. "Not that I recall, just people going about their business. Nothing else I can remember."

"Thanks Charlie, you've been very helpful. Now, William, what do you remember?"

William straightened in his chair. "The same, really. There was a bearded man looking at a newspaper. And there were two guards talking at the entrance about their shift patterns, and how the union needed to do something about it.

"Charlie got on the escalator first, and I followed just behind him. I glanced over my shoulder looking for Linda, and noticed that she was a couple of steps behind me, standing on the right. I was going to tell her to stand on the left, but got distracted seeing Charlie walking down the escalator steps. I turned back again to talk to her, but she was looking over her shoulder, then she fell forwards. She bumped into my right shoulder. In fact, I was glad I had a grip on the handrail or I could have followed her.

"She fell forwards down the steps, bumping into Charlie – he managed to stay on his feet, too. She continued to fall, hitting both the left and right hand walls of the escalator as she tumbled over. She landed at the bottom. We both rushed to help her. Charlie got there before me. The guard had shut off the escalator. When we got to the bottom he was there with Linda, telling people not to move her.

"He said the emergency services were on their way, and shortly after that we heard sirens in the distance, then the paramedics arrived."

The Inspector looked at William. "Did you see anything else, anyone acting suspiciously at any time?"

"No, not then."

The Inspector looked up and tilted his head. "What do you mean, not then?"

"Well, it did occur to me that a man we'd seen earlier in the day was a little odd. He was sitting on a bench on the platform at Paddington Station, reading a newspaper, when we arrived. Actually, he was staring at the sports page at the back of The Sun, so to be totally accurate he wasn't really reading and it wasn't really a newspaper.

"We saw him again at Holborn tube station after our appointments. It was definitely the same man who picked up the Standard at the news stand, and I wondered why he'd be bothering with it when it would have had the same news in it as his copy of the Sun newspaper from earlier in the day."

"Can you describe the man for me please, William?" asked the Inspector.

"Yes, he was tall, stocky, and had a distinctive bushy beard. He was wearing a casual light coloured jacket, dark blue jeans and black trainers, I think."

The Inspector reached into his inside pocket and took out a photograph that was obviously taken from CCTV footage. He slid the photograph across the table towards William.

"Was this the man, William?"

William looked at the image for a few seconds, and shared it with Charlie.

"Yes, I'm pretty sure that was him."

The inspector put the photograph back in his

pocket.

"Do you recognise him, William? Have you ever seen him before yesterday?"

William didn't have to think about his response. "No. I've definitely never seen him before."

The Inspector lent forward in his chair.

"So you can't think of any reason why he may have wanted to harm you?"

William shot a glance at Dan.

"Harm me? Certainly not! Why do you ask?"

Inspector Dhillon hesitated; he didn't want to overstate his suspicions, but he did need to explore them further.

"We are investigating the possibility that this was not an accident, and that Ms Bridges was deliberately pushed. When we looked at the footage, the man you have just identified can be seen deliberately lunging forward and pushing Linda down the escalator."

They looked at each other, incredulously.

"Why would anyone want to hurt Linda?" asked William. "She's lovely, one of the kindest…" his words trailed away.

Dan picked up on the inference immediately. "But Inspector, you asked William if he knew why the man might want to hurt him. Why did you say that?"

DC Allen spoke for the first time.

"The CCTV footage clearly shows the man lunging for Mr Wright, here. Linda stepped into his path at the wrong time and caught the full force of his attack."

The Inspector glowered at him.

"Thank you, Constable, less of the detail if you don't mind."

Suitably chastised, Allen put his head down and continued making notes.

'We're still trying to identify this man. It was a very serious assault, and we need to catch the person responsible. If you remember anything that might help our enquiry, no matter how insignificant it may seem to you, please contact me."

He passed his card across the table to Dan.

"Thank you for your time, gentlemen. I'll be in touch if there are any developments."

Dan put the card in his jacket pocket and stood up. He was shaking hands with the Inspector when there was a knock on the door and it opened abruptly. A very worried-looking Layla was standing there. She didn't even acknowledge the others, and just said in an urgent tone, "The hospital on line two for you, Mr Grant."

Dan picked up the handset, jabbing at the flashing button with his thumb.

"Hello, this is Daniel Grant." The others watched his facial expression to see if the news was good or bad.

He simply said "thank you for letting me know," and put the handset back on the cradle. He sat down heavily in his chair and exhaled.

"That was the surgeon dealing with Linda's case. She passed away twenty minutes ago."

Inspector Dhillion looked at his DC.

"Welcome to your first murder enquiry, Allen."

13

Shady Fields, 22nd March 2018, 11am

The news about Linda had spread quickly and everyone seemed subdued. And as Hilary worked through her tasks for the day, it made her realise how little she knew about the people here. She didn't know their back stories; why they were here, who their friends were, and who mattered to them. One thing was clear, however, and that was the respect and warmth felt by everyone for their deceased friend and colleague.

Bernard Cummings arrived at exactly 11am, with his usual flourish. His immaculate grey pinstriped suit was complimented today with a snow-white shirt, a green and silver paisley silk tie, and matching pocket square. Hilary was in the library preparing a window alcove for the consultant interviews that afternoon and saw him get out of his official black Jaguar saloon.

His driver had clearly been told to wait, and manoeuvred the car into one of the reserved spaces as Bernard approached the building, taking the steps two at a time before pressing the intercom buzzer for access. It struck Hilary as odd that he would make his driver stay in the car while he completed his business.

She walked out of the library and met him just as he was about to mount the stairs. She wondered who had let him into the building.

"Good morning, Bernard. I'm sorry, but Dan is in a meeting at the moment and can't be disturbed. Can I help?"

He turned, and flashed her his best wolfish smile. It began and ended at his mouth.

"Good morning, Hilary, and who might Dan be meeting with?"

Hilary swallowed her dislike of this man and said politely, "There are two police officers with him at the moment. They're gathering information about Linda Bridges' accident yesterday."

He stepped off the bottom step and came towards her.

"Yes, I heard about that, it sounded terrible. How is she doing?"

There was clearly no genuine concern behind the enquiry, just someone asking what he thought he should.

"She's still in a critical condition, but the doctors are hopeful. The next few days will be crucial."

He continued to feign interest.

"Well I hope she makes a speedy recovery. Was she alone when it happened?"

"No," said Hilary "She was accompanying two residents who had appointments in the city." She couldn't be certain of the expression on his face, but he seemed to hesitate.

"Well I was going to meet with Dan then stay for the final interviews this afternoon, but in light of what's happened you probably don't need me hanging about like a spectre at a funeral! I need to make a call, though. Is there somewhere private I can use? Then I'll get out of your hair." The false smile flashed again.

"The small office in the corner should be free."

Hilary ushered him towards a discreet door beneath the stairs. It opened into the porter's office and was normally used for deliveries and luggage. Bernard entered, and closed the door behind him.

The cleaner, Eileen, came stomping along the corridor and headed straight for Hilary. "I want to complain! Someone has been in the supplies cupboard again and stuff is missing. It's my responsibility and if I can't account for the stock it's my head on the block. This is the second time in a week that things have been taken and I know the door was definitely locked."

Hilary sighed. "What exactly is missing, Eileen?"

"A box of soda crystals, some micro cloths, a pack of latex gloves, and a five litre container of ammonia! What good are they to anyone else? You have to nail things down in this place!"

"Leave it with me please, Eileen, I'll investigate. I've arranged to have combi-locks fitted to the supplies cupboards, but that won't be done until tomorrow. Let me know if any of it turns up in the meantime."

Eileen wandered off back down the corridor, muttering.

Once alone, Bernard took out his mobile phone and selected the speed dial he wanted. It was answered before the first ring had stopped.

"What the bloody hell happened? You were meant to make it look like an accident! … Well, the police are here now, so there is bound to be an investigation… Okay, well get over to the hospital. See what needs to be done and meet me in the 'canteen' in an hour. Don't be late."

He scrolled through his contacts, selected another number, and waited for someone to answer. "Hello, Shannon? Slight change of plan. We have to find something serious enough to close this place down for good. I don't care what it is, but it's imperative that your report recommends immediate closure. Do you understand? … Good."

Bernard turned off his phone, opened the door and saw Hilary loitering a couple of feet away.

"Thanks for that. I can't wait for Dan. I have to get back to London, something's come up. Can you tell him I dropped in and I'll telephone tomorrow morning after the draft report is complete? Oh, and I do hope Linda is okay," he added as an afterthought.

14

London, 22nd March 2018

Bernard was irritated by the recent sequence of events, and felt he had to take matters into his own hands now. He strode out towards the car park and found his driver reclining behind the wheel. He was listening to some god-awful cacophony that passed for music. Bernard opened the rear passenger door and the driver shot up in his seat, annoyed he had been caught unawares. He immediately re-tuned the radio and a soothing aria flooded the luxury leather interior.

"Back to the office, Mr Cummings?"

"Yes, but we need to do a detour to Westminster first, St Ermin's Hotel."

Heading along the A20 towards London, Bernard struggled with his current predicament. There was no doubt that things were getting out of hand. This retirement home for loose-tongued has-beens had become a thorn in his side.

He reflected on a time when things were much simpler. Agents understood the precarious nature of their work; the risks, the thrills, the rewards and the consequences. An agent knew his life was always on the line. One mistake and you could lose everything.

When he'd run agents he had always cleared up his own mess, secure in the knowledge that his secrets remained safe. That was until William Wright turned up as a resident at Shady Fields.

If Bernard had known Deni Dokka when they were in Tbilisi his current problem would not exist. He could have sorted Vlasta and William at the same time. Unfortunately their paths didn't cross until a few years after.

 Bernard had been stationed in Chechnya during the first War of Independence in the country, in 1994, using his covert position with a mining company to gathering intelligence. The brutal battle of Grozny was a turning point in the war and one of its veterans was Deni Dokka. He was just eighteen, and had seen things that damaged him irreparably. He began hiring out his services to the highest bidder. He didn't care who his victims were, as long as he got paid. Bernard appreciated this entrepreneurship, and quickly established a connection with him for under the radar operations. Dokka liked the fact that their agreement paid well, and Bernard liked the fact that Dokka's actions were untraceable back to him.

Bernard's career was built on nerve and a willingness to do whatever was necessary to protect national security. He understood people, what made them tick, and how they could be exploited. That had been the basis of his success, but times had changed. Currently there was a wave of bleeding heart liberalism sweeping through the corridors of power. People no longer had the stomach needed for the game. Dan was a classic example. He had gone soft, believing that the service had an obligation to former agents. In Bernard's opinion, they knew the stakes were high when they joined the service. They knew that you could find yourself isolated, without backup.

The bread and butter of spying was about acquiring secret information from your assets. A good intelligence officer could be so close to a target within an hour of meeting them they'd know their sexual preferences, their hobbies and their shoe size. They needed to understand what motivated people. They had to discover what their vulnerabilities were, and what would make them betray their employer or country. Agents needed to be master manipulators; they had to be able to lie easily, and to spot another liar a mile off. They needed to be cool in a crisis, and to blend in. And they had to be able to do all of it without drawing any attention to themselves. The best agents could pass for a second hand car salesmen.

Bernard's chief talents lay in picking and turning

good assets, and Tbilisi had produced one of the best he had ever run. Vlasta had given them some of the most valuable intelligence to come from the Eastern Block. And he'd been able to use William's genius for eavesdropping and surveillance into the bargain. Luckily, William never sought the limelight for his triumphs, leaving Bernard to pick up the accolades. It was an arrangement that suited them both.

In the early days he had liked William Wright. He'd been good at what he did, partly because his geekiness made him almost invisible. There was nothing remarkable about his physical appearance, but he had a razor sharp mind, a talent for technology, and a love of his country. William was not married; his bachelor lifestyle was common in the service. Many agents were unable to live a double life and cope with all that that entailed. And Bernard's mistake had been to miss the signs of emotional attachment from William. He had broken the basic rule, and fallen in love with the asset's wife. When Bernard challenged him, he'd denied it, but Bernard was no fool. The idiot had put the whole mission in jeopardy, so he had no choice but to act.

He had reassigned William to a desk job in London. He had been compliant and seemed to understand the reasoning for it. Besides, his real value lay at home working on gadgets, not in the field.

Bernard's career had blossomed after Tblisi, and he continued to receive promotions. The double life came easy to him. He had a wife and a son at home, and a mistress in every city he had been posted to. His marriage became a convenience, rather than a love match. It had ended nearly 10 years ago, when Stella left him for her tennis coach. She had taken the family home, a chunk of his salary and his son, Tristan, and still surfaced occasionally, when she wanted something. The possessions she'd taken were one thing, but he could not forgive damage she'd inflicted on the bond with his son. She had poisoned Tristan against him and they hadn't spoken for five years now.

Bernard sighed.

He had made the assumption that because William had ultimately left the service under a cloud, he would be not be eligible for residence at Shady Fields. But Dan took him in anyway, because of his run in with the journalist. Then recently, the threat of his memoirs had surfaced. That's when Bernard thought of Dokka, who'd just finished a job for him in Ireland.

Bernard 's driver interrupted his thoughts.

"We're about ten minutes away from the hotel, sir. Do you want me to park at the front, or in the car park?"

"The front will be fine, I won't be long."

The imposing hotel stood at the end of a tree-lined courtyard. Its decorative entrance was framed by a wrought iron, art deco portico. A smartly liveried doorman moved briskly to open the car door, but Bernard was out and up the steps long before he touched the handle.

As he crossed the threshold, Bernard immediately felt at home. He was fundamentally a traditionalist, comfortable with locations that held echoes of secret service glory days.

St Ermin's Hotel had been at the centre of British Intelligence since the thirties, when it was known to agents as 'The Works Canteen.' It was the worst kept secret in the Service. It seemed everyone knew its prominence as a meeting place without ever openly acknowledging it.

Famous intelligence officers such as Ian Fleming and Noel Coward drank in the hotel's Caxton Bar, while Winston Churchill allegedly conceived the idea of the Special Operations Executive over a glass or two of his favourite champagne. Bernard felt connected to the service's rich history whenever he was here.

He crossed the mosaic marble floor and walked up the staircase onto the mezzanine. The figured stucco walls and gilt-decorated ceiling added an old world elegance to this public meeting place, although it was a little vulgar for his personal tastes. He made his way through the archway into the tea lounge, scanning the room for his contact, safe in the knowledge that it would be fairly quiet at this time of day.

Dokka's thickset frame was clearly too big for the chair he was sitting in. Bernard made his way across the rich carpeted floor, signalling to the waitress that he would have his usual. He sat down but offered nothing to his companion.

In a low but determined voice he said, "Well that was a bloody farce! I told you it needed to look like an accident. How difficult could it be? He's an old man, for Christ's sake! The police are crawling all over this." His tea arrived. He dropped a twenty pound note onto the tray, and waved it away.

Dokka 's accent was thick. "She stepped in front of him. There was nothing I could do. She was falling before I knew what had happened."

He shifted uncomfortably in his seat.

"I can have another go in a few days. I will not fail again."

Bernard glowered at him. "Don 't be ridiculous, they'll have images of you now. I'll handle it myself. I do hope you are not losing your touch, Deni. It would be a shame if I had to seek a younger man who's a bit quicker and sharper. You need to disappear for a while. I can 't have any loose ends on this one."

Dokka was not going to mention that he visited the hospital and learned that the woman was dead; working with the Englishman had proved very lucrative over the years. Changing the subject, he asked "What about the manuscript? He wasn't carrying anything so I assume he either left the copy with the solicitor, or that she still had it in her bag."

Bernard took a drink. "It must have been in her bag. I know they left nothing with the solicitors. I have a plan to recover it. For now, keep out of sight. I'll be in touch when I need you again."

Dokka got up to leave, and Bernard caught his arm. "And for god's sake, shave the beard. You look like a bloody hipster! You might as well be wearing a guilty sign around your neck."

Bernard took the time to finish his tea. He knew he needed another solution; there was someone he had in mind, but it was risky. This asset would not be usable again if his plan succeeded. He made the call from his phone.

Dokka pulled the collar of his leather jacket up around his ears. He walked down the hotel steps and along the drive that led onto the main road, cursing under his breath. He was annoyed that he had missed his mark and that he had disappointed the Englishman. He needed to find a way of making it up to him.

He stopped suddenly, looking around behind him. There was no-one there. But he couldn't shake the feeling that he was being watched. He'd had the same feeling for a couple of days now. Each time he checked, he saw no-one. He needed a quiet drink. The Feathers was only around the corner, an evening haunt for people who wanted to socialise before they went home. At this time of the day it would be virtually empty.

The pub had dark wood panelling and red leather seats that reminded him of a film he had seen about the Kray twins. He would feel safe from prying eyes in here. He ordered a pint of cask ale and a vodka shot. He paid, and took the drinks to a booth in a dimly lit corner. Training his gaze on the pub entrance, he unzipped his jacket and took a long pull from the beer.

The door opened and a couple walked in. The woman went to find a table, while the man walked up to the bar. He returned with a bottle of red wine and two large glasses. He sat down, poured them both a drink, and they toasted each other. Deni watched them. He guessed it was a business arrangement, but there was a definite attraction between the two; they were probably work colleagues out for a quick drink, and perhaps a shag. They started chatting, and he quickly lost interest.

He finished his drinks and rose to leave. As he passed the couple, he noted that the man had an earbud in his left ear. An alarm bell began to ring in his head. He needed to get a grip. This was just nerves because his job hadn't gone to plan. He walked out of the pub and back onto the busy London street, checking behind him again, but no-one had followed him out of the pub. He was being ridiculous, no one even knew he was in the country. Perhaps the Englishman had a point, though, perhaps he was getting a bit too old for this.

Deni didn't see the bicycle courier on the other side of the road. He touched his ear as he mounted his bike. Then he pulled his black crash helmet onto his head and spoke softly into the receiver. Slowly, he set off in the same direction as Dokka.

15

Shady Fields, 22nd March 2018, 4pm

The two older men were back in Dan's office, still looking dazed and bewildered as the tragedy hit home. The police had completed their interviews and left just after lunch. William and Charlie had believed that Linda would be fine, both certain that she would rally and be back at work in a few weeks.

Dan walked over to his desk drawer and took out a bottle of Highland Park single malt. He returned to the table and poured three good measures into the glasses that sat on the tray.

He passed them out.

"I know it 's a bit early in the day but…" he raised his glass, "To Linda." He took a sip, and the men responded by raising their glasses. William added "God bless her," as he took a sip of the warming spirit.

Dan spoke again. "William, when you called me on Linda's phone, can you remember what you said?"

William stared at his glass. "Not really, it all happened so fast."

A deep furrow appeared on his brow as he tried to recall the details. "I think I told you that she'd had an accident. I told you where we were, and that she was being taken to the hospital. I think that's all."

Dan wondered if now was the right time to be having this conversation, but he realised that it might be a mistake simply to assume dementia-related paranoia.

"Yes, you did tell me all of that, but you also said something else which struck me as curious. You said *"It was meant for me. He was trying to get me."* Do you remember that?"

William looked stunned as Dan's words hung in the air.

"The man in the photo! I remember now. I had seen him before. He was at Paddington station when we arrived in the morning. Then I saw him again outside Holborn. As I turned to tell Linda about standing on the wrong side of the escalator I caught sight of him again. He was behind her but he was looking directly at me. She just sidestepped at the wrong time. He was moving towards me, and she got in the way."

The realisation hit. "Oh my god, it's my fault. She's dead, and it's my fault."

William cradled the glass with shaking hands and bowed his head.

"Of course it's not your fault, William, but it is

important to understand why anyone would want to harm you."

He was visibly shaken. "It just doesn't make sense. Why? What have I ever done?" His voice trailed off. Suddenly, he looked up.

"It's my book. It's the memoirs. Someone knows about it, and doesn't want me to publish. They want to shut me up. It's the only possible explanation."

Dan sat back in his chair. "I think that might be a bit of a leap, William. After all, you won't let anyone read them, so no-one knows what 's in them."

William didn't look convinced. Dan decided to follow the train of thought to see where it might lead.

"Okay, if that was true it would narrow it down distinctly to two groups of people. Someone linked with the journalist who wrote about you, or someone linked to Shady Fields."

The implication hung in the air like an old London fog.

William thought for a while. "Well, hypothetically, if it's linked to my book there are three possibilities. It might be connected to a mission I was involved with. Or it might be payback for something I've done personally. Or it's about information I know but don 't realise the significance of."

Dan nodded slowly. He was right. There may be something that William knew or had in his possession that could incriminate a third party.

"How are we supposed to know what it is?"

He really didn't want to acknowledge the next thought that came into his head, but he had to.

"If this was an attempt on your life William, they may try again."

Whatever the reason, the stakes were obviously very high for whoever was behind all of this. How could Dan keep him and the other residents safe from that threat, particularly when he didn't know where it was coming from?

"Where's the manuscript now, William?"

"It's in my room. The draft is finished, although I need to do a bit of editing on one particular chapter. When we saw Mr Erskine yesterday I told him I needed more time, but that was because I was still unsure about handing it over."

"You have an excellent laptop; why are you using that old typewriter?"

Recognition dawned on Charlie's face.

"Because he doesn't want his files hacked, do you William? You use your laptop for everything else, but storing your memoirs electronically would make them vulnerable."

"Exactly. I'm not taking any chances. The world has moved on since I worked in cyber security, and hackers are even more sophisticated now. I don't want to risk it."

William downed what was left of his whisky. It was obvious that he was wrestling with a decision, but Dan didn't want to put any undue pressure on him. He stood up to leave. "This has really shaken me up. You think you are doing something for the right reasons but you never know the lengths others are prepared to go to stop you. We can justify our actions to ourselves, but it's the victors that write history. The vanquished are forgotten, regardless of their virtues." He left the room.

Dan turned to Charlie, "How are you coping, Charlie, are you ok?"

Charlie nodded. "I am, but listening to all of this leaves me with a very uncomfortable thought."

Dan cocked his head slightly, encouraging Charlie to continue.

"If the man who pushed Linda was indeed after William's manuscript, then whoever was behind it must be linked to Shady Fields."

"What makes you say that, Charlie?"

"Because the journalist lost interest and moved onto her next story. She wouldn't know he came here after her story was in the paper. Even if she did, old men's reminiscences hardly matter when they live in a care home, do they? We aren't seen as a threat by the majority. Only someone who knew that he had written something incriminating would see it as that."

Dan had to admit that Charlie's words made a lot of sense.

"We have to help him, Dan, and we have to find out who's behind it all. Linda should have justice. She helped me come to terms with my lot from the day I came here. We can't let her death be for nothing… and we can't let it go unpunished, either."

Dan returned to his desk and watched Charlie leave, a smaller, more vulnerable man. The file he was working on lay open, and the planned savings proposals Linda had made sat looking up at him.

He was really going to miss her. She was often the voice of reason, and a passionate defender of this place. He remembered her easy way with the residents. He had once asked her what on earth she found to chat about with them. She had laughed, telling him that ordinary people would never ask you what your second favourite weapon was, or if you could remember where you had your first knife fight. He would not let her death be in vain; he needed to deal with this, and quickly.

He had re-read William's file and the scant details of his assignments, and the name that kept coming up was Bernard Cummings. It was clear that there was no love lost between the two men, and he knew he would have to tread carefully. Bernard was a powerful man who did not take well to being challenged. He had to be sure of his facts. In the meantime, he also needed to keep Celia appraised of recent developments.

The call went through Celia's PA and she picked up immediately.

"Dan, what the hell is going on?"

Dan told her about the accident and Linda's death. He'd wavered about sharing the threat to William, but on balance had decided she needed to know. She listened carefully without interruption and when he had finished she said simply, "So what's your plan?"

"We're upping the security around here for the foreseeable future. Hilary will see that William doesn't go anywhere without an escort, and I thought I'd ask Mitch to help us identify the man from the escalator. I feel he must be known to us in some capacity."

"Well that's a start, Dan but I think it might be helpful to delay the final evaluation report for a couple of weeks too. I'll speak with Bernard, I'm seeing him later this evening."

Dan hesitated at the mention of Bernard's name, but decided not to share his misgivings with her.

"Thanks, Celia, that's one less thing to worry about. We're liaising closely with the CID officers in charge of the investigation. Obviously they're not privy to William and Charlie's service backgrounds. I'd like to keep it that way."

"Agreed. How is Hilary shaping up, by the way? Not the ideal start to a new job. Is she coping ok?"

Dan noted that Celia had asked after Hilary by name.

"She seems to be handling things well. She grasped the big picture at once when we had the visit from the police. Since then she has increased security checks and procedures, particularly where visitors are concerned. I really think she was an excellent appointment.'

"Good, I'm pleased." She paused. "Dan, there was something else I wanted to talk to you about. As you know, I'm retiring in a few months. And I've been asked to draw up a short-list of possible replacements.

"I want to know if you have considered throwing your own hat into the ring?"

To say Dan was surprised was an understatement.

"I gather from your silence that you haven't."

"Well, no, I hadn't even considered it. I just assumed that it would automatically go to Bernard."

He could almost hear her smiling at the other end

of the line.

"The new Home Secretary is clear that all future appointments should be made on merit rather than 'dead man's shoes', as it were. That doesn't mean it won't be Bernard. It just means that we want a pool of suitable candidates to choose from. Have a think about it, and let me know in a day or two, will you?"

"Yes I will, and thanks Celia. I really appreciate your faith in me."

"Faith has nothing to do with it! If you were not the right calibre of leader we wouldn't be having this conversation."

He replaced the receiver and sat back in his chair. That was definitely not the way he predicted that conversation would go.

He had huge respect for Celia. She had come into the job at a very difficult time. Terrorist activity was difficult to predict, and the technological improvements she had made to track suspects were very effective. She'd been the one to knock heads together over information sharing between MI5 and MI6, and she could hold her own with the Americans as well. People messed with Celia at their peril.

There was a sharp knock, and Hilary popped her head around the door.

"Are you free for a quick catch up, Dan?"

"Yes, in fact I was just talking about you. Come in, sit down."

Hilary sat across from Dan at the desk. "I hope it was all positive," she smiled.

"Yes, it was. Celia was asking how you were getting

on. I told her that I thought we'd made an excellent appointment."

Hilary looked pleased.

"If I'm honest I didn't think the threats were as real as you made out to begin with. But since I've met with the residents, it's very clear why this place is necessary.

"I wanted to update you about the security improvements I've made. I've set up secure cloud storage for all CCTV footage, and William helped me to identify CCTV blind spots, so I've ordered the installation of a couple of extra cameras. All visitors and delivery drivers will automatically be digitally photographed. ID checks will be validated, and no service or delivery personnel will be allowed into the building unescorted. I've set up a duty rota for that. I also had a chat with Charlie and William about putting RFID trackers on them. They both felt it was unnecessary, but they've agreed to use the GPS tracker function on their mobile phones."

She smiled.

"What 's funny?"

"William told me that in the old days if they wanted to keep tabs on him he would have had radioactive dust sprinkled on his clothing so that he could be tracked with a Geiger counter."

Dan looked serious.

"Hilary, he wasn't joking. That 's how the Russians tracked double agents in the sixties and seventies. It was a dangerous game back then."

"Damn, and there I was thinking I was getting a handle on secret service humour."

Dan smiled. "That will take a bit longer than a week. I think you're right about the GPS tracker though. Until we know who and what we are dealing with, I think it's a sensible precaution to take."

He stood up and stretched, he'd been sitting too long in the same position. At times like this he missed active postings. A desk job was the price he'd paid for losing his temper in Aleppo.

He looked out of the window.

"My real concern is that whoever tried to get to William could try again. This is our first real test, and we can't afford to get it wrong, Hilary. Celia has suggested that we extend the deadline for the evaluation report and I want you to take that over. It would give you an opportunity to get even more up to speed on the workings of this place. With your previous experience it should be a walk in the park. And it will leave me free to deal with other things. Are you ok with that?" He walked over to the meeting table.

"Yes Dan, that's fine. Can you let me see a copy of everything that's been prepared to date?"

Dan pointed to two large blue box files on the end of the table.

"All ready for you. Plenty of light reading in there, and I've included a copy of the original brief, along with the winning bid from Maguire's."

He tapped the top box absentmindedly. "If you have any queries don 't hesitate to ask, but I'm handing it over to you as of today."

She thanked Dan, picked up the boxes and left the

room.

He walked back to his desk, picked up the phone and dialled a familiar number. It was answered quickly.

"Hello, this is the King speaking. I'm sorry I can't take your call now. Please don't leave a message after the tone. Beeeep."

"Peter, stop buggering about. I wasn't sure you would still be there at this time."

Peter King gave a laugh of derision.

"You must be joking! I don't work part time like you. I saw your number on the caller display. You never call for a social chat, so what do you want?"

Dan smiled at his old friend's candour. He'd known Peter since his early days in the service, and he was the best data analyst Dan knew. He had an eidetic memory and the ability to sniff out a problem like a scent-trained spaniel.

"I need you to build a full history of an ex-agent, William Wright. I want his missions, personnel record, whatever you can get, really. I know he joined the service in 1970 and left in 2006 after an unfortunate incident."

Peter replied almost instantaneously. "That would be Operation Greenday."

Dan was impressed. "How do you do that, Peter? It's very unnerving, you know."

He laughed. "I take it as a personal challenge to keep people on their toes, but I have to confess that the only reason I know is that I was asked to pull some of that stuff together by someone else already."

Dan's heart rate quickened. "Can you tell me who

asked, Peter? It's important."

He heard Peter tapping on his keyboard. "Sure, the request wasn't restricted. Mitch Bennett asked for it. The request came through normal channels and I sent the data over to him. Do you want a copy?"

"Yes, please." Almost as an afterthought, he added "Was there anything that jumped out about the information? Any anomalies?"

"Nothing, really, although I only gave it a superficial read through. Why is this so important?"

Dan briefly explained the attempt on William's life. "There's something going on here that I can't see yet. This man, in his seventies, who has given a lifetime of loyal service, is suddenly a target. I'm missing something, Peter."

"Leave it with me, Dan. I'll do another sweep and see what I can come up with. Oh, and by the way, William's wasn't the only file Mitch asked me to compile. He also asked for information on Charlie Bingham and Rita Hayward."

"Can you include those as well then, Peter? I really appreciate it. And contact me if you find something of interest."

Dan put the phone down and began to think. What was Mitch doing looking into three of their residents? He had been right to call Peter. If there was anything to find, he would find it.

16

Shepherds Tavern, Mayfair, February 2017

Jodie was a hack. As tabloid reporters went, she had a well-developed nose for a story, but she was a hack none the less. Fellow hacks described her as 'mercenary'. She accepted that dubious honour, but she often wondered where her once noble journalistic aspirations had gone. She smoked hard, drank hard and played hard. She had a nose for the sensational. She knew her big break would come. But she didn't realise that it would be in the form of a septuagenarian with a dull personality and a questionable memory.

She was supposed to be ghost writing a book for Toby Stevenson, a senior civil servant who had his own theory about a sixth man in the Cambridge spy ring. He had given her William Wright's name because they'd worked together briefly in London in the '70s. Her background checks had uncovered a dedicated man who had left the service under a cloud. She decided it was worth having a chat to see if he had anything worth saying. She knew from Toby's notes that William had been involved in the electronic archiving of the files linked to Philby. It wasn't much of a stretch to think that if there had been a cover-up, William would know about it. Toby was convinced that the unnamed spy had been a member of the royal household, and that sort of sensationalism was too good for Jodie to pass up. This meeting would tell her if there was anything in that theory.

When she contacted the old man to set up the meet she introduced herself as the author of a new book about Kim Philby and his friends. He agreed to lunch at the Shepherds Tavern in Mayfair. She entered the public bar and spotted him alone in the corner, recognising him from an old photograph.

Jodie motioned to the barman and ordered two double scotches. She waved at William to attract his attention and mimed 'do you want water?' at him. He nodded. She took the drinks over to the table. He had an empty glass in front of him and was reading Stalin; the Court of the Red Tzar.

"Is it any good?" she asked.

William closed the paperback and put it on the table. "It is one of the most civilised and elegant chronicles of brutality and evil I have ever read. I have only ever seen ruthlessness to rival him once before."

He blinked at Jodie and accepted the drink.

"You know he wasn't Russian. He was born in Georgia."

Jodie feigned interest.

"No, I didn't know that."

"He transformed Russia from a peasant society into a military and industrial power, killing millions in the process."

Jodie sat and dumped her bag on the floor. She removed a small Dictaphone from her pocket and placed it on the table, then set her mobile phone to record too.

"You don't mind do you? I can't remember details, and I want to get this right."

"No, I don't mind." He casually angled an empty foil crisp packet in front of the devices just enough to interfere with the built in microphones. The quality of the recordings would not be good enough for her to quote from.

"It's really good of you to give up your time. I've read a number of your pieces about whether the spy ring should have been detected earlier than it was. I particularly enjoyed your hypothesis that Elliot knew about Philby all along."

William looked at her without any emotion. "Suspected. I never said he knew."

She nodded. "No, you're quite right, sorry. He suspected. But that makes sense of Philby's defection though, doesn't it? Several people have suggested a sixth man, but I'm working with Toby Stevenson, and he's quite certain that there was a very senior public figure who was the final piece of the puzzle."

William shrugged, and swallowed a mouthful of the blended whisky.

"Ah yes, Toby. Proof that artificial intelligence is no match for natural stupidity.

"What makes you think that if there was a sixth man, he was British? He could have been American. Recruited much later than the others, when the US became a strategic player in the arms race."

He looked around the bar; the lunchtime crowd was quiet and happy to keep their chat to a low murmur. He dropped the volume of his voice and leaned towards Jodie.

"What are you really looking for? No-one is interested in Philby and co. It happened lifetimes ago. The public have forgotten about it. The security services are still trying to forget about it, and I'm not sure anybody that matters really cares anymore."

Jodie wanted to keep him talking.

"You're absolutely right, William. All of this happened a long time ago. But I'm interested in the human cost of espionage. The toll spying takes on relationships. Not knowing when you'll get caught. The pressure on loved ones must be terrific. It must change you as a person."

"Of course it changes you!" snapped William. "You're chosen because you don't have any ties. There is no wife or husband in the picture when you start out. They tell you rule number one is never to fall in love!

"The problem is that it can happen when you are not expecting it. That's when you put those you love at risk simply by doing your job. You stand by and watch powerlessly while their world falls apart. Then you have to acknowledge your part in their downfall. That's the hard part."

"You never married, William?" She was keen that he should feel relaxed around her, otherwise he would not drop his guard.

"No. Some people can lie and cheat their way through life, but I could not. I only ever loved one woman, and that was doomed to failure. She loved someone else. She didn't know how I really felt about her."

As they chatted William played a skilful game, suggesting things but never giving Jodie anything tangible. After their third double whisky, he was more relaxed and talkative.

Jodie wanted to stop the verbal dance and get to the nitty gritty stuff.

"So what went wrong, William? How did you come to leave the service under such a cloud?"

"Is that what Toby said? What would he know – he was a pen pusher. His job involved counting paperclips. He was never at the sharp end, although he desperately wanted to be. I was collateral damage to save someone's shining career. I had the integrity to take responsibility for something that happened on my watch. I fixed a problem. We learnt from it so that it could never happen again but that wasn't enough for some people. When you are working on the edge of knowledge with ridiculous expectations and impossible deadlines, mistakes happen. Do you know they took my pension?"

He banged the table and the glasses shook. He leaned across, and whispered through gritted teeth. "I know we were hacked, but as soon as I found out, I fixed it. No one complained when my software gave us the edge to eavesdrop in other countries. They could have let me leave quietly. I could have retired early with my pension. Reward for a lifetime of keeping this country safe. Not too much to ask, is it?"

Jodie sat back. Bingo. The mother lode.

William realised he had said too much. He began to pull back.

They talked for another ten minutes, but she knew she would get nothing else. She kept up the pretence, explaining that she would send him a draft of the chapter he would feature in and that he would have editorial control over what was included.

At three o'clock she said her goodbyes and left the pub. He noticed that she nodded to a lone drinker standing at one of the tall tables by the door. He realised he was probably a photographer, judging by his state of the art phone he held in his hand.

He could have kicked himself for saying too much, but with any luck she wouldn't be able to piece the whole thing together.

William had forgotten about the detail of the meeting until three weeks later, when he opened a copy of the Sunday Times to see a photograph of himself in the pub chatting with an out of shot Jodie.

The article described how many of today's cyber-attacks were made possible because of the early hacking software the secret service had developed. They alone had created some of those hardwired back doors hackers were so fond of. She cited him as the expert who had told her about the hacking that had been carried out on British soil against foreign powers. The Americans would be very pissed indeed.

There was nothing factual in the piece, only inference and suggestion. But dangerously, it was enough for the media to sense scandal.

The next two days were a nightmare. He had been doorstepped by all of the major tabloids, hounded for a follow-up story. They took to following him around, wanting comments and pictures. He knew if this continued he would have a visit from the service. He cursed his own stupidity, and his taste for whisky.

17

The visit had come two days after the story had broken.

His life had been turned upside down. The press were relentless, and he cursed himself for letting the journalist get so much information from him.

There was a knock on the door. William stiffened; he had no intention of answering it. It would only be another bloodsucker journalist wanting more dirt. He would wait it out. They would get bored before he did. The knock on the door came again, and this time it was followed by a single- folded sheet of paper being slipped under his front door.

He walked over to retrieve it. He didn't recognise the handwriting, but he did recognise the name at the bottom: Daniel Grant.

He had worked with Dan when he was new to the service and had briefly been seconded to William's team. He was surprised he'd lasted; men with his integrity were few and far between. He waited. Another tap came on the door, this time followed by a question.

"I know you're there, William. I just want to chat about your current predicament. I want to help. Can I come in, please?"

William took the bolt off the door and unhooked the chain. He opened the door a crack and saw Dan's tanned smiling face looking back at him. He opened the door wider. "You'd better come in before anyone sees you."

Dan sidestepped into the hall, and William closed the door behind him.

"You're the last person I was expecting. Did the farm send you?"

Dan shook his head. "I thought a friendly face would be a nice change after the last couple of days. And no, I wasn't sent. I am here of my own accord, and alone."

Dan took a look around the dingy hall. The place was dismal. It had not been decorated for at least 30 years, and the smell of old age floated around like fumes from an old tractor. He followed William into the tiny sitting room. The only furniture in evidence consisted of two fireside chairs, a coffee table and a radiogram from the sixties.

William looked over his shoulder. "Can I get you anything?"

Dan nodded. "Coffee, please."

He moved the pile of newspapers and magazines from one of the chairs onto the floor and took a seat. The kitchenette was just off the sitting room, and he could see William moving around, boiling the kettle and getting the cups ready. He watched him as he sniffed a plastic milk carton.

"I take mine black please, William."

He felt really sad that someone that someone so technically gifted had been reduced to such a life. He didn't know William 's full story but he did know that this was not right. If he could help William, he would.

William came back into the room with two steaming mugs. He placed them down on the table and pushed a battered biscuit tin towards him, before taking the other seat.

"So what's this about? Am I in trouble?" William held his mug and blew on the contents to cool it down.

"I am here with a proposition, William. I'm heading up a new venture for the service. We've set up a residence for ex-agents who have retired from active service and need a place of refuge. Some come because they have medical needs, others because they're struggling with their memories. They come because we can offer a safe environment away from the public eye, where they can live the rest of their lives without worry. There's a place for you there if you want it, William."

William eyed him with suspicion.

"So you're here to arrest me, then. To make me disappear."

Dan couldn't help laughing out loud.

"William, I'm not the KGB! Shady Fields is exactly as I've just described it to you. A residential home that offers a safe space to people like you who have devoted their lives to the security of our country. The nature of what we have done in our careers means we have secrets. And there are people, like your journalist friend, who are only too happy to exploit that and benefit from those secrets.

"Why don't you come and take a look around? We can be there in an hour. It's a large converted house in its own grounds. Each resident has their own apartment. They're free to come and go as they please. And in your case, accommodation costs would be covered by a pension grant. Come and take a look. You've got nothing to lose, other than the pack of hyenas camped on your doorstep."

William relaxed a little. "And what do you get out of it, if I come?"

"Honestly? The service gets to manage the fallout of the story, and we'll know if a journalist gets too close in the future. We are not the enemy William. I really would like to help."

William bowed his head.

"I'm tired of struggling, Dan. When I joined the service there were rules that everyone understood and played by. There were no suicide bombers or beheadings plastered over the internet. All of the countries that used spies knew where the boundaries were, and there was a weird sort of gentleman's agreement in place that gave integrity to the work that we did. Like honour amongst thieves. I don't remember the level of violence that we have now."

He shook his head and sighed. "I was treated very badly by the service. I didn't deserve to be the scapegoat, and yet I've ended up with virtually nothing. I'm not even sure I could afford your place. I'm writing my memoirs to set the record straight, and to try to earn some money. Really, I just want to be left alone." He fought back a tear.

Dan had reached a decision.

"That is it! I will not leave you here one more night. How long will it take you to pack? Just bring your clothes and personal belongings. We can come back for the rest if you decide you want to stay. Please come back with me, William."

He looked up at Dan. There was no fight left in him.

"All I have of any value will fit into two suitcases."

Dan smiled at him.

"Well, how fortunate. I have room for two suitcases in the boot of my car."

18

D an rose to greet Mitch Bennett. They shook hands, and Dan gestured to the armchair at the other side of the fireplace. He was keen that this meeting should have an informal feel to it, so they were in the library. No one used it on Friday evenings, when everyone was at the other end of the building for movie night.

Tonight's film was the latest Jack Reacher blockbuster. Not 20 minutes in, and the residents had already decided it was far too 'Hollywood' for their liking. They were busy critiquing the flaws in the plot and the ridiculous physical abilities of the agents. This inevitably led on to real-life one-upmanship conversations.

"Do you remember Moscow in '76, when Ivanovic

caught it with a blunt dessert spoon?"

"When I was shot in the arm it put me on the floor for an hour!"

"Flesh wound, my arse, still hurts like a bugger!"

"I was on Waterloo Bridge in '78 when Markov had his run in with the umbrella tip!"

Movie night post mortems usually went on until after 10pm. They wouldn't be disturbed here.

Mitch's favoured tipple was Jack Daniel's. A bottle of it and a glass stood on the table to the left of the chair. Dan preferred vintage single malts, and tonight it was a 15 year-old Dalwhinnie, taken with just a single drop of spring water.

Dan studied Mitch as he poured himself a decent slug of JD, undecided about whether he should be direct or diplomatic. He let him settle and take his first sip of the honeyed spirit.

Mitch was forty two. He had wide-set blue eyes, a nose that had been broken more than once, and a scar that ran across his chin, giving him a horizontal dimple. He was a powerfully built man, standing six feet and two inches tall. His substantial neck was not accentuated with a collar and tie (except on formal occasions). Women seemed to find him attractive, which Dan concluded was probably more down to his warm personality and self-deprecating humour than his physique.

The two men sat in silence for a few moments until Mitch broke it.

"Well this is very pleasant, but I can't imagine there isn't some sort of ulterior motive for inviting me tonight, Dan. What's going on?"

"I just thought a catch up might be nice, it's been ages. How are things? Anything hot off the press?"

"Not much," said Mitch.

Dan tried again.

"I wondered if Bernard had mentioned anything about taking over from Celia when she retires?" He studied Mitch 's face to read any tells.

"There's been speculation, but he hasn't said anything to me. Why would he? I'm only his deputy."

Dan changed tack again. "As you know, he's leading our evaluation, and with everything that 's happening here I can 't help but feel a degree of anxiety. Have you been involved in the process?"

Mitch gave a wry smile. "My God, Dan, you really are out of practice with your interrogation technique! Stop fishing, and ask me what's really on your mind!"

Dan put his glass down. "OK, Mitch, I've known you for a long time and I trust your judgement so I'd appreciate an honest opinion. What's Bernard up to? I don't understand why he's taking such an interest in what happens to us here. We're insignificant in the grand scheme of things."

Mitch shook his head. "You are insignificant from a financial perspective. A drop in the ocean compared with other departments and service budgets."

"Exactly. So why put us under scrutiny? It was his

idea, you know. The consultants doing the report were recruited by him, and the brief has his name all over it. Why would he get so involved if he thinks we're insignificant?"

Mitch thought a little. "I really don't know, but I think you're right to be concerned, Dan. He does have a real bee in his bonnet about this place. I did originally think it was his 'milk of human kindness' approach to old agents. You know, 'let 's just do away with them if they are a risk.' But it doesn't explain the priority he has given to this place." Mitch looked to Dan for a response, but none was forthcoming, so he continued.

"We've been fairly busy recently with the increased activity of the Russians and all the ISIS stuff, but he hasn't put you on the back burner like I would have expected him to. In fact he asked for detailed updates on some of your residents. I was asked to pull some background files together for him, but that's as far as my involvement goes.

"I do agree with you – he does seem to be showing disproportionate interest. Does he have an old score to settle with you? I only ask because it sort of feels personal."

Dan looked up at Mitch. "Well, you know how much Bernard and I have always respected each other." A smile broke out on his face. "We've had a few run-ins with each other, but nothing that would count as a grudge or a score to be settled. Obviously, with his history he's come into contact with most of our residents at one time or another. He helped with the logistics when Charlie was assigned to South Africa back in the seventies, William Wright worked directly for him on a couple of occasions, Rita was intelligence gathering on a mission he was involved with in the Middle East, and most of the others have had contact with him at some point in their careers. Usually when he was on his way up and they were on their way down."

Dan took a sip of his whisky, letting the warm spirit deposit its full hit.

"I spoke with Celia earlier. Between you and me, she's asked me if I would be interested in applying for her job."

Mitch's expression didn't give anything away.

"Does Bernard know that?"

"I don't think so. She said they wanted a meaningful process with a field of candidates rather than the next in line appointment we normally get. I haven't given her my reply yet."

Now Mitch smiled. "My guess is that if Bernard knew that, you would have heard him from here. He sees the job as a shoo-in, which is probably why he hasn't spoken to me about it. I'm not high up enough up the food chain. Look, all I know is that he seems too interested in this place for no good reason. I just can't see what he has to gain if Shady Fields were to fall."

Suddenly the library door opened and Layla walked

in. "Sorry Mr Grant, I didn't know anyone was in here. I just came to straighten up before I go off shift."

"That's fine, Layla and please call me Dan. What are you doing with the rest of your evening then, or what's left of it?"

"Nothing much. I'll go home and probably watch some TV." She hesitated, then added, "You know how terribly sorry we all are about Linda Mr, ah, Dan. She was so kind. She helped me so much when I first came to work here. We're all really shocked."

"Thank you Layla, I know how much that would mean to her family and I will pass on your comments." she nodded and quietly left the room.

Mitch looked at Dan.

"She's new. Do I detect the hint of a Russian accent?"

"Yes. Layla is originally from one of the Balkan states, I think, but she's lived here a long time."

"I heard about Linda's accident too, Dan. I'm so sorry."

"In all honesty Mitch, they don't think it was an accident. They think it was an attempt on William Wright's life."

Mitch laughed, until he saw Dan't expression. "Oh my god, you're serious."

"Yes, I'm afraid I am."

Dan gave Mitch the details of the investigation, while Mitch listened carefully. He shook his head.

"Something doesn't sit right, Mitch. And I think the

reason for it all is that William has threatened to release a tell-all memoir, even though you know as well as I do that there are enough checks and balances in place to ensure that nothing of any real sensitivity could be published, anyway. Whoever was responsible is connected with Shady Fields in some way, too, I'm sure of it. I asked Peter King to pull something a little more detailed together for me, so I can see if anything stands out."

Mitch looked into the depths of his glass.

"So he must have told you about the files I asked for?"

Dan nodded. "He did, Mitch. And I want your help – two heads are better than one. Can I ask if we can compare notes? I mentioned it to Celia and she's happy if you are. I don't want to put you in a difficult situation with Bernard, but..."

Mitch interrupted. "So let's not tell him. I'm happy to do this on my own time. Send me what you've got so far, but use a courier rather than sending it electronically. And let's keep everything between us for now.

"I didn't know Linda very well, but she had a good reputation. If you're an agent, you know the risks. She wasn't, and that made her vulnerable. What happened to her was not right. I'll be happy to help, if it brings her killer to justice."

"Thanks Mitch, I really appreciate it. Now, I have another favour to ask. We have a CCTV picture of a person of interest who was involved. Do you think you could run it for me and see if anything turns up?"

"My pleasure," said Mitch.

Mitch thought further about their discussion as he drove home.

Bernard was a difficult character to like. He was very traditional, and he liked things to be done to the letter. Except of course, when it was about him. Then there wasn't a rule that couldn't be bent or broken. His one fatal flaw was his over developed sense of entitlement. That was what Mitch struggled with the most.

Bernard was charmingly patronising to everyone he met, which meant that any dismissal of one person was not personal. He felt sure Bernard knew nothing about Dan potentially becoming competition for Celia's job. That would have been an insult he would take personally.

The information Mitch had gathered so far showed that the three agents Bernard was interested in all had operational links to him. None of that was unusual – someone with Bernard's length of service and career trajectory would have come into contact with all sorts of missions across the world. The coincidence was simply that all three former agents were now residing in Shady Fields. He wasn't sure if there was any other link, but he was determined to find out.

19

Amman, Jordan, 1998

Rita Heyward was bored with her life as a supermodel. She had used her physicality and sexuality to make love to photo and film cameras, and they had become enslaved.

She had mastered the art of using men to give her the experiences she craved. Like the chance meeting with a music impresario in 1982. That relationship had catapulted her onto the celebrity A-list. Her brain and ambition had screwed (literally) every last opportunity out of it too. She had carefully crafted a persona that led others to believe that she was an open book. As far as most people were concerned, she was beautiful, self-absorbed and of basic intelligence. A slightly bad good-time girl.

But for Rita, that life was not enough. She needed risk and danger to make her feel really alive. So when a recruiter approached her to 'work for the government' in 1985, she jumped at the chance. The characteristics that they coveted were quite different.

She had become an MI6 agent. They used her talent for mimicry to become a master of disguise. Her quick thinking and nimble fingers were trained to crack locks of all sorts. But her real value came from her nerves of steel, and an underlying psychopathy that made her a deadly assassin. Her preferred method was a blade. She liked the intimacy of the weapon.

She had a natural affinity for sex, and used the bedroom like Bond used his Beretta. In short, she was an excellent operative.

Until she met Saleem Al Baadini.

In a bid to foster economic development, the Jordanian Government held a trade summit in Amman in 1995. Their intent was to boost tourism, the minerals industry, energy and telecommunications. The event was a great success, and established significant trade agreements with emerging African economies as well as the big three of UK, America and Russia. By 1998 however, the country's UK and American partners felt that they were losing out on some of the more lucrative deals. They knew that corruption and bribery was playing a part in the awarding of contracts. So Rita was sent on a mission to discover who was channelling the contracts to Russian companies.

For the Jordanians, the second summit was an exercise in global image polishing, and the whole of the royal family were included in what was a month long programme of events and seminars. The King saw it as an opportunity to promote the country's democracy and pluralism.

The opening was marked with the Ambassadors' banquet, and it was a supremely lavish affair. Held in the Basman Palace in the Royal Court Compound in Amman, the magnificent building was decorated traditionally, with no expense spared. About two hundred guests attended. Every Ambassador was present, supported by their trade delegation. Business leaders rubbed shoulders with members of the Royal household, and the odd celebrity put in an appearance, too.

Rita found functions like this boring, but necessary. In her experience, they were attended by overpaid, officious civil servants who handed the real work to their minions. The only reason she was attending was to try and make the connections she needed to do her job. Just like every other spy in the room.

A livered waiter handed her a glass of champagne and directed her to the seating chart so that she could find her table. A small commotion had broken out between an Arab man in a western style dinner jacket and one of the senior embassy staff. The Namibian Ambassador, a formidable mountain of a woman in a technicolour ceremonial dress with an enormous headdress stood to one side, with an amused look on her face.

Rita smiled and introduced herself, reminding her where they had met before.

"What's all the fuss about?"

The Ambassador chuckled. "It seems no one

informed the organisers that I am a woman, and it has thrown the seating plan into all sorts of difficulties. This gentleman is attempting to find a solution."

The Arab turned to face them. "A thousand apologies, Ambassador, we have a solution. You can take my seat at the Crown Prince's table, and I will take yours."

She chuckled again. "Then let me introduce you to your companion for the evening, Saleem. This is Rita Heyward, fashion model and film star. I was going to be sitting next to her at dinner. Rita, this is Saleem Al Baadini."

She winked at Rita. "I think you have the better deal," she said, and wandered off to find her seat.

The Arab was incredibly attractive, with dark eyes that flashed intelligence, perfect teeth, and a lithe physique that carried a dinner jacket better than anyone in the room. In fact, Rita thought, he was almost her male equivalent.

He reached out for her hand and bowed over it, barely brushing the back of it with his lips. "I am very pleased to meet you, Ms Heyward. I am a bit of a fan."

"Really? I wouldn't have guessed that you subscribe to Harper's Bazaar."

He smiled. "I do not, but I would have had to live the life of a hermit not to know who you are. Shall we be seated?" He gently took her arm and guided her through the sea of people until they reached their table.

He drew out the seat for her.

"So you have the advantage over me. You know me, but I do not know you."

"I am Prince Saleem Al Baadini, third cousin to the King and a minister in our department of trade and industry."

"Then it is my turn to ask for forgiveness, Your Highness. I had no idea."

He flashed another smile. "Well, I must extract a forfeit from you for such an oversight. Have dinner with me tomorrow evening."

From that moment on, they were inseparable. They shared each other's company, each other's beds, and each other's secrets.

As the summit drew to a close there was no turning back. In three short weeks they had fallen deeply in love. It felt like a sort of madness, where logic and reason played no part. The affair consumed them with a frightening intensity. It dragged them in, and pulled them under. It was beautiful but messy. They had both lived colourful lives, and found each other when they were not looking for permanence in their lives.

They were brutally honest with each other. She had learned about his playboy lifestyle, and discovered it was Saleem who was awarding the most lucrative contracts to the Russians. Being a junior member of the Royal family gave him a unique ability to favour contractors, and if they wanted to show their appreciation, then who was he to stop them? It was the way business had been done for thousands of years.

He had been in charge of screening attendants for the summit, and had wondered as he was doing so why a model of her fame should be an increasingly present figure in diplomatic circles. With the resources of the

Jordanian secret service at his disposal he had been very thorough in his checks. Before they met, he knew she worked for MI6, and of the extent of her activities.

When they met for the first time he was intrigued by her. Her history, her intelligence and her sense of fun made her even more attractive. She came along at just the right time, and scratched an itch he wasn't even aware he'd had.

A week before the summit ended he organised a special day out. He had a traditional costume delivered to her hotel the night before, asking her to wear it. It was a cream, full-length shift dress with collar and sleeves decorated with delicate gold embroidery, accompanied by a cream silk thobe headscarf, expertly sewn with tiny gold discs that framed her face. He had sent his car to collect her at dawn. The chauffeur drove through the dessert for three hours before they came to a deep valley with mountains either side. They cast deep shadows in the morning sun, causing the rock walls to glow red. Up ahead she spotted a tent with camels waiting outside.

The chauffeur came to a halt, and Saleem emerged from the tent entrance in a white flowing robe, with a traditional red and white shemagh scarf held in place with black silk circular cords. He flashed a smile, and she felt her heart lurch.

The door opened and she stepped out onto carpets laid on the sand. He wrapped his arms around her, and kissed her longingly before leading her inside.

The billowing fabric ceiling made the space seem enormous. She was surprised by the opulence of such a simple structure. There were low divans covered in cushions of rich red and gold fabrics and ornate silver tables dotted around. More patterned carpets provided a soft floor, and a huge potted palm tree stood to one side, its fronds touching the textile roof. It reminded her of a film set she had worked on a few years ago, but this was no movie.

A manservant moved around the tent, serving them hot sweet tea, and offering dishes of dates and candied nuts.

"Well if today is about impressing me I will give you six out of ten so far."

She smiled at him, and took a sip of her tea.

"You cut me like a knife with your heartless words, but you are so beautiful I will forgive you."

"Thank you for the gift, I love it."

She twirled around, and the bottom of her dress fanned out and she flopped down onto the seat again.

He waved her comment away. "It was a poor attempt at gilding a lily."

Saleem walked over to a wooden desk set up behind one of the divans. He opened a draw and took out a large blue velvet box. Walking around to where she sat he offered it to her.

"It is customary to give tokens of love that have significance to the receiver. I hope you like it."

Rita opened the box and let out a faint gasp. Nestled in blue silk sat an exquisite dagger and scabbard. About ten inches long, the scabbard was engraved with Arabic patterns and symbols, and the end of the handle was carved into the shape of a delicate crown. Three sizeable cabochon rubies were embedded in the hilt.

Saleem took it from her and pressed the central ruby. A quiet click released the scabbard, to reveal a deadly blade engraved with flowers and leaves.

"Do you like it? It is called a shibryia."

Tears welled up in her eyes. "Saleem, it is truly beautiful. I don't know what to say. Is it tradition that I give you a gift? I didn't bring anything with me."

"Yes you did, but that can wait. I want to ask you something, but not here."

He pulled her up from the low divan and led her outside, where his bodyguards stood, holding the bridles of a pair of camels. With a flick of the harness the animals knelt. Saleem placed a stool for her to mount her ride. Once seated on the colourful saddle he placed her feet in the stirrups. He gave her instruction on how to move as the camel stood, to ensure she remained in the saddle. Then she was ready to ride. Rita had ridden horses before, how different could it be?

Saleem mounted his ride and they set off towards the foot of the cliff, his shadows following at a discreet distance.

She noticed what seemed to be a crevice in the rock face that she had not seen before. They headed directly for it. It took them into a natural pathway, with walls of rainbow-coloured stratified rock that towered high above their heads. The wind whispered around them as they made their way around a bend.

As they emerged into the sunshine beyond she blinked to adjust her eyes to the light. Before her stood a temple, carved into the mountainside. They were in

Petra. Its magnificent pink sandstone facade towered above them, taking her breath away.

Saleem dismounted and lifted her down onto the sand. "It was built by the Nabateans, nomads from the desert. They built it from the profits of the incense trade." He led her up the stone steps and into the cool temple entrance. The shadows stood sentry. Saleem was proud of his heritage, and his knowledge was impressive. He guided her though the corridors and rooms, pointing out features and recounting stories of its history.

When the tour had ended, Rita stood at the entrance once more, drinking in its raw beauty. She really didn't want this day to end.

"I would have thought it would be busy with tourists."

Saleem smiled. "I had it closed for the day so we would not be disturbed."

"Of course you did. Now, you wanted to ask me something?"

"You know that I am in love with you." He looked down for a second. "I have decided that I do not want to live without you, but my position creates an obstacle.

"To remain as a member of the royal house I would have to keep you as a mistress and marry someone of my cousin's choice. That is not what I want for us. I am asking you to come away with me. I have money, enough for us to live a life in Europe without tradition or restriction. I want you to marry me. I know we have only known each other for a matter of weeks, but I have never felt so sure about anything."

Rita caught her breath. "I love you too, Saleem but have you considered what it would really mean? You would lose your family, your birth right, your position in society. There would be no coming back from a decision like that."

He pulled her close to him. "But I would have everything I desire. My life has had little meaning up to now. I love you completely. I have not worked out all of the answers, but I know that I cannot go back to what I had before. I want to spend every minute of the time I have left on this earth with you."

20

London, 25th March, 2018

There were many in the service who thought that Peter King's job was boring. He wasn't at the sharp end of things, he didn't conduct clandestine meetings, or have anything to do with spying or subterfuge to set the pulse racing. But what he did was necessary, and made everything else possible.

He explained his function to others who were more action-oriented than he.

"I do not trade in guesswork and gossip. We live in the age of information where evidence is always at our fingertips if you know where to look for it, and I do."

Peter's ability to remember things after one look was a natural gift. As he studied information, he could spot how disparate facts fitted together long before others saw a connection. He used this laser focus to critically analyse data then produce insightful observations. He spotted red herrings a mile away.

When he first worked with Dan Grant at counter intelligence in the Middle East in 1998, their job had been to track the escalation of Islamic extremism. There had been a series of kidnappings by foreign extremists groups at the time, with a group calling itself the 'Islamic Army of Aden' claiming responsibility for the worst of these – a seizure of twenty five western tourists. Peter had pinpointed their location using data from their phone signatures. Dan had outlined a plan to secure the release of the hostages, but as a junior member of the team his advice had not been prioritised. The terrorists had killed five hostages by the time Yemeni forces launched their rescue mission. The remaining hostages were safely reunited with their families, but Dan had taken it hard. Peter had seen the lengths Dan went to to get the best results. He was definitely one of the good guys. Their efforts in the Yemen were noted by their bosses, and promotion duly followed for Dan. Peter, though, chose to stay where he was, with the data.

At this precise moment, Peter's instincts were fizzing. Two seasoned operators like Mitch and Dan concentrating on an old agent's history was unusual. And the fact that the agent in question was William Wright made it all the more intriguing.

Peter remembered the fallout from Operation Greenday. It had not made sense at the time. When he examined the incident at the time, he could see that the team had been under terrific pressure. They had been given unlimited resources to build hacking software that gave the UK and its allies an edge.

He had pulled together the files Dan had requested, and reviewed them in conjunction with the information he already had. It was obvious that William 's talent for tradecraft had been extraordinary. He designed and built his own equipment, miniaturising cameras to the point where they were virtually invisible. His work got him noticed, and when he returned home he was invited to head up the department's in-house technical team.

He had devised algorithms that allowed anonymized IP addresses to be traced back to geographical locations. He had also been largely responsible for mitigating the impact of the Millennium Bug Y2K; thanks to him and his team, none of the apocalyptic predictions became a reality. As the dawn of a new millennium broke, William had kept every major communications, security and financial system operational. All in all, a major triumph.

His biggest breakthrough however, had been much more far-reaching. He spearheaded the mission to remotely exploit the vulnerabilities present in commercial hardware and software, and as a result, Operation Greenday had changed the face of espionage. He had been able to hijack internally built-in devices, and used them to spy for the security services.

His software could remotely turn on a computer camera or microphone to record conversations and meetings in the finest detail. They could access public surveillance cameras, national and international communications networks, and use the feeds to monitor phone calls, text messages, and email to identify trigger words that could indicate potential terrorist or criminal activity. He was without a doubt the biggest technological genius of his day.

What didn't make sense to Peter, therefore, was why the service had been willing to lose such an incredible asset without a fight.

When he examined the account of Operation Greenday there were conflicting versions of events. A disciplinary hearing run by Bernard Cummings had found William guilty of gross misconduct, and he had been retired from the service with a reduced pension. The internal report conducted by William 's own team was completed but was never formally logged as an official document.

After some digging, Peter had managed to locate a copy. It made for interesting reading.

The report described the software breakthrough of building back doors into hardware to allow for undetected access. It was part of an alternative arms race, as both the Americans and Russians were trying to do the same thing. And once success had been achieved, the person who gave the order to move on to another system was Bernard Cummings.

It concluded that in the drive to move forward, one of Wiliam's younger team members had been given the task of closing the vulnerabilities in MI6's own systems. They had added additional security layers to prevent a breach, but what no-one could have foreseen was that an update of the security program had also inadvertently reopened the backdoor. Remote access to confidential data from MI6 had been enabled.

The person that made the discovery was a PhD computer student at Minsk University by the name of Gregori Yeslikov. He had been working alone late one evening, testing a hacking program he was developing, and gained access to the MI6 personnel system accidentally. The list he downloaded stayed on his hard drive for months, but once he realised what he'd found it went straight to the KGB. The Russian secret service began to liquidate British assets who were still in play immediately. Fortunately, many key people had been reassigned to posts in other countries which limited the damage, but still, three agents had lost their lives.

William 's internal review pulled no punches. He was objective and honest in his assessment, accepting responsibility for the actions of his teams.

In contrast, the report of the disciplinary hearing was subjective and scathing. Authored by Bernard Cummings, it recommended that William should be demoted and forced to take early retirement with immediate effect. It suggested that William had a record of poor judgement and insubordination that made him too much of a risk. But Peter had been unable to find any evidence of a poor service record. In fact, the opposite was true. It was almost as if the report was describing a different person.

He could not reconcile the incident with the punishment. In his experience, never had anyone suffered this kind of degradation and humiliation.

Most people who screwed up were promoted out of an embarrassing situation. It reduced the risk of questions being raised about the role of their supervising officer.

He felt irritated. He could not see any direct connection or glaring fact that justified the action taken. He had also discovered definite omissions in the official documentation, which had either been classified above his pay grade or redacted completely. That made no sense in a disciplinary report.

As he went on to review Rita and Charlie's files, he discovered that the links there were even more tenuous. Bernard had never managed a mission that involved either of them directly. All that Peter could say for sure was that Bernard Cummings was the common factor between the three ex agents.

He decided that his next step should be to cross-reference the major events with Bernard's personnel records, but he wouldn't be able to do that without raising a flag. Key people would want to know why he had strayed so far from his original brief. He needed to talk to Dan before he made his next clearance requests.

Dan answered his mobile after the second ring.

"Peter. You do know it's Sunday, don't you? Don't they give you a day off?"

Peter ignored the joke.

"I might have something for you, but I'm in a bit of a quandary. I can't complete the search you asked for unless I stray into higher clearance territory. I believe there's a missing piece of the puzzle, and it's definitely worth further digging, but I'm not sure I can do that without tripping alarms. I have a plan, but it's risky.

Just how important is this?"

Dan phrased his next statement deliberately. "To be honest, Peter, I think William Wright is in real danger. If I'm going to protect him, I need to know who or what is at the bottom of all of this. Looking for something in his past is the logical thing to do. What's your plan?"

"Bernard is the only link I've got so far, but I think he may be the key to finding out why William has been targeted. I know I'll be asked to review candidates' personnel files for Celia Browning's replacement. Bernard is obviously one of those in the frame, so as soon as I get the formal request, it will give me a justifiable reason for digging. The delay should be minimal – perhaps a week, ten days at most. Will that be ok?"

"This is urgent; there's been one attempt to kill William already, and I think there may be another, so as soon as you can please, Peter."

"OK, let me see what I can do." He put the phone down.

Dan sounded genuinely worried. Peter knew his reputation gave him some scope for a fishing trip, so he would speak to his boss and offer to get the ball rolling whilst things were a little quieter than normal. After all, the best place to hide a match is in a box of matches. He just needed to be careful that he didn't start a fire.

21

Elliot Park, London, 25th March 2018, 9pm

Hilary sat in her living room with a glass of Malbec and Madeleine Peyroux playing quietly in the background. The large french windows looked out into her lit courtyard garden. It was too cold to sit out, but she enjoyed the feeling of serenity the space gave her.

She had bought her basement flat in Elliot Park before it became fashionable. Her mother had wanted to buy it outright for her, but Hilary's stubbornness kicked in and she accepted only the deposit as a 21st birthday gift.

When her father had passed away two years ago, she had been able to pay off her mortgage and do the renovations it so badly needed to make it more comfortable. He had been generous in death in a way he had never been in life.

The real luxury she had invested in had been in the courtyard. Her aunt had helped to plan it out. After the work was done they had enjoyed the all-weather seating on summer evenings, relaxing away from city noise and bustle.

"You work long hours, Hils, and you put so much of yourself into your work," Ada had told her. "You need a space that feeds you. A garden is a place to find yourself when you've lost yourself."

She was right.

That was just before her aunt had the cancer diagnosis. She had thought Ada had looked tired when they had spent that Christmas together at her cottage in the Dales, but had put it down to her age. The tiredness, the loss of appetite had taken its toll physically. Hilary felt guilty that she hadn't paid enough attention to the signs. She had been too wrapped up in the project she was working on.

Ada had been the single constant person there for her when she was growing up. Both filling the unspoken gaps in each other's lives. Her love of jazz and swing music, visits to the theatre, galleries and the ballet, of good food and wine, and her strong sense of values and social responsibility, all of it was down to the time spent with Ada. She had shaped the adult Hilary had become, and the job she was now trying to get to grips with had come around because of Ada, too.

Hilary had always suspected that her aunt had lived

a colourful life before settling down. She had not been able to fully work out her connection to the secret service, though, and Ada had been evasive when she had asked.

Now here she was, on a dark and wet Sunday evening, poring over boxes of information about this extraordinary residential home. This was the most exciting thing ever to happen to her.

Dan fascinated her. She knew very little about him other than what she had observed in their brief meetings so far. He was attractive, and looked younger than his years. He had a dry sense of humour, and a compelling turn of speech. She felt he was a natural leader, an easy man to like and respect. The fact that he had given her the evaluation project to run after a couple of weeks demonstrated his confidence in her ability, and gave her the chance to show him what she could really do.

She plunged back into the contents of the open box. It was obvious that Shady Fields was not exactly the cheapest solution to this particular issue. Normal residential care for people with dementia was costly, but even at the top end of provision, this place still looked lavish.

If the consultants wanted to argue that the residents could go into a normal residential facility once they had lost their faculties, it could be framed as a measured risk. It would be unlikely that anyone would take any notice of them at that point, so their stories may just be taken as the normal delusional behaviour of dementia patients.

But Shady Fields residents were unique. Rita, for example, was skilled in hand to hand combat and using a blade. On several occasions she had startled Hilary by appearing behind her without having made any noise to announce her appearance. She was also a consummate thief, and Hilary had wondered if she was the culprit liberating the cleaning materials from Eileen's cupboard, although quite what she wanted them for was unclear.

They also had several ex-SAS operatives on the top floor that were still physically strong but psychologically spent most of their time reliving their missions. And they had to deal with residents who wandered off, and some of whom were frequently sexually inappropriate. It was fair to say that staffing on the upper floors was a challenge.

Ultimately, they were offering excellent care to people who might otherwise have to be cared for in a high security unit, making their conditions deteriorate even faster.

She scanned through the draft findings that Sarb had pulled together; it made for difficult reading. The report outlined three messages. First, this was the most expensive model of care for their residents and an unnecessary indulgence. Second, it was poorly run, with civil servants in charge who lacked basic business acumen. Third, it was not core business, and could be more efficiently delivered by a private sector contractor. Hilary could find no reference to the risk assessments highlighting national security as a consequence. The findings were skewed and subjective.

She reached across for her laptop and googled 'Maguire's'. The company's website was suitably corporate, and emphasised its work with national and local government. There were sophisticated marketing messages that said absolutely nothing about the effectiveness of the business.

An extremely flattering picture of Mike Shannon, probably taken a decade ago, identified him as a partner and head of the public sector division. In his blurb, he offered a number of case studies that demonstrated his team's ability to save money. There were links to an online library of their position papers supporting particular legislation. All in all, it made up a typical management consultancy's digital shop window that Hilary was all too familiar with.

After exploring the site she was in no doubt as to why they had been successful in winning the contract. They were self-declared experts at moving services away from public sector and into the hands of private business. Several of the non-executive directors on the board held top positions in some of those private companies, and their chairman was well connected.

She knew that Maguire's were hired guns meant to discredit the work of Shady Fields, and shift residents into private residential care companies. When she read the original brief that Bernard had written and the successful Maguire's bid, the link was as clear as day.

They were so close in language and presentation style they could have been written by the same person.

She looked again at some of the data that she and Linda had produced with Sarb. It was difficult to see how so much of it could have been ignored in what was supposed to be a balanced analysis. Sarb had been more objective and sympathetic in his approach, but he was fighting a losing battle. The conclusions and recommendations would be to recommend closure with immediate effect.

If this were the only data she had sight of, she would come to the same conclusion. She wasn't sure what her next move should be. Dan clearly expected her to pull a rabbit out of a hat, and counteract the bias in the report. But she had no idea how she was going to do that with such short deadlines. The final draft would be submitted next week.

She had to face the fact that she may possibly be looking for a new job before she collected her first pay cheque from this one.

Hilary felt very angry. The report suggested that the residents could be treated like every other older person with diminishing faculties. That they should be put somewhere out of view, with their basic needs met but not much else. The more challenging residents could be medicated into compliance so they could be managed by staff in ordinary facilities. The whole thing ignored the fact that if you took away independence and mental stimulation for dementia patients, it would trigger a downward spiral from which there would be no coming back.

She was puzzled by the original tender document. Why had Bernard written it himself? He was Director of Operations for MI5, for goodness' sake. It was also particularly strange that many of the residents may well have worked for him in the past, so he must be aware of the risks to national security, but hadn't mentioned that at all.

There was an extremely short lead time from the date of the tender to the beginning of the work. In her experience this could only mean one thing. It was a stitch up. The bid was written sympathetically to the chosen company, with a token gesture being made of comparing the returned bids before the contract was awarded.

She looked at the sums involved and felt the tendrils of doubt creep in. This approach was common for high value contracts, but for a project of this size the reward would have been peanuts. There must be something else she was not picking up.

If they stood any chance of survival at all, they needed someone else on their side. An internal advocate, a champion with real influence. Particularly if they were going up against the big guns.

Big projects that she had managed previously had been successful because she had controlled the game, and set the rules. In this situation, Shady Fields was an outlier. Seen as a drain on resources that produced nothing of any value to its host. They were being painted as a parasite. She had to change the rules of the game.

As soon as she got into her office the following morning, she made the call. It was answered after the third ring.

"Good morning, Jean Terry speaking." The tone was 2 degrees below 'frosty'.

"Good morning, Jean. It's Hilary Geddes here from Shady Fields. I'm the new manager here, and Dan has asked me to lead the evaluation."

"Ah yes, he mentioned that he had appointed someone. What can I do for you Hilary?"

Hilary sensed the opening of a window of opportunity.

"I thought it would be useful for me to understand the financial pressures the service is under so that we can make our contribution to the required savings plan. Are you free sometime this week to come and visit us? I know how busy you must be, but it would give you a chance to put some context to what we do, and maybe you could offer us some pointers at the same time. What do you think?"

Hilary felt a distinct thaw in Jean's tone.

"Well it's not very often we are invited in, we normally have to beat the door down! Let me check my diary."

Hilary knew time was against them. "I know it's short notice, but I want to make sure our figures add up, and being new, I could do with some pointers from someone with real expertise in service finances."

She heard keyboard strokes, before Jean replied. "Actually, I've just had a cancellation for tomorrow morning. I have got an appointment just after lunch, but I can reschedule that. Send me a meeting request with directions for your place and I'll see you around 10am. Is that ok?"

"Yes, 10 is fine" said Hilary, trying not to sound too pleased with herself.

She was struggling to get her head around the complexities of her new job, but her transferable skills were working fine. Influencing others had always been her strong point. It gave her a day to build a case that would turn Jean into the advocate they desperately needed.

22

Ben Faulkner and Bill Tandy had been friends since 1972, when they became Royal Navy recruits. They were inseparable and enjoyed distinguished careers, serving together in the Royal Marine Commandos and the Special Boat Service. Bill had exhibited a flair for explosives and Ben earned a reputation for his complete fearlessness. After they left the service they set up a business together.

It was Dan who had given them their tagline of 'Bill and Ben the Dynamite Men,' and helped establish their business by recommending them to his contacts in the CIA, FBI and MOSAD. They went on to build an enviable reputation for doing jobs others would not even consider, and consequently made themselves a small fortune. In 2015 they sold their business and embarked on a world tour where they simply visited places as tourists rather than members of a fighting force.

Bill Tandy had been diagnosed with stage two Alzheimer's just eighteen months later, and that was when they realised that their lives would have to change. Dan understood that they came as a pair, although no-one had ever described them as a 'couple' and survived.

Ben was tall and sinewy, but despite his advancing years, he was still in excellent physical condition. Now sixty-two, he still had a still punishing fitness regime. Bill was shorter and solidly built. A rugby fly half who could have played professionally had it not have been for his career choice, he was a powerhouse in his day with enormous strength and agility. He was also an exceptional swimmer.

They shared a strong bond, and it was clear to his friend that Bill's condition was deteriorating. Ben had reached out to Dan when he learned of Shady Fields. An assessment for Bill was arranged with Dr Arnott, and when they realised the seriousness of Bill's condition, they decided to become residents, moving into apartments one and two at the front of the building just a couple of days ago. Ben had hoped they'd have longer to enjoy their retirement.

Dan knocked on the door of number two, and it was opened by Ben. He liked them both enormously, due to their dark humour, their clear thinking under pressure and their loyalty. These were two of the good guys.

"I just thought I would drop by and see how you are settling in. Is there anything you need?"

Ben gave him a broad smile, "Thanks Dan, we're fine. I was just helping Bill to find his strongbox. He keeps his papers and valuables in it and he's put it somewhere safe. Come in, he'll go mad if you don't say hello."

Dan entered the room and looked at the chaos. There were clothes strewn across every flat surface, packing boxes open in the middle of the room and a guitar on a stand by the window. Having known how pedantic Bill had been about order and tidiness, he realised how much more advanced his Alzheimer's must have become. His face gave nothing away, though, as he greeted his old friend.

"Hi Bill, just checking you've got everything," he called.

A damp head popped around the bathroom door.

"Hello Rocky, you old bugger. How are the devil are you?" The grin was genuine.

Dan walked across to him. "Good to see you, Bill." He shook his hand, and noticed the strength was still there.

"Will you both join me for dinner tonight? We can catch up, and I have a fresh bottle of Balblair 99 we can knock the top off. Downstairs in the restaurant at 7.30pm, ok?" Dan made his way back towards the door.

"That would be great. We'll look forward to it. In

the meantime let me get back to unpacking. Ben means well, but he's bloody useless. I can't find a thing when he's been here." He disappeared back into the bathroom.

Dan looked across at Ben, who was trying to find a chest of drawers underneath a mountain of coats and sweaters. There was a fleeting glance of sadness before the smile was back in place.

"What's with the 'Rocky' greeting?" Dan asked.

"He's started calling all the blokes he meets Rocky. I think it's because he can't recall names very well at the moment." He smiled an apology. "Dinner sounds great. We'll see you then."

Dan closed the door behind him. He was pleased that they had come here; at least he knew they would get the support they needed without judgement.

When Mitch arrived he went straight to Dan's office. Hilary was already there with papers strewn across the meeting table. Dan had his own files in a neat pile at his side. They were already deep in conversation. Dan acknowledged Mitch. "Thanks for coming. I thought it would be good for us to meet and compare notes. Hilary has been digging into the evaluation project, and I've bought her up to speed on what we have done so far."

Hilary picked up a wad of papers, and waved them at Mitch.

"I was just taking Dan through what I've found out, too. Let me summarise for you. Essentially, I think

Bernard is using the whole evaluation thing to shut us down. It's clear that Maguire's had advanced knowledge of the project and tailored their bid to get the contract. Quotes were received from four companies, but despite Maguire's being the most expensive they were the only ones to be invited for interview."

Hilary pointed at highlighted paragraphs in the bid document, and Maguire's final bid, and continued. "Bernard has handled the whole thing himself. He's even carried out some of the resident interviews, although none of them have made it into the draft findings. I know he's been meeting with Mike Shannon to discuss the final report, and even though it's Sarbjit who has been doing most of the analysis, he's been left out of the loop."

Mitch rubbed his chin, "Are you sure about that? None of those meetings were recorded in Bernard's diary, I would have seen them."

Hilary began tidying her papers. "Sarbjit told me that Bernard met with Mike on at least two occasions, and each time he took our file with him.

"I don't understand what he would get out of Shady Fields closing, though. We have nothing to do with active agents or ongoing missions that he's in control of. If we're to stand any chance at all, we have to balance what goes into the final report. I think we need an ally, so I've invited Jean to come down tomorrow to see what we do at first hand. If she sees it for herself, she'll be able to judge how subjective the Maguire's report is."

"That's a good idea Hilary, well done. She would be great to have on side if we can convince her of our value."

He grinned at her. "So no pressure!"

He turned to Mitch. "How about we compare notes on the files that Peter sent across then, Mitch. Was there anything that stood out to you?"

"There were several things, actually. The first was in Rita's file. There was something about the mission in Amman that didn't feel right."

He looked directly at Hilary. "Contrary to popular belief, we are not in the habit of assassinating people. There was a trade delegation in Amman in '98, attended by Bernard, amongst others from our side. During the summit, a trade minister by the name of Prince Saleem Al-Baadini was found just outside the grounds of the American Embassy in Amman with his throat cut. He was a member of the Jordanian Royal Family. A known playboy, he loved spending time with the Americans. Saleem had also been suspected of selling information to the Russians.

"Rita had been sent to discover who was working with the Russians, and had been seen in the Prince's company several times. Local police had swiftly identified and apprehended a local thief and pickpocket, Farik Al-Salik, as his murderer, beheading him just two days later. Rita was recalled to London with immediate effect and that was her last active mission. After that, she worked at the home desk doing a mundane job, and dropped off everyone's radar. Her file shows that she was an excellent operative. She was first choice for honey-trap missions or anything that required burglary because she was a gifted safe cracker. So why would you bury that sort of talent behind a desk? You have to remember that Arabs have long memories and short fuses; if there was a suspicion that Saleem's death might have involved the British in some way, relationships would cool very quickly."

Something was swimming around in Hilary's head, just out of reach; she was sure it would come to her.

Dan consulted his copy of Rita's file. "I totally agree. I knew her from the training we had done together. She was so useful because of her talent for disguise. She didn't just change her physical appearance; her walk, her stance and her accent all changed. She was able to create believable characters, a real chameleon. I met her again after that mission and something had changed. She seemed to have lost her spark.

"Her knife skills were her trademark. If she had taken Al Baadini out, that is the definitely the way that she would have done it. I checked myself, and no action was ever sanctioned against the Prince. If Rita was responsible, then it was either a result of a situation that had gone badly wrong, or a Black-Op. There's always the possibility that Bernard may have wanted to cover up something like that if it happened on his watch."

The thing that had been irritatingly out of reach in

Hilary's mind suddenly came into focus, and she took a sharp intake of breath.

"Why didn't he recognise her?"

Both men looked at Hilary. "Recognise who?"

Hilary thought back to her first meeting with Bernard.

"On the day Linda died, you were in here with the police, Dan. Bernard came, do you remember?"

Dan nodded.

"Rita was in the entrance hall when he arrived, and I saw them talking briefly, but when I spoke to him a few minutes later, he didn't acknowledge that he knew her at all. It was as if they were complete strangers."

Dan thought about it. "That's certainly a bit strange. She was probably in one of her many disguises, and the incident in Amman was twenty years ago. Perhaps he genuinely didn't recognise her."

Hilary was determined to be useful. "It's worth having a chat with her to see if she recognised Bernard. I'll see what I can find out over the next few days."

Mitch left the thought hanging in the air, and picked up Charlie 's file.

"I suppose we know for sure that Charlie isn't really Lord Lucan, do we?" He smiled. "Because if Bernard had been complicit in helping one of the century's most notorious murder suspects escape a trial it wouldn't look good for him."

Dan looked across at Hilary 's shocked face.

"Stop it Mitch, this is serious. From what I can see, their work together in South Africa was all above board. Bernard had contacts there and used them to set up meetings for Charlie when he first arrived. All of that was arranged from London, and they never actually worked together in Johannesburg."

Dan picked up William's file; it was by far the thickest.

"There's obviously a lot of history between these two, and William definitely suffered badly as a result of their work together. Operation Greenday finished William 's MI5 career. It would be handled differently today."

Hilary poured herself some water. "What do you mean, Dan? In what way would it be different?"

"Well for a start, the investigation would not be conducted by William's immediate line manager because he would be considered too close. There would be an independent review headed by an officer from a different department, and everyone directly involved would have completed statements which would be kept on record as part of the process. What I thought was interesting was that William conducted an internal review of the failings of the operation, but it was never referenced or even acknowledged as part of the investigation. It was as though it never existed. The copy Peter found was registered after William had left the service."

"I spotted that, too," added Mitch. "What happened to William's team was unfortunate, but it would be hard to argue intent or even incompetence.

"My gut tells me something happened before

Greenday, but it was the excuse Bernard needed to get William out of the service. Hindsight is a wonderful thing, but it sends in expensive bills. I couldn't see how the outcome of Greenday was in any way predictable."

Dan nodded in agreement. "They were working on the leading edge. Ground-breaking stuff, when the internet was in its infancy. If anyone could have predicted what might have happened, it would have been William's team. Bernard had put them under ridiculous time constraints to get results, and frequently bypassed established protocols. William was not always sure who was working on what, such was the level of confusion Bernard was causing. From a strategic viewpoint, it could be argued that it was poor leadership on Bernard's part, not William's."

Mitch thumbed through his notes. "So I decided to look at the earlier stuff as well, and I reckon the Tbilisi operation looks more of a possibility. Bernard led that team, it was his first time in charge, and he had specifically requested William, presumably because of his reputation as a data analyst. He was experienced in cyphers and code breaking, and would have been a great addition to have in support. They lost a valuable asset just around the time the Berlin Wall fell."

Dan checked his file. "Yes, a young Georgian nationalist. They'd been running him for months and he'd produced some high value Russian intelligence. The head of the service had taken note of the asset, because it was felt that he was giving them the inside track on the stability of the USSR. Coincidentally, the asset was murdered the day after the wall fell. William was redeployed back to London within a couple of days of that, and Bernard followed him three months later. He was originally meant to come home at the same time, but the section head delayed it, as he felt someone had to monitor the nationalists to ensure the movement for independence gained momentum."

"Did they know who murdered the asset?" The words felt strange, almost ridiculous, as Hilary uttered them.

Mitch checked the details. "They didn't have a name, but it was recorded as most likely a KGB hit. The report also suggested that the Russians had discovered they had a spy in their midst, and had identified him by a process of elimination. He had worked largely unsupervised for nearly a year. None of the equipment we had provided him with was ever recovered, and his wife and child disappeared too. It was like someone had erased the whole family. Their baby was just six months old."

Dan looked directly at Mitch. "Does that sound right to you? The KGB take agents alive for interrogation. They like to know what they have passed on and to whom before they kill their traitor. It doesn't sit right, does it?"

Mitch shook his head. "No it doesn't."

"The rest of the details in the file are sketchy at best. It seems he was killed making a routine drop. The documents went missing and his body was discovered by a baker doing his early morning deliveries. He had been knocked off his bike by a car, or perhaps a van, judging by his injuries, which then reversed over him just to make sure. The case was never followed up, because the fall of the wall threw everything up in the air. The Georgians began to mobilise their nationalist supporters. To be honest, everywhere was a bit chaotic. It could be that family and friends rallied to protect the wife and baby, and took them into hiding. Alternatively, the Russians could have got them, but again that doesn't make much sense. They usually only take family members to use as leverage when they are interrogating someone. But in this instance Vlasta, their traitor, was already dead.

"The trail goes cold there."

Dan made a suggestion. "We could ask Peter to track the wife and child. See if they surfaced afterwards, and where."

Hilary was trying to keep up. "So what happened to Bernard after that?"

Dan looked at Mitch, and something silent but important passed between them that she couldn't understand.

"We don't have Bernard's file, so we can't tell exactly. It seems that it was around time that his career took off. An asset that good gets you noticed in the service, and his death was a golden opportunity to move him onto a new role. The asset was no longer in play, so nothing was lost by moving him."

Hilary shook her head, an unconscious gesture to clear it.

"Hang on a minute. If this was a success as far as everyone was concerned, Bernard would have nothing to be reproached for. William gets a new assignment, Bernard gets a promotion, everyone's happy. So in fact there's nothing untoward going on here, is there?"

Mitch pulled a single sheet from his file. "The only other thing linked to their time in Tbilisi was a separate investigation that Peter found. A report that cited William, and the last thing he did from the embassy before he came home.

"He prepared a shipment, a small crate of documents and papers, to come back to London in the diplomatic bag. The crate was meant to be collected by Bernard when he got back, but as we know, he was delayed. When he did return three months later, it had gone missing. The investigation drew a blank, because nothing could be traced."

Hilary felt like she was playing catch up again. "But if it's a diplomatic bag, surely there would be a reliable paper trail for it?"

Mitch looked up. "You would think so, but back then the volume of stuff being shipped around was higher than you would think.

"It wasn't unusual for things to be misplaced. They were usually misfiled. They turned up eventually, but often months later. I think it was assumed that that's what happened to the crate. It was at least a couple of months before Bernard went to try to collect it, and it couldn't have been that important, because he didn't try that hard to track it down. It is unusual for it to have been a crate, though. That would suggest something bulkier than paperwork."

Hilary threw another thought into the mix. "Could it have been tradecraft equipment?"

Mitch looked impressed, and nodded "Yes, it's possible, but it could also have been contraband.

"Some people will bring back all sorts when they are coming home. Things they have bought on assignment, and don't want to ship back through normal channels. I can't see Bernard smuggling drugs or booze through the diplomatic bag, though. He's far too straight laced for that."

Dan thought for a moment. "It might be useful to have a chat with William about Tbilisi, and see if he has any recollections about what happened. His long term memory is still very good and he may be able to shed more light on the crate.

"If he did send it, he may even have packed it. It's a bit of a long shot but it might yield something new. I'll go and chat with him later today. Hilary, can I ask you to talk with Sarb about the draft report? I want to know what your version with his full analysis included would look like." She acknowledged his request with a nod.

"Is there anything else?"

Mitch waited for Dan to feed him the line, then stretched back in his chair.

"Well, there was just one other thing…" he paused, for dramatic effect.

"I spoke with Bruno Gomez from the CIA a couple

of days ago. I sent him the image of the bearded man, just in case he was known to them. Well he is, and they've managed to ID him. He's a 41 year-old Chechen called Deni Dokka, a freelance hitman used by the Russians in the past for punishment beatings and killings. He is definitely a person of interest for them, and for Interpol. There's an international arrest warrant out for him and they've been keeping an eye on him since he turned up in London. Last week he was spotted arriving at St Ermin's Hotel in Kensington, shortly before Bernard Cummings."

23

Thames House, August 2006

Willlliam waited patiently in the artificially-lit room. It was cold and impersonal. The ideal place to receive a dressing-down for the mistake he had made. The furniture consisted of a metal edged table and three steel chairs. It was the kind of room that interrogations took place in.

He reflected on the reality of his predicament. Three agents were dead, and it was his fault.

A female representative from Human Resources sat next to him. He could sense the anxiety rolling off her in waves. She remained silent, only speaking to introduce herself by name and rank. He felt reassured that he had remembered to bring a small recording device into the meeting. It sat in his pocket, capturing every word.

Some viewed the work they did as a dark art, but he was hugely proud of the team he'd built. They spoke a different language, had their own rituals and trusted no-one outside their inner circle with details of their work. They understood the true potential of the internet at a time when few could. They had predicted the growth of near-instant messaging and communication and its impact on society, culture and commerce. They knew that entrepreneurs and innovators would develop software to exploit the private, personal details that millions of individuals happily provided to social networking applications, believing they were just innocently chatting with each other. Meanwhile computers were now smaller and more powerful than ever, and even phones had internet access. It seemed that the march of technology was unstoppable.

William's team had specialised in the development of applications designed to exploit these modern-day phenomena. The security services could look at or extract whatever they wanted, whenever they wanted, and no one had the slightest idea that their system security had been compromised.

They were not the only service working on hacking protocols, but nevertheless, if the perpetrator that had hacked MI6 had been an agent from another country, they would probably have seen it coming.

William's nemesis was in fact a nineteen year old student at Minsk University, studying for his doctorate. He had inadvertently gained access to their system using what was in effect his experimental hacking software. To prove that it worked, he'd downloaded a list of names and details, not knowing that they belonged to active British agents. The student didn't realise the significance of the data he had stolen at the time; it was only some twelve months later, when he submitted his thesis for evaluation, that his supervising Professor saw the list and immediately handed it over to the KGB. The information was mostly out of date by then, and many agents had been redeployed, but the valid intelligence was still acted on, and three agents were liquidated before the breach was discovered.

The heavily reinforced door opened, and an impeccably dressed Bernard Cummings strode into the room. He took the remaining seat across from the pair and slammed his folder down onto the metal table, causing William to recoil.

William was worried that Bernard was conducting the hearing. He didn't like him, and he didn't trust him. Bernard used his power and position to bully and intimidate people. Someone famous once said that that the eyes are the gateway to the soul. Bernard's eyes certainly revealed his true nature. They were sly, furtive and cold.

He opened the file and began to read it, flipping through pages of reports, and occasionally glancing up at William just to increase the tension in the room a little more.

Bernard removed a single sheet from the folder and began reading aloud. William sat very upright in his chair.

"These are the grounds for the disciplinary action we are taking today. Do you understand why you are here, William?"

William nodded, and Bernard continued.

"William Wright, you are accused of committing a very serious offence. Namely, one of enabling a breach of National security to transpire, through your clear and inexcusable dereliction of duty. Should the charges against you be proven, the consequences will be significant. This offence is categorised as Gross Misconduct, and is punishable by dismissal with immediate effect. Do you understand what I have just said?"

"Of course I do!" William snapped, thanking his maker that he wasn't Russian. They would have shot him already, after a lengthy period of torture.

He felt absolutely wretched, and launched into his mitigation immediately.

"As soon as we discovered the problem we closed the vulnerability. We also acted immediately to update security protocols to prevent anything like this ever happening again. But yes, the fact remains that people died as a result of my error."

Bernard returned to the files, scrutinising the data in front of him.

"That's not enough! I want the name of the person responsible for this catastrophic mistake." He banged the table to emphasise his point.

"It doesn't matter which of my team was

responsible. I'm the head of the team, so the responsibility lies with me."

"So there is no doubt then, that the security breach was only possible because of the back-door that you built into the system and failed to protect?" He looked over the top of his silver-framed reading glasses and glared at William.

"That's only partially correct. The gateway was secure. At least, it was until we did a software update that deleted the security protocol. You will no doubt recall that we were under huge time pressures to get results. That meant that we were not perhaps as rigorous with our testing procedures as we should have been. The glitch was missed. I'm not trying to make excuses, I am simply describing what happened."

Bernard let out an irritated sigh.

"Sounds exactly like an excuse to me. The reality was that your team got sloppy. It was your job to ensure the security of our systems, and you failed. Lots of teams work under pressure but they don't cut corners in key areas. It's not much of a defence for the loss of three lives, is it?" He spat the last words out.

William winced as if he had been physically slapped. "No. You're right. It's no defence, and I'll have to live with the knowledge of that for the rest of my life. May I presume, therefore, that you will be recommending I leave the service, take early retirement?" He looked utterly crestfallen.

Bernard stared at him.

"No, you may not presume that. I'm going to

recommend you are dismissed with immediate effect for gross misconduct, with complete loss of pension entitlement. This incident was so serious that anything less would be a dereliction of duty on my part, and disrespectful to the memory of the people that died."

He flashed a malicious smile at William. "You could always appeal, but your team members would come under scrutiny too, and there could be serious implications for one of them."

William visibly deflated. It looked like the air had been squeezed out of his body.

The HR advisor shifted uncomfortably in her seat and spoke for the first time. "Mr Cummings, whilst you are within your rights to make that decision, it is normal practice to consider extenuating circumstances such as previous record, length of service and conduct. You have made no reference to any of that."

William looked sideways and noticed that her left hand was trembling. She covered it with her right hand to steady it.

Bernard flashed a look of pure hatred at the young woman and spoke aggressively. "Last time I checked, young woman, I was in charge of this hearing. You are here purely in an advisory role. When I want your opinion, I will give it to you. Do you understand?"

William watched an angry rash of embarrassment on her neck turn deep red. It travelled upward towards her face, spreading slowly across her cheeks. Her eyes were glassy.

She took a deep breath. "Unless you follow service

procedure, I have to urge caution. If we do not follow policy, then Mr Wright could not only appeal your... the decision, he may also wish to make a formal appeal at tribunal for unfair dismissal. It is my job to keep the service out of the courts, Mr. Cummings. Procedure requires you take his service record into consideration."

She opened William's personnel file in front of her, and swallowed deeply.

"He has received two commendations for his work, he has a perfect attendance record, and testimonials from no less than five Heads of Service as character references. To take the action you are suggesting may appear to be personally motivated, which would make it unsafe."

William was impressed. It took a lot of chutzpah to stand up to Bernard. He looked across at a man that was about to explode.

Bernard spoke through gritted teeth.

"Thank you for your opinion, but I have to say that this is my decision alone. If I choose to take the risk of a legal challenge it will be my risk, and I will ask you to keep your mouth shut."

William thought it was over with this, but she came back again.

"I must say one thing before I 'keep my mouth shut,' as you so nicely put it. You are not my boss, and while I am here to protect the service I am also here to protect William's employment rights. If there is a tribunal as a result of this decision, you will find yourself as one of the defendants. I would guess that it's not a role you are familiar with. It would be an unusual precedent to dismiss someone without their pension and could be interpreted as a particularly punitive measure, bordering on maliciousness." She emphasised the last s, letting it fade…

Bernard paused for a few seconds, weighing the pros and cons.

"William does have an acceptable record and we must not appear to be operating a blame culture. So, on reflection, I think a more reasonable decision might be that we apply a demotion to his rank, to the reflect the serious nature of the security breach. I will then recommend early retirement with immediate effect. I think we can allow him to keep his reduced pension, in recognition of his long service."

The woman looked at William.

"I think that's a far more reasonable outcome, William. I would advise you to accept Mr. Cummings' judgement."

William felt numb. He knew he needed to be punished. He simply nodded, and slumped down into the chair.

Efficiency took over. "Right Mr Cummings, I will record that judgement and prepare the paperwork." She stood up to leave. "Come with me please, Mr Wright. I'll take you back to your office. I need you to clean out your desk and hand in your security badge before I escort you from the building."

Bernard stood. He displayed a sickly smile and

reached a hand out to William.

"I'm sorry it's come to this. No hard feelings?"

"Go fuck yourself, Bernard!"

When they were out in the corridor, William looked at the woman. She looked grey. She suddenly made for the toilet opposite, and William could hear the sound of her vomiting. He was slightly confused by what had just happened. The disciplinary hearing was a farce. He had not been allowed to submit the findings of his own internal inquiry in mitigation. Bernard obviously didn't want those findings made public, as they clearly showed that some of the errors were down to pressures he had placed on the team himself. He'd been desperate to give his department a head-start on cyber espionage. He was going to have that feather in his cap, and he had cut corners to get there. Now William's team was taking the blame.

William felt bruised by the whole thing. He had dedicated his career to keeping his country safe. Meanwhile, he'd seen the incompetence of others getting swept under the carpet, their mistakes and poor judgement deliberately expunged to safeguard senior figures. Yet here he was being hung out to dry. Something was indeed rotten in the state of Denmark.

The door opened and the HR advisor appeared looking pale, but ok.

"I am sorry about that. I struggle with conflict."

"Well after your performance in there I would never have known."

"I hate bullies! He obviously has a personal issue

with you, William. I'm surprised he was allowed to conduct the hearing if I'm honest. There is an appeals process should you want to go down that route; I'd be happy to put you in touch with one of my colleagues."

William felt numb. He was about to be shown the door from the career he had loved, and all because of a vindictive fop! He thought about Bernard 's veiled threat, and he realised that he had no desire to prolong the fight.

"No, I just want to see the back of this place, and him."

The woman touched William's arm. "I understand. It's a battle you're unlikely to win, but I have to offer you the choice."

"Then I choose my integrity."

24

Shady Fields, 27th March 2018, Morning

Hilary was standing in reception watching the CCTV security monitor when Jean Terry's Toyota hybrid pulled up next to the intercom at the entrance barrier to Shady Fields. She opened her window and pressed the call button. There was a short buzz, before she introduced herself. "Hello. Jean Terry, here for a meeting with Hilary Geddes."

Hilary held down the 'speak' button.

"Hi Jean, glad you could make it. Just follow the signs to the visitor's car park and pull into the first bay on the left, please." Another buzz, and the metal gates slid open. Jean drove though the barrier and out of sight of the camera as the gates closed firmly behind her.

Hilary needed this meeting to go well, and had spent hours making sure her case for the continued operation of Shady Fields was a convincing one. She wanted Jean to understand the importance of maintaining a secure facility for former agents, to balance the viewpoint that Maguire's was putting forward. She selected a different camera on the security console, and watched as Jean 's car pulled carefully into the designated space.

Hilary went to meet her as she entered the hall.

"Jean, welcome. I'm so glad you could make it. Did you have a good journey?"

Jean was looking around, obviously impressed by their surroundings.

"Wow, this isn't quite what I was expecting. The journey was ok, thanks."

"I thought you might like a guided tour first, then we can look at the figures. Will that be ok?"

"Yes, that sounds fine, but I have to be away by half past one at the latest. I'd like to make notes as we walk, is that ok?"

"No problem," replied Hilary, guiding Jean to the elevator.

They started their tour on the top floor of the building, where residents with higher dependency needs were housed. This floor consisted mostly of single rooms, which resembled the sort of facilities one would find in a top-notch private hospital. Beds were situated in private cubicles with large smart-glass observation windows set into the corridor walls. All doors and windows were wired with sensors that triggered alarms at the nurses station when they were opened. Two additional high-security rooms were located at the far end of the wing.

Two uniformed orderlies were completing paperwork at the nurse station and greeted Hilary and Jean as they passed. Security was evident, with coded swipe pads on every door. A nurse wearing a yellow tabard with the words 'DO NOT DISTURB' printed on the back and front was dispensing medication from a secure drugs trolley. As he approached the door to a resident's room, the electronic entry mechanism detected the proximity card built into the pocket of his uniform, automatically unlocking and opened the door.

Jean was fascinated by this. "Why don't staff use lanyards or badge clips?"

Hilary noted Jean's observation skills. "Some of our patients with challenging behaviour could use those things as weapons or steal them to try to leave unescorted. We find the proximity card to be the most secure option."

Hilary gave Jean a brief description of a couple of the current residents who had advanced needs, stressing the implications of trying to care for them in a non-secure facility. "They would pose a significant risk elsewhere. These ex-agents are still physically strong and possess the skills to be able to attack carers or other patients and do serious damage unless they're handled skilfully."

Jean was trying to process what she was witnessing.

"So this place allows the service to offer advanced levels of care in a secure environment that protects everyone, but that comes at a price?"

"Spot on. Some need help with eating, washing and dressing, whereas others may only require limited support and the opportunity to engage in meaningful activities."

Jean stopped. "What do you mean by 'meaningful activities'?"

"We provide residents with stimulation and engagement through structured activities: arts and crafts, a technical workshop to make and repair things, physical exercise, and sports, all of which keep the degradation of their condition at bay for a little longer."

"I see. But the residents on this floor must be much more demanding than most?"

"Yes. Staff working here face the biggest challenges, so we ensure regular rotation, shorter shifts, and extensive training for them. Please say if I'm going into too much detail."

Hilary watched for Jean's response.

Jean hesitated. "No, I get it, and I want to hear it. But what happens when they near the end? Can they die here, or…?"

"Oh, yes. Palliative care is vitally important. It might sound callous, but we know what 'dying well' means for people, whether that's just being pain free, or not dying alone. The key thing is to understand their wishes before they lose the ability to express them. Everyone who comes here completes a living will so that we can do what they want when the time comes."

The security door closed behind them with a solid click as they exited the secure area.

Hilary was grateful that Jean seemed to grasp the diversity of care they offered, and inwardly chastised herself for her stereotypical view of accountants.

The two women walked down the staircase to the floor below, where the atmosphere lightened considerably. Discrete cameras and tracking technology was not as evident here.

"Some of our residents are insomniacs, prone to wandering. For that reason they carry RFID chipped devices that allowed their movements to be tracked if we need to. The system is programmable for each individual through their tracker device. For some residents this device might be an item of jewellery, while for others it could be a wallet or a watch they always wear. The identification tag means their apartment door only opens for them or a member of staff, and not for any other resident. It also means we can see their location in real time. And just as helpfully, it can monitor their vital signs, and alert staff members if they are unconscious, or have had a fall."

"It seems very intrusive," said Jean, looking a little uncomfortable.

Hilary smiled reassuringly. "Strict protocols govern how we use it. It's there to enhance residents' daily lives, not to spy on them. Some of our former spies find the irony of their situation quite amusing."

As they walked past the communal lounge, Jean

noticed an elderly lady sitting in one of the tall armchairs wearing a handbag on her head. The flap on the front pocket had been pulled down to form the peak of a hat, and the handle was pulled under her small face to make a chin strap. She made a low purring noise.

Hilary popped her head around the door.

"Good morning, Sylvia. This is Jean, she's with us for a short visit. What are you up to this morning?" She spoke in a matter of fact way as Jean looked on.

"Well, I've found the helmet, but I seem to have lost the goggles! I can't go out without them – the dust blinds you." The old lady blinked, expecting Hilary to solve her problem.

"I'll get a couple of the mechanics to have a search around and see if they can't find you a spare pair."

A smile spread across the old lady's face. "Thanks, I knew you would help."

They continued down the corridor until they were out of earshot.

"Who was that?" Jean asked, puzzled by the old lady's behaviour.

"That, Jean, was Sylvia James.

"Imagine this. It's the height of the second world war, on the darkest night possible: pitch-black, with no moon, and no street lighting. A pre-emptive blackout that precedes a German bombing raid. A dispatch rider has an urgent message that must be delivered to an SOE Commander some 200 miles away. This courier rides a 342cc Triumph motorcycle with a top speed of

70 mph. Bombs are dropping on the London outskirts. The courier has a near miss and crashes, badly damaging the bike. After patching a punctured tyre, the rider fashions a makeshift headlamp from a torch, before getting back on the bike and continuing the journey. They navigate across Dartmoor before reaching Plymouth. The trip takes a gruelling 10 hours. The message arrives safely, despite the rider's broken wrist. The courier – in case you hadn't guessed – was Sylvia. And for that journey she was awarded the British Empire Medal. On days like today, she prepares for the mission again."

Jean was silent.

They walked along the corridor, stopping at apartment twenty six. Hilary knocked on the door, tapping out a sequence that sounded like a code. There was a muffled noise on the inside of the room before the door opened to reveal Rita standing in the doorway with a huge smile on her face.

Today she was distinctly Russian, with a glossy black bob, heavy black eyeliner and bright red lipstick. She wore a black turtle neck jumper and tight, leopard skin pedal pushers with flat, black pumps.

"Vot do you vant?"

Hilary smiled, and took a step backwards and to the side so that she could introduce Jean.

"Hello Rita, this is Jean. She's visiting us to have a look at what we do here. I wanted to check that you were ok and see if there was anything you needed at the moment?"

Rita blinked at them both.

"I vas looking for Linda earlier, but couldn't find 'er. Do you know vere she is?"

Hilary glanced at Jean.

"She isn't here today, Rita. Why did you want her?"

"I don 't zink it vos fair that she vent out viz Charlie and Villiam and I voz not invited. I could 'ave gone shopping or gone for lunch. But she never ask me."

Rita looked much younger than her advancing years. Like a small child, petulant, with a bottom lip that stood out in a pout. "I haf to get home. My muzer vill be vorried."

Hilary brightened. "Oh Rita, I'm so sorry, I forgot to tell you! Your mother sent a message. She says it 's ok if you want to stay an extra day, then you can go home tomorrow instead."

Rita seemed to relax. Hilary continued.

"Layla is finalising the details for the concert in the library, would you like to help her?"

Rita rushed back into the room and grabbed a bright red fedora which she put on at the exact jaunty angle that made it look stylish.

"That would be simply lovely, darling. I'll go right away." Her English accent was firmly back in place. She closed the door behind her and hurried towards the staircase.

Hilary looked at Jean's mildly amused expression.

"And that was Rita Hayward. Do you remember the face that launched Hot Chocolate? *'You sexy thing'* in the seventies?" Jean looked vague, as though a memory was stirring.

"No, nor me. A bit before my time. But she was a bit of a celebrity back in her day. A beautiful and intelligent woman who moved in all the right circles. She joined MI6 in the eighties. She had a distinguished career as a field agent, but her health began to fail. She injured a resident with a knife at the facility she was staying at. Her physical health was deteriorating and she needed more intensive support than they could give her, so Dan bought her here.

"Like many agents, she has no family and never married. She needed a stable environment with people who understood her needs. Since being here, her violent episodes have decreased, and what you see today is how she is for about fifty percent of the time. There are days when she is just like you or me. Her condition is managed without medication, and she enjoys a quality of life with us that she couldn't get anywhere else. I would say that she is typical of the residents who live on this floor."

Morning coffee was due to be served at 11:00 so they made their way to the restaurant. There were already more than a dozen people seated and chatting in the large dining room when they entered. Hilary noticed Dan sharing a table in the bay window with William.

"Let's sit with Dan," she suggested, and walked across to where the men were sitting. Jean was clearly amused that they both stood up until she and Hilary were seated.

"What do you think of our little 'experiment' then, Jean?" Dan asked.

"Well, Hilary has been showing me around, and I must say I have learnt an awful lot this morning."

"We met Sylvia and Rita on our travels," said Hilary, by way of an explanation.

William adjusted the manuscript in the crook of his left arm. "Are you coming to stay here then?"

"Oh no," said Jean. "I'm here to help with the business side of things. Hilary and I will be going over the figures after coffee, then I must get back to the office."

Suddenly a muted, heavy thud resonated through the building. Cups and saucers on the tables rattled and clinked. It was hard to tell if the noise was from a distant part of the house or outside in the grounds.

"What on earth was that?" asked Jean looking around.

Dan returned the remainder of his pastry to the plate in front of him. "Our gardener has been tackling a stubborn tree root for over a week now. He's probably decided that more drastic action is required, but I'll go and check just to be sure." He looked at Hilary. "You haven't seen Bill and Ben around recently, have you?"

Hilary smiled and shook her head.

His coffee break prematurely ended, Dan left the restaurant, but William lingered to treat his new audience to the facts about his memoir and how sensational it was going to be. Jean listened patiently and remembered that Dan had mentioned William and his book at the meeting in London a few weeks ago.

"So is it finished, William?" she asked.

He became defensive. "No. Not yet, but it's nearly there. Then people will see! I will make people pay the price for their dirty dealings!"

"Dirty dealings?" Jean 's interest was aroused but Hilary decided to stop William before he said anything else.

"William, Mr Erskine rang yesterday and said that we need to get the manuscript to him by this weekend if possible, or next week at the very latest. Do you think you can do that?"

"Well only if you stop wasting my time and let me get on with it!" He pushed his chair away from the table, stood up abruptly and strode out of the room and across to the stairs.

"Right Jean, I think we have some work to do. Let's go up to the office."

Seated at her desk, Hilary pressed a button on her keyboard and a multicoloured spread-sheet appeared as the screen burst into life. They looked at the rows and columns of figures in the spreadsheet that held the future of Shady Fields somewhere in its formulae. Hilary pointed to some totals highlighted in yellow on the screen.

"If we put the current development plans on hold and include the new residents' fees for the rest of this year, we can break even by the deadline you first mentioned."

Jean studied the lines of numbers and nodded. "Yes, but the running costs are still very high for so few residents. How can you make economies to get that down below the two million figure?"

"There are a number of things we are working on. Our carbon footprint is significant. If we install low energy lighting and heating, the savings will be considerable.

"We've also put forward a proposal to both service heads to create a specialised safe-house environment here that they could use for 'special guests'. So if, for example, you wanted to hide a someone waiting to go into witness protection, this is the almost certainly the last place anyone would think of looking. We would run it like any other safe house, with an annual lease to secure it and then chargeable services when it was occupied. If you look at line seventeen of the proposed budget, we think it would generate a reasonable income and move us into a financial surplus. What do you think?"

Jean studied the figures. "This is very impressive, Hilary. I really don't know why you asked me to come and advise you, you're doing fine on your own."

She looked at her watch.

"I have to make a move now, but thank you so much for inviting me down today. I really didn't know what to expect." She gathered her papers together. "You know Hilary, you are running an expensive operation, but at least I now understand why there's a need for Shady Fields to exist." She looked intently at her, with a gaze heavy with meaning.

"There are some who would be happy to see you fail. Make sure you fully cost alternative solutions and include those in the evaluation report, too."

Hilary was left wondering exactly what she had meant by her parting comment but knew instinctively that Bernard Cummings was in the mix somewhere.

25

Shady Fields, 27th March 2018, Afternoon

Dan walked along the main corridor towards the East wing to visit William. Apartment fifteen was on the first floor, and was one of the smaller studios. It had good views of the extensive grounds at the side of the building, and William had been perfectly settled here since he moved in. Dan realised with some surprise that it was the first time he had visited him at home. He knocked on the door, and after a little while it opened. William stood there looking slightly dishevelled.

"Oh hello, Dan. What can I do for you?"

"William, when I saw you earlier at lunch today we agreed that that it would be good to have a chat about recent events and we said about 3pm. Is it still ok to talk now?"

William blinked. "Yes, of course," and hurriedly

added, "I hadn't forgotten. Please come in." He opened the door and stepped aside for to Dan to come in.

It was a quiet space with all the basics but no ornaments or embellishments. The furniture was practical, the television was small, but the bookcase was large and overflowing. An expensive DAB radio stood on a table next to a winged reading chair. A small two-seater sofa sat in the middle of the room.

Through the open bedroom door he could see a single divan made up with sheets and blankets rather than a duvet. There was a plain teak dressing table and chair in the small bay window. The only decorations were a wooden icon that stood in the centre of the table, its doors opened to reveal a painting of a Madonna and child, and a small frame with a faded picture of a young woman in front of that.

Dan was surprised. He'd never thought of William as religious, or of having a private life, but these two objects stood out sharply against the impersonality of everything else.

William gestured for him to sit down on the settee. "Would you like a cup of tea? I've just made a pot."

"No, thanks, but don't let me stop you."

William disappeared into the studio kitchen and came back a few minutes later with a mug in his hand. He sat opposite in the armchair, put his mug on a coaster on the side table, and looked at Dan, unsure of what was about to come.

"We're trying to understand why someone might want to harm you, William, so Mitch Bennett and I have been reviewing what we know about your service career and we have a couple of questions that might help us to find the answer. Is that ok?"

William shifted slightly in his seat, making himself more comfortable.

"Yes, that's fine."

"We know you were stationed in Tbilisi in the late eighties. You and Bernard ran a high value asset called Shura Vlasta. Do you remember that William?"

"Of course I do, I'm not senile yet!" William gave a slight smile as he spoke.

Dan continued. "So, can you tell me about the events that led up to you being redeployed back to London?"

"I should've thought that would be in my file. I found him you know. Bernard ran him, but I found him and turned him. He was married to the most beautiful woman, Milena Vlasta." He let her name roll off his tongue, and sighed as her memory revisited him. "She loved him and supported him, stood by him even though she knew the danger it put them both in. When they had a baby she worried about being caught.

"Shura was feeding us high value intelligence right under the noses of the Russian military and they didn't have a clue. We set up a dead drop system, and used the Metekhi Bridge. We thought it would be difficult to launch an ambush there, clear lines of sight, you know, the usual.

"That last drop, I was there. Bernard had asked me to do surveillance on the family when Shura first came on board, but I carried on long after the routine had been established. The drop was early in the morning, just after 5.00am, I think. I was testing out a new version of my digital camera, and wanted to see its capability in low light. The street lights were pretty poor there, even when they were working. I saw it all. I saw Shura come across the bridge on his scooter. I saw the car swerve right into him and knock him over. I saw the driver get out and take the pannier with the papers in it, then reverse over him, killing him." William was so matter of fact. He never hesitated or baulked at the description he had just given.

"All I could think of was how devastated Milena would be. It was horrible. I watched the car drive off, then went to check on him, but of course he was dead. I waited until the delivery driver found his body, then went into the office as normal. I couldn't even report it. I had no reason for being on the bridge at that time in the morning. It would have raised all sorts of questions, so I stayed quiet."

William picked up his tea. His hands were shaking. As he raised his mug he spilled some of the contents on his trousers. Dan knew he was on the edge. If he pushed too hard it could trigger a reaction that might render William useless for days. He went into the kitchen for a cloth.

William took the cloth offered by Dan and began dabbing at the patch on his trousers. He reached into his trouser pocket for his silver hip flask and took a slug. It calmed him, and the shaking lessened. Dan waited until he had regained his composure.

"So how do you think the Russians found out?"

William looked at him and blinked.

"Oh, it wasn't the Russians. It was us. We killed Shura Vlasta, or rather Bernard did. It was his car on the bridge."

Dan didn't quite know what he was expecting William to say, but it certainly wasn't this.

"William, can I just check – are you absolutely sure it was Bernard driving? It was a dark morning, and you must have been some distance away. How can you be certain?"

"Because he told me later that morning that he'd done it," William blinked again as if what he had just said was completely normal. "And later when I developed the photos I could see it was him."

"What exactly did Bernard tell you?"

William paused for a moment, remembering the conversation. "He was already in the office when I got in, which was unusual as he never normally came in until after 10 o'clock. There was a sealed crate by the side of my desk, and he'd left me a handwritten memo asking me to complete the paperwork and get it into the diplomatic bag back to London. He said he would collect it himself when he returned home.

"I did that, and then he took me into the secure comms room. He told me he'd received orders from London that Shura had to be removed. Apparently, London had known for a few days that the Berlin Wall was coming down and that Georgia would be plunged into a fight for independence. They couldn't allow the Russians to discover what Shura had been giving us. It would be like throwing petrol on a fire. With great reluctance, Bernard had agreed to take care of it himself, but it was top secret, so no-one else knew.

"I was shocked. I really liked Shura. He was an idealist, but he loved his country. He wasn't some shabby opportunist doing it for personal gain. My main concern was for his wife and child. I wanted to help them, but Bernard said it was too dangerous and in any case, I wouldn't have time, because he had orders for me to return to London for redeployment with immediate effect. I left on a commercial flight for home that evening."

William's shoulders slumped. "After that, I requested a move to MI5 scientific services. I couldn't deal with the matter-of-fact way they dealt with death. I wanted to stay in London, removed from that world. I wanted to develop technology that others could use remotely to gain access to secrets. I thought it was a way of saving lives rather than being complicit in taking them."

He gave a hollow laugh. "I came home and developed a software package that could do that, and was responsible for the death of three agents. We were hacked and their details were stolen!" He shook his head. "I couldn't win, could I?"

Dan reached out a hand to comfort him, but William pulled away.

"William, you saved more lives that you will ever know. From what I've read, you were at the forefront of the technology. Your work gave us the capability to eavesdrop electronically, protecting agents."

He wanted to keep William focused.

"Tell me about the crate, William. Did you know what was in it?"

"No. Why would I? That's the point of a diplomatic bag service, the contents are anonymous. The crate was already sealed when I got it. I was just following orders. I completed the paperwork and it went off the same day. The next thing I heard about it was months later when I was working for the surveillance equipment team and got hauled in to an inquiry because it had gone missing.

"Actually, that's not strictly true. They found the crate, but the contents were gone. No one had called to collect it, and when Bernard finally came back, he was too late. Whatever was in it was long gone. That could never happen nowadays – CCTV, biometric identifiers, and audit trails all make the diplomatic bag service unbreakable, but that wasn't the case back then."

A smile crept across William's face. "He was furious when he realised the contents were gone. I think he even suspected me, but because I was meticulous in following procedure I was cleared. The enquiry found that it had probably been misfiled. Wouldn't be the first time, so everyone carried on as normal. After that, things between me and Bernard became strained. He would go out of his way to make my life difficult. A couple of times he was managing my team or an operation I was working on. I could never do anything right as far as he was concerned. He would make ridiculous demands, and if I failed to meet them it was always my fault. Not good enough at my job or leading my team. The Operation Greenday fiasco was the opportunity he needed to get rid of me once and for all. I did think he was particularly vindictive about all of that. I was the only employee ever to have been downgraded before I was forced to retire. All those years of faithful service, and all I got was a reduced pension and a blemished service record. I didn't deserve that."

"I can see why you would feel like that," Dan sighed. The more he heard, the more he was beginning to realise how unpleasant Bernard was. He had never really got on with him. They had rubbed along because they had to, but this was revealing a much darker tale of manipulation, vindictiveness and a cavalier approach to the rules. The biggest difficulty he faced in following through with any action, though, was that Bernard's position gave him a huge degree of protection. To investigate him would ring alarm bells. It could potentially smack of undermining or trying to discredit him.

Dan was also starting to understand why Bernard saw Shady Fields as a threat. If what William was saying was true, and if it became public knowledge, Bernard could kiss goodbye to ever becoming Director General. His subsequent knighthood would evaporate, too.

Dan also considered that Bernard might well be behind William's attempted murder to protect himself. He would have dismissed the idea as absurd a few weeks ago, but now he began to wonder just what Bernard might be capable of.

He left William to rest, and returned to his office to call Mitch and update him. As he relayed their conversation, he realised that William's version of events was potential dynamite.

"To be honest, Mitch, when you told me about Dokka I thought it was a coincidence, but now I'm not so sure. We have to find out if there's anything that corroborates William's account of events, but we'll need to tread carefully. If we take this to anyone at the moment, they'll simply put it down to William's history with Bernard, or his dementia making him paranoid."

"Do you believe him, Dan?"

Dan hesitated. "For the most part, yes, but I did get the impression I wasn't getting the whole story. The trouble is, I don't know if William is holding something back or just has holes in his memory."

"What's your next move, then?"

"I don't really want to say. The less you know, the safer you'll be, but I think I know a way of checking some of this detail out without raising a red flag. I'll be in touch."

26

The Reform Club, 29th March 2018, lunchtime

Bernard looked at his watch. Charlie would be here shortly. He had managed to get hold of his mobile phone number when he last visited Shady Fields, and he reasoned that he could use him as a possible player in his little drama. He called him with an invitation to lunch at the Reform Club.

"Look, Charlie, I don't want to beat about the bush, but I heard about what happened to poor Linda and l wanted to check that you were ok. It must have been a terrible shock. I wondered if you would like to lunch with me at The Reform Club on Thursday. They do a simply wonderful roast beef, and I thought it might help to lift your mood a little. My treat of course. What do you say?"

Charlie had been flattered. "I would love to,

thanks."

Bernard had helped Charlie big time when he had arrange the posting in South Africa. His gambling addiction had racked up thousands of pounds of debt. His marriage had broken down, and his wife was granted custody of their children. Even his father had practiced 'tough love' by cutting off his access to family funds. He had been mixing with some very unsavoury people, even owing the notorious Richardson brothers a five-figure sum. Their reputation for violent debt collections was legendary.

One of Charlie's favourite haunts had been the KitKat Club. He'd gone there to drown his sorrows one night, and had met Bernard. Bernard bought him a few martinis, and he had confided his predicament. "If this gets back to my section head, I'm finished," he'd slurred.

Bernard knew that any agent in this situation could be exploited. They were prime blackmail candidates who could be coerced into spying for the highest bidder. He liked the power that having people in his debt offered him, and he always played a long game with it. Favours he granted now could be called in whenever he needed them.

He clearly remembered his offer to Charlie. "There's a diplomatic posting coming up in South Africa, on a trade delegation. It involves high-level negotiations, designed to bring the country into this century. With your background I think I could persuade people to give you a chance."

He knew Charlie's family had significant mining interests in the country and those might create useful connections for the mission.

"Bernard, that would be great. It would give things a chance to blow over here, and I could get my act together. Will you do it? Will you recommend me for the posting?" Charlie was virtually pleading through his drunken haze.

"Leave it with me. I'll put a good word in for you and see what I can do."

Bernard had already heard Charlie's name being put in the frame, anyway. A small nudge from him now, and the deal would be sealed. If Charlie's connections worked as well as he thought they would, Bernard would take the credit. And if they didn't, Charlie could carry the can.

In fairness, Charlie took the second-chance he had been given and turned over a new leaf. The posting to South Africa had saved his life and his family reputation. He felt indebted to Bernard. Of course, Bernard had been incredibly modest about it all. He made sure he never accepted thanks or even kept in touch that much, although he kept a watchful eye on Charlie. Knighthoods were given by recommendation, and it would not hurt if his recommendation was supported by an old and respected aristocratic family who owed him a favour.

Yes, it paid to play the long game.

It had occurred to Bernard that he could use Charlie to solve his current predicament. It was indeed fortuitous that both Charlie and William had ended up at Shady Fields. If handled in the right way, this may even provide him with the means to close the place down completely.

Sometimes, fate was on your side.

Charlie saw Bernard's car pull into the collection zone at the railway station, a discreet placard bearing his name on its dashboard. He stepped forward, catching the driver's attention. The driver got out and opened the rear door for him. He slid across the luxurious leather seats and inhaled the unique smell of new car. The journey around Hyde Park and along Piccadilly towards St James Palace was smooth and quiet. London was dreary at this time of year, and he compared it to the warmth and light of Johannesburg. It fell considerably short.

They arrived outside the Reform Club just before 1.00pm. Charlie smiled to himself as he stepped out of the vehicle and made his way to the entrance. It bought back memories of life as a spy in London in the swinging sixties. The Reform Club was an old institution, but it had reinvented itself quite successfully.

Bernard was waiting for him in the club's impressive atrium. He loved this part of the building. It was both spectacular and imposing, with its glass roof visible three stories above them. Bernard watched Charlie take the steps confidently and enter the inner sanctum looking for his host. He had a fawn Gannex raincoat on, with a simple but well cut suit beneath. Bernard moved towards Charlie, extending a hand. "Hello, Charles. So nice to see you again."

Charlie shook his hand. "Bernard, please, only my mother and my bank manager ever called me Charles. Charlie is fine."

Bernard gave Charlie a brief guided tour. "How was your journey?"

"It was ok. Train travel isn't what it used to be, though. It's too cramped and too quick for my liking. I had the worst cup of tea I have ever drunk, served by a teenager dressed like a Butlins' Red Coat who was welded to her mobile phone!"

Bernard smiled in agreement.

A porter took Charlie's coat and motioned them into the 'Coffee Room', which was actually the restaurant.

A table had been reserved for them in a quiet corner of the room, and an immaculate waiter showed them to it now. Both men took their seats, menus were produced, and Charlie took his time to read through it all before making his selection.

Bernard took a breath. He needed to be patient, so let Charlie read without interruption. After a few moments, his guest chose a dover sole and the roast beef. Bernard ordered the same and selected a mid-priced Burgundy to accompany the main course. Napkins were unfurled and water was poured before the waiter took his leave.

Bernard began. "So, Charlie, how are things?

Linda's tragic accident must have been a great shock to you all, but worst for you. You were there when it happened, weren't you?"

"I was. She was such a lovely person. We miss her a lot. The police don't think it was accidental, though. They think it was an attack, intended for William. They have footage of someone intentionally going for him, but Linda got in the way at the last minute, and she was shoved down the escalator instead."

Bernard feigned shock. "Goodness me, Charlie, that'sterrible. Do they have any idea who it was?"

"They're looking into it at the moment, but I'm sure if he's in the system they'll track him down. I really hope they do, anyway."

The fish course arrived and the two men savoured the succulent lemon flavoured fish in relative silence. While their plates were being cleared, Bernard ventured a little farther.

"And how is my good friend William doing? It can't be easy for him. I would think he's blaming himself, isn't he?"

Charlie took a sip of water.

"He did to start with, but now he's just angry. He hasn't had it easy, you know. He felt badly let down by the service when they retired him early. No one else had ever received that sort of treatment. He lost a lot financially, too. I don't think he has much in the way of savings.

"That's the main reason he's writing his memoirs; he wants to make some money to supplement his pension. His legal advisor thinks that in the current climate and with the threat of another cold war looming, his book could be a Sunday Times bestseller. People love the cloak and dagger stuff, and it could become a huge success if it's professionally edited."

"I don't mind telling you Charlie, I was worried about him the last time we met. I took him down to the village pub for a chat. Just wanted to get a few quotes from him for this evaluation report we are all working on. Between you and me, he looked tired. I was surprised how much his memory had deteriorated. He exhibited some very odd behaviour when we were together."

Charlie looked puzzled. "I haven't noticed anything. Like what?"

The waiter returned with their main course. He positioned their plates and side dishes to perfection, poured them both a glass of wine, topped up their water glasses, and left as silently as he'd arrived.

Bernard raised his wine glass to Charlie and took a sip. It was a mediocre wine, but good enough for lunchtime. He didn't want to waste a good burgundy on his guest. At his age, his tastebuds were probably shot anyway, so what was the point? He wouldn't appreciate it.

Bernard continued. "William was mislaying things, then finding them in the oddest places. He thought he had seen and spoken with people that died years ago. He was forgetting his medication, you know the sort of thing. He was also very paranoid about his manuscript. Quite frankly, he thought someone was out to steal it to stop him publishing his story. I am not quite sure why he thought that. I understand that he carries it around with him everywhere and that it's never out of his sight. I suppose you've read it, though?"

Charlie smeared a forkful of beef with a dab of English mustard.

"No, he hasn't let anyone read it yet as far as I know. He did say that he was going to give Dan the manuscript for safe keeping until he can get it to his publisher."

He popped the beef into his mouth and winced slightly, eyes watering as the mustard burn took effect.

Bernard suddenly paid a little more attention.

"When did he tell you that, Charlie?"

"He mentioned it a couple of days ago. In fact, he gave the impression that it's almost finished. I understand that the final chapter is about an incident he was involved in years ago in Georgia. He said there was a cover up at the highest level.

"I popped round to his apartment for a drink and a game of cards one night and he was telling me he wants to set the record straight. Apparently, he has pictures and documents to prove his claims but he isn't sure whether they'll let him publish them."

Bernard almost choked on the beef he was chewing. He snatched the napkin to his mouth and coughed, then reached for the water. Photographs? It was the first he'd heard of any photographs! If there was visual proof he had to act now. He couldn't afford to delay any longer.

Despite the many delicious and tempting sweets on offer, they both declined dessert, but finished their meal with a large brandy. Charlie held the balloon glass between the palms of his hands to warm its golden contents.

"I would give my good knee for a cigar now, but Dr Arnot would go mad!"

Bernard signalled the waiter.

"What Dr Arnot doesn't know can't hurt him."

But Charlie declined the offer with a shake of his head. So instead, Bernard just signed the bill with a flamboyant flourish.

"Well that was most enjoyable," said Charlie, Bernard guided him out to the reception desk and the concierge retrieved his raincoat. As Bernard helped the old man on with his coat he chatted to distract him, and slipped something into his pocket. He walked him out and down the steps, where his driver was already waiting to take him back to the station. Charlie turned and shook Bernard's hand.

"Thank you, Bernard, I've really enjoyed today. Most kind of you to ask me."

"Well, I hope it did the trick and took your mind off things for a while. Please keep an eye on William and if there's anything I can do please contact me. I wouldn't mention our lunch today though if I were you, Charlie. I wouldn't want anyone to think I was showing favouritism, even though we do go back a long way."

He slid a business card from a silver card holder and passed it to Charlie. "This is my direct number. If I can help you with anything, please give me a call."

"Today will be just between us. You can rely on me, Bernard, and thanks again."

Bernard watched the car swing out into the main flow of traffic, then returned to the library to finish his coffee.

A quick phone call, then all he had to do was wait.

27

Shady Fields, 30th March 2018

William's eyes were tired. The drops Dr Arnot prescribed didn't seem to be helping at all, and today his headache was getting worse. To add to his frustration, his hands were becoming increasingly unsteady. Steve, his care assistant, had to help him take his medication last night and this morning. The physical discomfort he could just about deal with, but the loss of mental acuity he disliked intensely.

He hated how his age made him feel. His hips, knees and back constantly ached from the dull throb of arthritis. It limited the length of time he could sit at his desk and write. After just an hour he would stiffen up and then struggle to get out of his chair.

But it was the foggy head that troubled him most.

It seemed cruel that he could remember things that happened thirty or forty years ago as if they'd only happened yesterday, but when he tried to recall what he'd done a few days before, his memories were cloudy and confused. He had to finish his book while he still could.

He looked out of the window at the grey sky and the steadily falling drizzle. The rain made the trees glisten and the grass look fresh and clean. The spring bulbs had almost finished, and the rhododendrons were in full bud. Warmer and drier days were on their way, which raised his mood a little. He was trying to complete his account of events in Tbilisi. He owed it to them. His actions had changed their lives forever, and the guilt he felt weighed him down like an anchor. Time was no healer for him. As he grew older, he'd come to realise that he had fallen for Milena. He had not intended to get close, and had fought against his feelings, but even though he could only watch her from a distance, he was in love with her.

After Shura's death, his only contact with Milena had been by letter. He had tried to take care of her and the child as best he could, but he knew how deep her grief was, and he felt ashamed.

When he learned he was to return to London with immediate effect, he used the short time left to set up a go-between for the two of them. She was a minor official from the British Embassy who could get money to Milena; initially its purpose was to help with the funeral, but as the months passed it became a fund for living expenses.

When the civil war started he found a small Georgian community on the outskirts of London, most of whom had made their own way across Europe to escape the fighting. William arranged for Milena and her daughter to join them, finding a house to live in and giving her the chance to build a new life. She had learned English, qualified as a nurse and put Sykhaana through school, but she never remarried.

On the few occasions when he observed her from afar, William could see that the sadness of her loss still overwhelmed her. She laughed and socialised, but she'd lost the fierce spirit he'd first observed. The light in her eyes was gone, and that was his fault. His guilt was compounded because he had been forced to perpetuate the lie that it was the Russians that had murdered her husband. He had maintained the lie because he feared that if she knew the truth she would refuse to accept his help. She might even return to Tbilisi and be lost to him forever.

The papers and travel arrangements he had made for them were 'off-book' – obtained through favours he had called in. The service had no knowledge of the help and support he was giving the family, the money for which had come from the sale of one of the illicit Russian icons he had shipped for Bernard. When William had discovered that his superior had used Shura's money to purchase the paintings he was incensed. So it seemed like a perverse sort of justice that the proceeds from the sale of one of them – the

'John the Baptist' icon, which sold for £350,000 at Bonhams to a Russian Oligarch intent on buying back the Tzars' history – should be used to take care of his family.

William was not sure why he'd kept the second icon. He suspected that the image of the Mother and Child was a strong connection, but he was not sentimental as a rule. It was the most valuable of the two and he thought of it as an insurance policy to protect himself. When he really needed money, however, he found he was unable to part with it.

He knew his condition was worsening, so he decided he needed to write a will. In it, he had left the icon to Sykhaana as a bequest. She could decide to keep it, or she could sell it to provide financial security for her and her family. The market for Russian icons had increased beyond expectation, and a simpler example by the same artist had sold for two million pounds five years ago. It would definitely guarantee her financial future.

When he realised that Milena intended to return to Georgia five years ago, he had made contact arranging a meeting at her home. He wanted to finally set the record straight.

He wondered if she was happy now and whether she ever regretted returning home. He got up from his chair and stretched a little, his joints made loud clicking noises.

The photographs he had taken that fateful day were damming proof of the atrocity committed by Bernard, and he'd kept them locked away securely with other photographs he had taken in Tbilisi. He had decided to include some of them in his book and would need to sort and catalogue them when he delivered the manuscript to Mr Erskine. He crossed the room to the built-in wardrobe, slid open the louvre door and moved the shoe boxes in the far corner. Underneath them, a small security box with a five-digit combination lock was set into the floor. He opened the lid of a Churches shoe box, unwrapped the protective paper around a handmade tan leather brogue, and looked at the sole. Written across the instep in a shaky hand was the combination. There was a time when he could remember great strands of letters and numbers without any difficulty, but he knew that those days were long gone. He keyed the code into the lock and the heavy steel the door sprang open. He reached inside and retrieved a worn leather pouch. He kept all of his important papers in the box, but the pouch contained only photographs. They were another insurance policy.

He carried the pouch to the table and removed the wad of old photographs. The majority of them showed Milena and the baby but they were not family portraits. They'd been taken clandestinely, when she was out shopping, playing in the park, at a school recital. There were a couple of Shura, too; one with his family and the other in his military uniform. But the pictures William was looking for today were at the bottom of the pile.

Five slightly dog-eared black and white photos,

from the poorly-lit bridge, showing Shura's death in three stages. The first two depicted the initial collision and the man retrieving the documents. The third was the most shocking. It clearly showed the reversing vehicle, just before it drove over Shura's body. In the fourth, diplomatic plates were clearly visible. The final shot was a grainy image of the driver in an overcoat. Although it had been enlarged, it showed unmistakably that the driver was a younger Bernard Cummings.

William felt his anger begin to stir. He'd never questioned the orders he was given by Bernard, because he'd assumed that everything they had done was for the greater good. Sometimes it was difficult to understand the decisions taken in the name of national security.

He picked up a photographer's loupe and studied the pictures in more detail. What he had here was 'smoking gun' evidence. The discovery of the icons and the missing money from Shura's account had led him to the truth. These were not pictures of an officially sanctioned mission. He had eventually realised that it had been Bernard's clean-up job, and that he was eliminating the one person that could expose his activities.

Spying was a dirty business, and there would always be winners and losers. It had nothing to do with right or wrong, or justice. Agents knew that there were no rules in the field. It was ten percent preparation and ninety percent improvisation. You did what you had to do to survive. You made it up as you went along, and it was only hindsight that rewarded or punished you.

William had come to understand that Tbilisi was one of those situations. No one could have predicted events. It took William a couple of months to realise that, but once he did, he also knew that the explanation Bernard had given him for Shura's elimination could not be true. He still didn't have the full story, but he knew that Bernard had lied to him and to their spymasters.

He despised his own weakness, and the fact that he had never confronted Bernard with any of this. Even when his name and reputation had being dragged through the mud and his career bought to an untimely end, he had not shared the truth. No one would have believed him. By then he had become a joke in the service; undervalued, and even pitied. Meanwhile Bernard 's career had gone from strength to strength. His lying and cheating had been rewarded with promotion and praise. But it was built on the backs of others.

The bitterness festering inside William had given him the idea of writing his memoirs. It would be his ultimate revenge. Bernard had taken everything that had mattered to him. The happiness of the woman he loved, the recognition for his cutting-edge inventions, and even, William reflected, his self-respect. His explosive publication would redress that balance. At present, there was an appetite for prosecuting historical acts done in the name of Queen and Country. The public would demand all of the salacious details.

The timing couldn't be better either, as Bernard was being lined up to take over as the next DG, with a knighthood sure to follow. That was the pinnacle of Bernard's ambition. He needed recognition, he craved acceptance, and he wanted to be lauded by those at the highest levels of society.

Now William could take all of that away from him with the written word. The irony was delicious. Bernard had frequently put William down as a pen pusher, but his fate lay in the words that William had penned.

"William…William…"

He was being shaken awake. He eyes flickered open, and a blurry shape slowly came into focus. It was Steve. "Come on William, wake up. You'll get stiff sleeping at the table like this. Are you ok?"

William blinked his eyes.

"What time is it?"

"It's eight o clock, William. Time for your medication."

William tried to focus but his head was splitting. "Is that morning or evening?"

Steve walked across to the bay window and drew the curtains. "It 's evening. You were missed in the dining room tonight so they sent me to see if you wanted to have something in your room instead."

William felt a wave of nausea sweep through his body. He obviously hadn't eaten since breakfast. He took the tablets offered by Steve with a small glass of water. "I do feel hungry but I don't feel like going downstairs. Can I have some soup and a roll please, Steve? Maybe a pudding too?"

"No problem. Let me see what I can rustle up for you. There were some hot cross buns left – do you fancy one toasted with butter? I'll be back shortly."

Happy that William was ok, he headed off to the kitchen.

William felt his senses slowly returning. His photographs were no longer strewn across the table. He looked around and spotted the pouch on his desk next to the typewriter. He walked unsteadily across the room to pick them up. A quick glance confirmed that they were all still in there. He couldn't remember putting them away but he obviously must have done. He decided it would be best to return them to the lock-box for safekeeping.

28

The Bull's Head, 31st March 2018

Mike Shannon was blasé about his concerns. "There are only the three of us that know about it. I think you're being a little paranoid, Bernard."

He sat in the comfortable leather chair across from the senior civil servant. There was a low hum of discussion from the other customers in the bar.

Bernard looked at him in a dismissive manner. "I have learnt two things in my job, Mr Shannon. Just because you are paranoid doesn't mean people are not out to get you, and three people can keep a secret but only if two of them are dead."

Mike laughed nervously. He was regretting the day they had accepted this contract. His job was to produce reports that were argued over in a board room and where the most dramatic outcome was that people lost their jobs. The more he got to know Bernard Cummings, the more he disliked him.

It was clear from the preliminary work they had done that Shady Fields was doing a good job providing secure care for a unique group of individuals, but that was not what Bernard wanted to hear. Shannon knew that normal care facilities would carry a significant risk for these residents and whilst their current home was not the cheapest, it was probably the most effective. The early conversations he had with Bernard had left Mike under no illusions. Those would not be the findings of this evaluation report; it should lead to the single conclusion that Shady Fields should be closed with immediate effect.

Mike continued, "Sir Henry was happy to leave the details of the report to me. Sarbjit has done an excellent job gathering the right data, and although Linda's death did create a slight delay in the timetable I think we're back on track now."

He wasn't happy about having the meeting in such a public place. The Bull's Head was not crowded, but that meant you had to whisper lest your conversation carry around the bar. This was the third time they had met here and he knew the landlord had recognised them this morning because he had reached for Bernard's favoured tipple as soon as he saw them enter the bar.

"It was a shock when I heard of Linda's accident. She was a very capable manager. So capable, in fact, that it would have been difficult to get some of our assumptions accepted in the report if she was still around." Mike was feeling brave all of a sudden.

Bernard took a sip from his glass. "Do not underestimate her replacement, Mr Shannon. Hilary Geddes is a formidable woman. Her credentials are impeccable and she has friends in high places. Her last employer praised her strategic thinking and political acumen. Both are talents we need to be mindful of, if the report is to do its job."

Mike hadn't touched his drink. He didn't really want it. He just wanted to deliver the report and end his dealings with Cummings. He had been involved in political wrangling before and was no stranger to those that were hell bent on empire building. This was entirely different. He had not experienced this level of maliciousness and intimidation before. The fact that it was dressed up in a public school accent with a veneer of bonhomie made it feel all the more menacing.

He was struggling to get his imagination under control. He had thought about the ways in which he might be 'disappeared' if things didn't go to plan. He took a deep breath to calm his irrational fears.

"I emailed the draft report to you last night. Have a look at it over the weekend and let me have any notes or amendments. Then I can circulate the finished article in time for the evaluation meeting on Wednesday."

He pushed his untouched drink away, and rose to leave.

Bernard watched him go. The consultant carried too much weight. A sign of too comfortable a lifestyle without any real stress or pressure attached to it. He was weak and ineffectual too. In fact, quite a stupid man overall. Bernard truly hated management consultants. They were, he felt, without any redeeming qualities at all. He disliked the red tape and bureaucracy that people like Shannon represented. And he hankered for the days when his work was conducted on nothing more than a man's word. When operations didn't have to be evaluated, costed or have a benefits realisation exercise done on them.

He would be in a position to change things when he took over from Celia as Director General. He thought Shady Fields a complete waste of money, and felt those precious resources would be better deployed on the front line.

Having Maguire in his pocket helped on that score, of course. The report was just a formality so he could turn his attention to more important things. He needed to get hold of William's manuscript as a matter of urgency. At the moment his was the only copy, but once it had been handed over to the legal team an electronic version would be made, and that would be far more difficult to manage.

His phone pinged, telling him that someone had emailed him. He took it out of his pocket and clicked the flashing envelope. His contact had established that William did have a set of old surveillance photographs, and confirmed that Bernard was recognisable in them. Bernard cursed under his breath. He knew that whatever was written in the manuscript could be challenged and discredited, but it would be much more difficult if the claims were backed up with images.

He clicked the folder, and five photos appeared. He examined each in turn. He had never seen them before, but the fact they were in William's possession was serious. His contact had obviously been in William's apartment at the time and taken them in a hurry.

Bernard needed to be sure that these were the only copies, and that no others had been lodged with anyone else. As he re-examined them, something caught his eye. It couldn't be! But sure enough, at the top of the picture frame just through an open door he could make out the distinctive edge of one of the lost Russian icons perched on a set of drawers. His blood ran cold.

Bernard arrived at Shady Fields twenty minutes after leaving the pub, and parked at the front of the building. He was buzzed into the main entrance by one of the attendants, and as he walked into the hallway he cast his eye around, looking for William. Steve came down the stairs and crossed the hall, heading towards the kitchens at the rear of the building.

"Excuse me," Bernard called out. "Can you tell me which room William Wright is in, please?"

"Yes, Mr Cummings, it's number 15. First floor, through the doors at the top of the stairs and turn left.

Or you could go up in the lift and turn right, then it's down at the bottom of the corridor."

There was no thank you from Bernard, just a nod of the head as he walked towards the lift. He was not a fan of confined spaces but it was easier than climbing the stairs when he was in a hurry. The doors slowly slid open and he stepped inside. Hilary had spotted him and trotted the last few steps, making it just before the doors slid shut.

"Hello, Bernard. We weren't expecting you today. Dan isn't in at the moment. Can I help?"

Bernard was irritated. He'd wanted to get in and out without being seen. He thought fast.

"No, thanks, I was just passing and wanted to see William for a minute. All of this stuff with Linda must have rattled him. I just wanted to check he is ok – I've got a bit of a soft spot for the old guy."

"Well that's a coincidence. I was just on my way up to see him too. He's got something he wanted posting so I told him I'd collect it."

Hilary was relieved – pleased that she had spotted him come in. There was no way she was going to let him see William alone. The lift hummed to a stop and gave a very gentle wobble as the doors again slid open. Hilary stepped out first, and Bernard reluctantly followed. They reached apartment 15 and Hilary knocked lightly on the door. After a short delay she tried again.

"Perhaps he's somewhere else in the building," she said.

Just as they were about to move away, the door opened a crack and William's right eye glared through the gap. "Yes? What do you want?"

Hilary turned to him.

"Hello. You wanted something posting, William. I'm here to collect it."

"Well it's not wrapped or labelled yet, so you'll have to come back for it later."

"Yes, I can do that". Hilary stepped to her left so that William could see Bernard standing behind her.

"I met Bernard on the way up. He's just popped in to say hello. To see if you're OK."

William opened the door fully. Hilary was shocked at the sight. He was dishevelled and had a feverish look about him. He gazed at her, not even acknowledging his visitor.

"Well you can tell him to bugger off! I'm fine, and I don't need him to check on me. Besides, I've got a terrible headache. I was just going to go for a lie down."

Hilary was genuinely concerned. "Shall I get Dr Arnot to come along and give you a look over, William? You look a bit warm, not yourself at all."

"No," he said quickly. "I'm fine. I don't want any fuss. I'll be ok after a nap."

She noticed Bernard looking beyond William into the apartment, oblivious to his appearance.

"OK, we'll leave you to it, but it you need anything give me a call, I'm around all day today."

She ushered Bernard away, so had no choice but to go with her. "Not one of his better days, but in all honesty he hasn't been well since all this started. I'll keep an eye on him and get the Doctor to look in on him later this afternoon. Sorry it 's been a wasted trip for you."

"Well I wouldn't say that exactly," said Bernard. As soon as the lift door opened on the ground floor he was off across the hall and rattling the front door to get out. Hilary took her time and went to the porter's room to release the door mechanism.

Bernard glared at her. "Don 't forget the evaluation report will be out on Wednesday."

As soon as he was outside he took a deep breath. There was no unpleasant smell in the building, but he found the air inside oppressive and cloying all the same. He imagined that the odour of the elderly stuck to him when he came here, and the feeling remained for several hours every time he visited. He climbed into his car and drove through the barrier onto the main road. As he headed back to London he began to think.

Hilary had been right. William did look terrible, and her concern for him had given Bernard the opportunity he needed to look through the door at his apartment, unobserved. He had seen the icon! It was standing on the chest of drawers just inside the bedroom. Over the years he had stopped wondering what had happened to the crate, although he'd originally had suspicions that William might have had something to do with the disappearance of its contents. His explanation had been plausible, though. Bernard had ultimately had to give up; he was never able to track down what happened lest he draw attention to the true value of the contents, so the trail had gone cold.

Bernard honestly didn't think William had it in him. And the bastard had lied to his face on numerous occasions, doing it so well that Bernard had believed him. He felt his anger as a hard lump in the back of his throat. He had seen the Madonna and child icon but not the other one. Did he still have it somewhere, maybe in a different part of his flat that Bernard couldn't see? Had he already sold it? These artefacts were always valuable pieces, so if he had sold it money wouldn't have been a problem for him. That kind of money could set someone like William up for life. But he lived a frugal lifestyle. There was clear evidence of penny pinching. He would not have had to do that if he had sold it. It must still be there.

He had bought the pieces in order to earn money from their sale, but now he was financially secure he could appreciate their beauty, their rarity and their value. If they were in his possession now he would keep them and enjoy owning them.

Bernard raged to himself in the privacy of his car. Who the hell did William think he was, duping him for all these years? At that moment, he wanted to kill him. The bastard techie had been a thorn in his side for years. He'd been generous to him, secured good postings for him, looked after him, but every time, he'd found a way of screwing things up. He'd covered William's errors until eventually things caught up with him. Then he couldn't be helped. If Bernard had known the betrayal he'd show him he'd have done it sooner.

No one made a fool out of him.

He needed to be punished.

Bernard stopped his car when he noticed a telephone box at the side of the road. He called his contact and gave him three simple instructions. He would wait no longer. He would deal with William, and let the Shady Fields problem resolve itself.

Hilary wanted to let Dan know what was happening.

"We had a visitor today – Bernard dropped in. I told him you were in London. He said he would catch up another time." She shifted the phone to her other ear so she could balance it between her head and shoulder.

"It couldn't have been that important, otherwise he would have called me. And he knew I was in London today, anyway. By the way, I found out about the bang from the garden."

Hilary smiled, "Do I really want to know?"

"It seems Bill had decided to help the gardener out by packing the tree stump with homemade explosives and detonating it. Result – no more tree stump! Although in fairness, there's no more rose arbour or garden seat, either. I think we can safely say we know what happened to the missing supplies you reported, too. Ben had been on a run in the morning, so the first he knew about it was when he heard the bang. It left quite a hole. Luckily there was no one around at the time."

"Well the combi locks have been fitted today, and not before time by the sound of it."

"Thanks, Hilary. I had a feeling the dynamite men would be at the bottom of it somewhere."

He was finding it difficult to disguise the amusement in his voice.

"It 's not funny, Dan. We're supposed to be keeping a low profile. Jean could have asked awkward questions."

He cleared his throat. "You're right, of course, but you have to admit, they don 't let the grass grow under their feet do they? A UDI in the grounds and they've only been with us a couple of days!"

29

William had slept fitfully in the night; the room had been spinning, and the headache that had plagued the small hours was now a dull thumping that made his eyes sensitive to the light. He was obviously coming down with something. He couldn't bear people fussing over him. And he had no idea why Bernard had turned up out of the blue yesterday. He was the last person William wanted to see.

He suspected Bernard had discovered that the book was finished and wanted to know what was in it. He would be the last person to find out. If there was any justice, internal affairs would be knocking on his door with a list of questions for him to answer. William would keep his dirty little secrets no more.

The room started to spin again and he wondered if he had overdone things. He had been staying up late to get the final chapter finished. Well now it was done, and Dan would take it to Mr Erskine next week for them to begin work on it. He had already received favourable responses from two publishers in response to his tentative enquiries. They wanted to see a copy of the full manuscript first, of course, but it did look like he would see his book in print, after all.

He just needed to lie down for a while. He'd tried a little breakfast this morning, but as soon as he came back upstairs he had vomited, and he hadn't eaten again since. He walked across to the bed, took a few sips of water from the glass on the bedside cabinet, and just as he lay down he heard a light knock on the door.

"Go away and leave me in peace," he called crossly.

But the door was already opening, and Steve came into the room. "Sorry, William, but it's time for your medication." Steve went into the bathroom, and William heard him unlock the drugs box and take out what he needed.

"Are you in pain at all, William?"

"Only the usual. I don't need more tablets, if that's what you're asking."

"Shall I do your eyedrops, or can you manage them yourself today?" Steve realised this was a redundant question. William had never managed to administer his own drops, his hands were too shaky and the small bottle too fiddly. William blinked at Steve, and in a small voice said "I don't think I can manage. Would you do them for me?"

Steve pulled on some latex gloves, and took the top from the white plastic bottle. He tilted William 's head back and squeezed two drops into each eye. William flinched as the medication stung initially. Steve offered him a tissue to mop up the excess that ran onto his cheeks, then he took the used tissue from him, placed it in a clinical waste bag along with his gloves, and tied a knot in the top, ready for the incinerator.

"If I were you, William, I would have a lie down – you look really tired. I'll be doing my rounds in an hour, I can come and check on you then if you'd like?"

"Thanks Steve, but I'm ok, honestly. A little tired, that's all". He said it to a closed door. Steve had already left.

Perhaps he should put his other affairs in order now. He needed to have a conversation with Milena 's daughter and ensure she was financially taken care of. He had given it a lot of thought and realised he needed to do that with a degree of care. It would be her choice about what to do with the icon, but because of its value she would be able to make whatever choice made her happy.

He'd already added a codicil to his will five years ago, leaving it to her in the event of his death, but he really wanted her to have it now while he was still around to see what it could do for her. She could return to Georgia, or she could stay here and make a life for herself. Also, although she knew who he was and some of the history between him and her family, he needed her to hear the whole truth. He didn't want her reading that in his book.

His headache was getting much worse. Maybe he should have taken some paracetamol when he had the chance. He realised the pain was actually coming from his eyeballs. It really was most unpleasant.

William had no idea how long he had been asleep but he awoke with a jolt, and every muscle in his body ached, as though he'd been engaged in the sort of strenuous exercise that pulled muscles and strained joints. He could hear someone moving around in the kitchen and called out to whoever it was. Dr Arnot put his head around the door.

"Don't try to get up, William. I've called for an ambulance, they'll be here shortly."

Just then the door opened, and Hilary came in, closely followed by Layla and Steve.

"What can I do, Doc?" Steve walked into the kitchen and Layla made her way straight to William, who was lying propped up with pillows. He was a deathly grey colour.

Hilary joined the pair in the kitchen.

"What happened?"

Dr Arnot was looking very worried.

"I came this morning because I had already left yesterday when you asked me to call in, Hilary. I asked Steve just to check on him but you said he was fine last night."

Dr Arnot looked directly at Steve, who shuffled his

feet and looked at the floor.

"He was ok last night – a bit on the warm side, perhaps, but nothing like this."

"When I got here this morning we had an emergency and I came to see him as soon as that was dealt with. I knocked at the door, but got no answer. I could hear noises, so I knew he was in here. I used my pass and when I got in he was fitting. His temperature and blood pressure were extremely high. His pupils were just pinpoints, and he was calling for Layla. I stabilised him and called an ambulance, then messaged you.

"He's seriously ill, Hilary. We need to get him to hospital as soon as possible."

Layla sat on the edge of the bed looking really worried. "I'm here, William. It 's me, it 's Layla. Can you hear me?" She pulled on some disposable gloves that Dr Arnot offered her.

William's eyelids fluttered, and he struggled into consciousness.

He opened his eyes and saw Milena sitting there in all her beauty.

"Did you get my letter? I have wanted to tell you for so long how much I care for you, but …"

He lapsed into unconsciousness again, but his hands jerked, and he wrung them together like he was washing them to get rid of a terrible stain.

Dr Arnot took hold of William 's bony wrist to measure his pulse. "Where's that damned ambulance?" he said. He turned to Layla to reassure her.

"He's delirious at the moment, so what he says will probably make no sense at all, but he can hear you. Keep talking to him, try to keep him calm. I'll wait for the ambulance to arrive so that I can brief the paramedics. If you're going to travel in the ambulance with him, can I ask you to wear these, please?" He offered her a sterile pack of protective gown, mask and apron.

Layla looked worried but put them on, returning to the bedside and speaking to him soothingly.

Dr Arnot motioned for Hilary to follow him outside. Out in the corridor he gave her a direct look. "I'm extremely worried that William may not survive, Hilary."

"My goodness, I had no idea he was that ill. What exactly is wrong with him?"

Hilary needed answers. Had she missed something when she saw him yesterday? Should she have insisted that he saw Dr Arnot immediately? Twelve hours could have made all the difference.

Dr Arnot looked conflicted. "I am not sure what it is at the moment, but if I'm honest I have my suspicions. The sudden onset, the symptoms, the delirium – Hilary, I think William may have been poisoned."

Hilary felt the air go out of her, almost like she had been punched.

"Poisoned? How? Why? He's an old man, for Christ's sake. Who would want to do such a thing?"

"I don't know, but I need tests to confirm I'm right.

I've seen something similar before, you see. I've been in touch with CDC, and they're sending a team as a precaution. You need to give Dan the heads up that this is serious. We'll need to enact the quarantine protocols and possibly our critical incident plan as well."

Hilary couldn't believe what she was hearing.

"CDC? Isn't that the Centre for Disease Control?"

Dr Arnot nodded.

"And the Critical Incident Plan, too? What the hell are we dealing with?"

"I am not certain yet, but I think it might be some sort of a nerve agent."

The specialist ambulance arrived, but it wasn't needed. William died just 15 minutes later.

The next hours went by in a blur. All residents were confined to their rooms, and each was visited by a medic in a hazmat suit taking samples and readings. No one was allowed in or out of the building. Dan was still in London, so the only contact with him was by telephone. He was as stunned as Hilary was.

Hilary had not thought much about Dr Arnot since she had come to work here. She had made the assumption that he was a run of the mill GP with a specialist interest in geriatric conditions. This crisis told her that was a gross underestimation of his expertise and background. He had coordinated the operations and CDC staff hung on his every word. She was in the office when he finally caught up with her.

"Hi how are you doing?" he said, popping his head

around the door.

She could see he had a hazmat suit on, but the flexible Perspex helmet was missing. His face looked tiny above the bulky neck piece.

"I'm fine, thanks. Any news?"

"Yes. Luckily we're dealing with Tabun, a nerve agent that was popular in the 1980s. It was commonly used in the Iran-Iraq war."

He seemed very matter of fact, and Hilary was struggling to process the words he used.

"A nerve agent? How can that be lucky? Is anyone else likely to die?"

Dr Arnot walked across the office and pulled up a chair on the opposite side of her desk.

"Sorry, let me explain. A nerve agent is always serious, but in this case we've been lucky as we've managed to isolate the method used to administer it. It was in William's eyedrops."

He saw Hilary's surprise. "Yes, the ones I prescribed nearly a week ago. But strangely, the contaminated ones were found in the pocket of one of the other resident's raincoat. That's what gave it away. We may not have looked quite so quickly at that, because the ones we tested from William's drugs cupboard were fine. There will have to be a post-mortem, and it's likely that we'll conduct that internally through the security services coroner, given the circumstances.

"The DG has been informed. Due to the nature of Shady Fields and the extremely low risk of contamination to the wider population, it's likely that she'll order a media blackout, but luckily it's a national holiday so that'll be easier to manage. No purpose would be served by going public at this stage. It's a containable incident so there's no need to cause mass panic, particularly with recent events in Salisbury. The last thing we need is conspiracy theorists getting hold of this.

"It seems to be a very deliberate attack to target William. We don't think anyone else is at risk, but the testing and decontamination will be done as a precaution. It's a safeguard, and nothing more. Are you OK?"

Hilary felt she had slipped into an alternate reality.

"What a stupid bloody question! It looks like a resident in my care has been murdered. The means used to kill him most certainly point to an inside job. Meaning, it is quite possible that his murderer is still here with us now. Of course I'm not OK!"

Dr Arnot looked across at her sympathetically. "Please forgive me, Hilary. What a first month to have in a new job. Two deaths, both potentially murder. The use of a nerve agent in your facility which is under scrutiny from the head of the service. And all for someone without a security services background. It must feel like your world is falling apart."

Hilary sat up in her chair. "Please don't misunderstand me, Doctor. I am not about to fall apart. As the accountable manager I just need to understand the implications of all of this so that I can deal with it appropriately. I need to know that no-one else is at risk, staff or residents. I'll have to put together a detailed containment plan, and I need facts for that."

Dr Arnot nodded in understanding. "OK, so the CDC coordinator is someone called Marina Kinskey. She's just completing the risk assessment now, and I'll ask her to meet with you as soon as she's free. She can give you an update. She is one of the best in her field, so use her knowledge and expertise while you have her. She'll be able to help you cut through the red tape of an incident like this. I need to get back now, but let me know if you need anything." And he left.

Hilary should have been thinking about what was going on at a time like this but a passage from one of her favourite novels, Alice Sebold's *The Lovely Bones*, came to her, and rolled over and over in her head. *"Hold still," my father would say, while I held the ship in the bottle and he burned away the strings he'd raised the mast with and set the clipper ship free on its blue putty sea. And I would wait for him, recognizing the tension of that moment when the world in the bottle depended, solely, on me."*

30

L ayla sat and stared at the William-shaped blanket on his bed. She was sad that she hadn't had the opportunity to get to know him better, but grateful for the fact that over the last few months he had at least fed her pieces of a jigsaw puzzle about her parents early life in Tbilisi. He told her about her father, and the bravery and courage he had shown. He'd added colour and texture to the faded picture she had carried in her heart all her life. She felt she was meeting her father afresh, through the eyes of someone who respected and admired him as a man.

They'd left Georgia when Layla was a toddler, and the only home she remembered had been the Victorian terraced house with a narrow bay window and tiled front path they'd moved into in Lewisham on their arrival in the country. It had been an unfashionable district when they first moved in. Unusually, they didn't rent it or share it, it was theirs, bought for them by a benefactor who had known her father.

Her mother had made it a warm, happy place to grow up in, and while it looked like any other house from the street, its interior was typically Georgian.

The heart of the home was the kitchen. There was a bright check-patterned oilskin cloth on the table, and the smell of bread constantly wafted through the house. It was always filled with friends, laughter and colour. All this, and her mother's wonderful home cooking, created a sense of security that had made her childhood seem easy. She heard other Georgian children talk of their experiences as immigrants. They had faced discrimination and bullying. Layla had not been affected by such things. When she was only a baby her mother had changed her surname from Vlasta to Strong.

Her mother had helped other Georgians escaping war and poverty to settle here. Their home was like a community centre, there was always a pot of coffee on the stove, and help and advice on tap. Her mother used to say to her, "Layla, we are lucky, we have the bird's milk," meaning their lives were rich and they wanted for nothing. Except her father.

Her mother worked hard to support them both and had learned to speak English at night school as she trained to be a nurse. She made sure that Layla benefited from a good education and gained good qualifications at college. Layla wanted to care for people too, her specialism was caring for older people. She worked with people who had dementia and Alzheimer's. She loved her job, and could not understand why what she did was so undervalued by others.

Then suddenly, five years ago, her mother had announced that she was returning to Tbilisi to care for her Aunt, their last remaining relative. Layla had to decide whether to leave with her, or to remain in England. She chose to stay.

Lewisham had undergone something called urban regeneration. Their home had increased in value by a sizeable sum. They had converted their house into two spacious flats. Layla lived in the ground floor apartment, while Marcia and Susan, the architect couple who had done the house conversion, loved it so much they purchased the top floor apartment. The deal gave her mother enough cash to buy an apartment in Tbilisi when she returned home, while Layla had savings in the bank and no rent or mortgage to find.

Before her mother left, she told Layla about William. A few years after they had settled in England, he had written to her to tell her how he had arranged for them to escape to England, and how he had supported them financially, although she never understood why he had given them so much yet asked for nothing in return.

She had met him first on the only occasion he had

visited their house. It was when her mother was preparing to return to Georgia. He came one Saturday afternoon as she was packing boxes. They were briefly introduced, and then he and her mother disappeared into the living room and closed the door. She found this behaviour puzzling, and even mildly amusing. Layla was 24 at the time, so what her mother thought she was protecting her from she couldn't imagine. William stayed for just under an hour, and left without saying goodbye. He just slipped out of the front door.

William had written to her a couple of times after that, and sent Christmas cards, but she'd heard nothing more from him until about twelve months ago when she received a letter from him explaining how he knew her father back in Tbilisi. He told her that he had moved to a place called Shady Fields, a new residential home where they were looking for staff. There was a vacancy for a senior care assistant and knowing of her occupation he encouraged her to apply for the job. She sent her CV to Dan Grant, and to her surprise she got the job. Obviously it wasn't a run-of-the-mill care home. She had never been asked to sign the Official Secrets Act before, for one thing. Her security vetting was completed without a hitch, and she found herself working in a place where she could get to know William better.

In the afternoons she regularly spent time with William. They had chatted and he had begun to open up a little about her father. He spoke in generalisms about her parents, and she noticed that when he mentioned her mother, it was with real tenderness. She realised that he was in love with her. He had never mentioned it or tried to act on it, but his feelings were clear.

Layla looked again at where William's body now lay. The coroner would be here soon to collect him. She had not been allowed to touch him. That in itself was unusual, as she was used to the customary laying out of a body after death. At the very least she would have expected him to be washed and made presentable. Instead, there were express instructions that his body was not to be touched. There had been lots of activity, people taking swabs, bagging samples of food, drink and medications.

She'd even had to wear gloves just to hold his hand as he lay dying. It was clear to her that no-one believed his death was natural and that someone had hastened his end. She felt a jumble of emotion. She was angry that someone would want to harm him, and at the same time sad that she would never speak with him again.

She remembered fondly how William could be difficult, grumpy and rude with anyone but her. If someone had done something to him she wanted to know why.

The door opened and two men in sombre uniforms came in wheeling an aluminium gurney. It had a metal, coffin-like container on the top of it. She stood and moved respectfully to the side of the room while they carefully gathered William's body up with the bed linen he was lying on, laid it into the casket and replaced the lid. They wheeled him out into the corridor and towards the lift. It was only then that she began to cry.

Apartment 15 was quarantined with yards of yellow and black hazard warning tape to keep people at bay. Staff from CDC were still in the building, but they were no longer wearing hazmat suits. They had visited every resident to give them the all clear to leave their rooms, although no one could leave the building and no one could come in. Hilary had set up sleeping quarters for staff to stay overnight. The last message they received was that Hilary would address everyone in the dining room at 8.00am the following morning.

Life went on.

31

Shady Fields, 2nd April 2018, Morning

The dining room was filled with staff, residents and the CDC investigations team that had remained on site. Everyone gathered quietly together, waiting for further information. There was a muted hum of conversation as people discussed their theories about what was going on. Hilary felt exhausted as she entered the dining room. A disturbed night's sleep had been peppered with images of William dying, hazmat suits, and Dan looking disappointed. She needed to exude confidence this morning, to carry everyone through the next couple of days. "Pull up your knickers and box on!" her aunt would have said, so she took a deep breath and, metaphorically, did exactly that.

Casting an eye around the room, she signalled to

Layla that she wanted to see her after the announcements were over. Layla understood, and nodded back.

A hush descended on the room as Hilary cleared her throat. "Good morning everyone. I am sure you all know by now that our dear friend William Wright passed away yesterday afternoon. I want to be clear that what I am about to tell you must remain within these walls, and as former agents I'm sure you will have no problem with that. William's death was suspicious."

The murmur rose, then just as quickly subsided.

"Investigations will be taking place here for the next few days, and visitors will not be admitted until that process is complete. We have notified friends and family by email, citing a case of Norovirus so that people will not come here."

Another murmur travelled around the room like a ripple in a pond.

"I am unable to give you any specific details at the moment, but I want to assure you that after extensive testing the investigators from CDC are satisfied that no one else is at risk. I repeat: there is no danger to anyone else. We have to carry on as best we can. I will keep you informed when I have more information to share. In the meantime one or two of you will be asked some questions by the investigators working on this.

"Residents will have a senior member of staff with them when that happens, but if you have any questions or concerns please talk to me or one of the staff. Dan has been detained in London. He will return in a few days, so until then all queries will come through me. Thank you for your attention."

The low hum of conversation resumed. Layla got up and followed Hilary out of the dining room.

"How are you this morning, Layla?"

"I'm ok, thank you. How can I help?"

"You're one of the seniors on duty today, so I'll need you to accompany the investigators when they interview our residents. All you have to do is sit in with them, and make sure that they're not coerced or distressed at any point. Can you do that?"

Layla did not hesitate for a second. "Absolutely."

"Can I ask you to start with Charlie, please? The investigator wants to interview him first."

"Who are they sending to do the investigation?"

Hilary wanted to reassure Layla. "It's someone called Mitchell Bennett. You may have seen him around, he's been here a few times before – he's the Deputy Director. All you have to do is make sure that the residents are ok when he questions them. He's just trying to get to the truth of what happened to William."

Charlie must have been waiting just behind his door because he answered as soon as Layla knocked. "Layla, please come in. Mitchell is already here."

Mitch stood and offered his hand.

"Hello. I'm Mitchell Bennett, but people call me Mitch. I think we met briefly one evening when I was here with Dan a couple of weeks ago."

"Yes, I remember."

She did remember him. After all, who wouldn't? He was a very handsome man. Powerfully built, and with such an open face. Today he seemed different, more serious, and she detected an undercurrent of anger.

They sat in the lounge of Charlie's apartment. Mitch had placed his phone on the table and was using it to record the interview. He did the formal bit first.

"This is an interview with Charles – Charlie – Bingham, on 2nd April 2018 at 8.45am. Present are Charles Bingham, Layla Strong, a senior staff member supporting Charlie, and Mitchell Bennett, Deputy Director leading the investigation into William Wright's death.

"Charlie, I want to ask you some questions about William's death, to see if you can remember anything that might help us find out how this terrible thing happened. Will that be ok?"

Charlie was clearly upset. He sat in his armchair hunched forward with his forearms resting on his knees. He was rubbing his hands together as if he were trying to keep warm. His face was stony and pale.

"Anything I can do to help, I will. I liked William. He could be a grumpy bugger but there was no harm in him. He was a decent chap who hadn't had a lot of luck in his life. This is wrong, Mitch, it shouldn't have happened." He shook his head.

"I know this is hard, Charlie, but you may have some useful information that can help without realising it, so let's just see how it goes.

"When was the last time you saw William?"

Charlie thought for a couple of seconds, then his face acknowledged the memory.

"It was yesterday at breakfast. He seemed preoccupied. I assumed that was because he had finished his book. He didn't eat much, just toast and tea I think. As soon as he'd finished he went back up to his room."

"Where did he sit?"

"At his usual table in the bay window. I usually sit with him, but he was late arriving. I didn't think he was coming down. I sat with Bill and Ben, the two new blokes. We chatted, I introduced myself, and they talked about themselves."

Mitch opened a file and took out a photograph, which he passed to Charlie.

"Do you recognise this, Charlie? For the record I am showing Charlie a photograph of a small plastic medicine bottle recovered yesterday."

He took the picture from Mitch and examined it, reading the label that identified it as belonging to William. "Well, they look like William's eye drops. I saw Steve give them to him the other morning."

"Are you sure, Charlie?" Mitch took the photo back.

"Yes, I'm positive."

"Do you have any idea why we found this bottle in your raincoat pocket when CDC were searching your room yesterday?"

Charlie was shocked. "That's ridiculous. Why would I have them?"

"Had you loaned William your coat? Could he have put them in your pocket by mistake when he was going out?"

Mitch was being as gentle as he could, but he recognised that he was on dangerous ground.

"No! Absolutely not. William didn't have a coat like mine and I am not in the habit of loaning my things to other people. He never went out yesterday either, he stayed in his room all day. There must be some mistake!"

Mitch took a deep breath. "I need to know, Charlie, because we know that William died of Tabun poisoning and it was administered in his eyedrops. The only ones we found that were contaminated were the ones we found in your pocket."

Layla could not stay quiet any longer. She drew herself up to her full five foot three inch height and said firmly, "Mr Bennett, I think it might be in Charlie's best interests if he didn't say anything else until he has a solicitor present. He has a diagnosis of dementia, and may require professional support if he is going to be questioned like this any further."

Mitch looked at her with admiration. It took some bottle to challenge a senior intelligence officer in that way, but it was clear she was meant business.

"Please don't misunderstand me, Miss Strong. I need to know how these drops got into Charlie's raincoat, because I don't believe he put them there. They have been checked for finger prints and they're completely clean. If he had put them in his own pocket, his prints would almost certainly be on the bottle. I don't think Charlie had anything to do with this, but I want to find out who is trying to implicate him in William's death."

Layla nodded. Her gut reaction was that this man was speaking honestly. He seemed genuinely concerned about Charlie, who was not handling being questioned like this at all well by now. His hands were gripping his knees, and his knuckles shone white.

Charlie shook his head in disbelief.

"He was my friend. We were going to lunch together at the club. Why would you think I could do anything like that?" He was starting to sound agitated, and beginning to panic.

Layla knew that Mitch would need Charlie to be calm if he was going to get anything useful from the questioning, so she made a suggestion.

"Let's leave it there for now. Charlie, you look as if you need a cup of tea; I know I certainly do. Let's pick this up again this afternoon, Mitch, when Charlie has had a bit of a rest. Will that be ok?"

She looked hopefully at Mitch and he nodded. He turned off his recorder.

"That will be fine. I would be grateful if neither of you would discuss this with any of the staff or residents." They both nodded, and Mitch left the room in search of Hilary.

Charlie seemed to calm down a little after Mitch had left. Layla made them both tea. Charlie took a well-used hip flask from the sideboard and poured a small measure of amber liquid into his cup. He offered it to Layla, but she declined.

"It's a bit early for me under normal circumstances, but I've had a bit of a shock," he said by way of an explanation. "I really don't know how those eye drops got into my coat."

"Not to worry," said Layla. "Drink your tea, we can think about where you have been and when you last wore it."

At that moment, Charlie was clearly too distressed to remember anything.

32

Shady Fields, 2nd April 2018, Afternoon

Hilary looked at Mitch.

"We really need to know if Bernard would risk everything to keep William quiet. If he wanted him out of the way, surely he just had to wait? William was over seventy; how much of a threat could he really be?"

Mitch looked troubled.

"All I know is that Bernard is not who I thought he was. What our intelligence gathering has revealed so far is that virtually every mission he's been involved with has been suspect in one way or another. It might all be an effort to cover poor decision making on his part, but the more I continue to dig, the more convinced I am that something more sinister will be uncovered.

"William 's manuscript definitely interested

Bernard, but he would have known that any mission details could not have been published without the express permission of MI5 and MI6."

Something occurred to Hilary.

"Wouldn't security service lawyers need to read everything before publication was even possible? That alone may have been enough to trigger an internal investigation, right?"

Mitch nodded, so she continued.

"So, he wouldn't want to risk that with Celia 's job in the offing, would he?"

Mitch shrugged. "I can't see it. It seems like a massive risk to take for a job.

"Dan has asked me to speak with Rita today as well. He thinks there is more to the Amman operation than has been officially recorded. Rita was a top female agent. She had some spectacular successes in her early career, but all that changed after Amman.

"Dan wants to know why. And we know that Bernard was involved in that operation too, but we just don't know the details. I'm meeting her in the library, do you want to sit in?"

Rita entered the library. Today she was a strawberry blonde coquette with a slight Parisian accent. She was wearing a pink Chanel suit, a cream silk blouse and was sporting large dark sunglasses.

"Hello, Rita. Would you like to take a seat?"

She offered her hand to Mitch and he shook it.

"Oohh," she remarked. "I like a man wiz a strong

'andshake. Firm, very firm. Just like my vibrator." She smiled as though she had just commented on the weather, and sat down. Her shapely legs were covered with silk hosiery of the finest quality that whispered as she crossed them.

"Layla is bringing us coffee, will you have a cup?" Hilary willed Layla to come through the door before Rita's conversation became any more flirtatious; to her great relief it opened at that moment, and she entered carrying a tray of drinks. She set the tray down on the table; Hilary motioned for her to stay, so she drew another chair up and began pouring coffee.

Rita did not appear to notice the two women. Her eyes were firmly focused on Mitch.

"And you are?"

Mitch shifted slightly uncomfortable in his chair.

"My name is Mitchell Bennett. I am working with Dan and Hilary."

"Can you keep a secret, Mitchelle?"

He nodded.

"So can I. It's the people I tell that can't."

She threw her head back and a peal of laughter escaped.

"I was a spy in my younger days you know, and a very good one. I 'ave lived my life outside of normal society. Do you 'ave any idea 'ow lonely that is? Even I don 't know who I seem to be anymore."

Mitch looked directly at Rita.

"It's that part of your life we want to talk to you about. If you want to, that is."

She shrugged. "It really makes no difference to me anymore."

Mitch became a little more formal. "Can you tell us how you were recruited into the service, Rita?"

She smiled at him. "I was working as a model when I met Tony Bailey the music impresario. We were at a party one evening. 'E was looking for a face for a music video, 'e introduced me to Errol Brown from 'ot chocolat, and the rest as zey say is 'istory.

"Suddenly I am on TV, chat shows, and in all ze newspapers. I became an overnight success, cherie!" She leant across and rubbed her palm up Mitch 's thigh. He took it, kissed the back of her hand, and placed it on her own knee. He waited for her to continue.

"I was approached at one of zose parties, because zer was a Russian ambassador following me 'round London like a lost puppy. Ze service thought I could be useful. Zey trained me. Zey taught me 'ow to use a blade and 'ow to crack locks.

"I could carry much more tradecraft kit zan any of ze men, too. My 'airdryer and toiletries bag alone contained a full photographer 's studio and dark room. Zey let me loose around ze world: Paris, Italy, Russia, Ireland, even 'ong Kong once. I 'ad a ball, cherie!"

Mitch looked directly at her. She was still an attractive now woman, and she would have been stunning in her younger years. He could well understand how men would have been seduced by her attentions.

"What about the Middle East?" he asked.

"I met and lose ze love of my life zere."

"What happened?"

"Zey were holding a trade Summit in Amman, and zere was a lot of activity, so I 'ad been posted zere on a temporary basis. Zere was a lot of socialising, and at an embassy party I met Saleem Al Baadini, a Prince of ze royal 'ouse.

"He was tall, dark and very, very 'andsome. He was also incredibly charming, and it really was love at first sight. Ze kind of crazy love zat takes your breath away. It was ze same for both of us!"

Then Rita began to sing:

"I'm involved in a dangerous game
Every other day I change my name
The face is different but the body's the same
Boo boo baby I'm a spy
The things I know would make you stagger
I'm so cocky I could swagger
I'm ten percent cloak and ninety percent dagger
Boo boo baby I'm a spy…"

She stopped as suddenly as she had begun, and looked expectantly at the others assembled. She looked disappointed when she didn't get any applause.

Mitch was worried her mind was beginning to wander, so he asked a more targeted question.

"What happened the night Saleem died, Rita?"

Rita wagged her finger. "No, no, no. No jumping ze gun!"

She took a few sips from her coffee cup, then took off her glasses and laid them on the table. It was like watching a butterfly emerge from a chrysalis. Her posture changed, and she became an efficient secretary who would take shorthand and type at 100 words a minute. When she spoke again, it was with an upper-class English accent.

"Saleem felt the same way that I did, but our relationship was doomed from the start. With his lifestyle and royal freedoms, his dalliances were his business, but marriage was a different thing altogether.

"I had been asked to get close to him and find out what information he had been passing and to whom. They wanted me to share it with our lot and the Americans. I told them nothing! Yes Saleem had been selling information to the Russians, but it was nothing about national security. It was commercial stuff; contracts that were coming up, that sort of thing. He had built quite a nest egg and was going to use it to build us a life.

"We'd decided to head to Switzerland, and on the night of our departure the Americans were throwing an enormous ball. Everyone was invited. We waited until nearly everyone was drunk and left through the French windows, running across the patio and into the gardens."

Rita lent forward to take a sip of her tea, the cup rattled as she set it back on the saucer.

"Suddenly, four men jumped us. They'd been waiting. They knew our escape route. Two of the men held me, and the other two grabbed Saleem. They rifled through his pockets, then killed him. Right in front of me. They slit his throat like a dog in the street. Then they were gone. I went to him, but there was nothing I could do. He died in my arms."

They heard a sob catch in her throat. She took a deep breath before continuing.

"I noticed the weapon on the floor; it stood out, because professionals never leave a weapon behind. I recognised it immediately. It was the shibryia dagger that Saleem had given me. It had his blood on it, and the scabbard lay next to it. I knew that it would have my fingerprints all over it, while the men were all wearing gloves so wouldn't have left a trace.

"I was there, covered in his blood, with his body and my dagger also covered in his blood. I was meant to take the fall for it. I couldn't think straight, I was distraught."

Tears began to run freely down her face.

"Suddenly Bernard Cummings from our embassy was there. He had only come for the summit and he was leaving for England the following morning on a military flight. He said he had been walking through the gardens, heard the commotion, and came to investigate. He found me.

"The rest is a bit of a blur if I am honest. He took me back to the hotel where our delegation was staying. He had fresh clothes there for me, so I got cleaned up. He said he could make everything ok, but that I would have to leave with him later that day.

"I wasn't thinking straight. My Saleem had been killed, and I was angry. I wanted to go after his killers! I wanted to inflict pain on them, like they had on me. Bernard explained that if I stayed, my life would be forfeit. The King would demand justice.

"Something broke that night. I had never loved anyone like I loved Saleem. I couldn't function, couldn't think straight, and I hurt all over. I left with Bernard and came home, but my life was never the same. I go through the motions. I laugh at people's jokes, I eat and drink, I chat with people on a bus, but something is missing."

Her voice trailed off and she sat there looking genuinely broken.

Mitch reached across and covered her trembling hand with his.

"You were lucky Bernard came along when he did. You may not have been here now if he'd not been the one to find you."

Rita slowly raised her head and a look of hatred settled on her face.

"Lucky? It was no coincidence! He knew I would be there, because he was the one that had tipped off the Americans about Saleem. The Yanks had lost untold millions in contracts to the Russians and with the agreements from the summit, they stood to lose even more. They had to stop him, and they did. I didn't know it at the time, but Bernard already knew we were going to run away. He had overheard us planning our escape, and he tipped off the Americans. He could have told them Saleem was no longer a threat, but he didn't.

"When I got home I truly went off the rails. I was drinking, taking drugs, having sex with anyone. I even went through a period of cutting myself! In fact I tried everything to dull the pain. But it didn't work and I became too much of a risk to post abroad, so I stayed at home and simply desiccated. After that I did little jobs for Bernard, off the books obviously. A safe to crack here and there, the odd house breaking. I even did a couple of safe deposit boxes for him, and they are not easy!"

She had diminished in stature as she had been speaking. She was now slumped in the chair, looking every bit her age, tears coursing down her face. Her immaculate makeup had streaked, and black mascara stains dripped onto her silk blouse.

"I hate Bernard Cummings with a passion, and he doesn't even know who I am. I was here the other day when he came, but the bastard never even recognised me! How can you ruin someone's life and not know them when you see them again?"

Hilary motioned to Layla, who stood and walked over to Rita.

"Come on Rita, let's go back to your room. You can wash your face and change your clothes."

Rita stood without any resistance and allowed Layla to lead her from the room.

Hilary let out a sigh as the door closed behind them. "Dr Arnot said her dementia had probably been made worse by her lifestyle when she returned in 1995. I had no idea what had happened to her. No wonder she was different when she came home."

Hilary looked across at Mitch. Rita's story had obviously affected him too.

"That still tells us very little about Bernard, though. Rita is making an assumption that Bernard was behind it, but there may not be any proof of it. All it demonstrates is how ruthless he can be when it suits him."

Mitch reached for the Amman file and scanned the top sheet.

"It says here that the thief who was found guilty and executed for the crime was found in possession of Saleem's wallet and passport."

"Does it say anything else?" said Hilary.

Mitch took a breath. "It says the murder weapon was never found."

33

Shady Fields, 3rd April 2018, Morning

Once again, Dan sat in the plush anteroom on the eleventh floor, waiting to give the update they had requested. He tried to remain focused on the report, but the reality was that he was still processing William's death.

He couldn't believe that this had happened at Shady Fields. The sheer audacity of such an act enraged him. It was reckless, malicious, and spoke of a dangerous character without any consideration for collateral damage. It was a miracle no one else had died or been affected.

Celia had asked him whether there might have been Russian intervention, it was their usual M.O., after all. Could Shady Fields had been infiltrated? Dan had initially dismissed this but he had to explore the possibility that they may have an active spy working or living there in plain sight.

His mobile phone rang and he looked at the number. He answered it immediately.

"Hello Bruno, what can I do for you?"

"Hi, Dan. It's more a question of what I can do for you," he said with his Texan drawl.

"The boys from the Met have dragged a body from the Thames, early hours of this morning. It was a classic hit, single round in the back and one in the head. We've identified the victim as one Deni Dokka. I thought it was a bit of a coincidence, as Mitch was asking about him only a couple of days ago. He said you might be interested, I just wanted to be the one to break the good news."

He laughed, and hung up.

Someone was getting rid of loose ends.

Dan needed more time. If Celia decided to go with the final report from Maguire's, they could shut him down with immediate effect. Recent events would be taken into consideration, too, and both deaths needed to be explained. This was supposed to be a safe facility, where risk was identified and managed.

They had no proof of who was behind everything that had happened, or why. Dan, Hilary and Mitch had strung together a series of events that suggested Bernard's possible involvement, but they had nothing concrete. Dan was sure they were on the right track, but he couldn't take that to Celia without proof; Bernard would dismiss it as sour grapes because of the upcoming DG job, and he could make life very difficult for staff and residents at Shady Fields as well. But all of this was academic unless he could get a stay of execution from this meeting.

The intercom on Anna-Marie's desk buzzed and she told him to go through. He entered the large meeting room and was surprised that Bernard was not there. Just three people formed the panel; Celia, Mike Shannon, and Jean Terry. Normally Dan would have been encouraged by this development, but today he couldn't help wondering where Bernard was, and why he wasn't here to make sure he got the outcome he so clearly wanted.

"Dan," said Celia. "Come in and sit down."

He took the seat she indicated and put his copy of the report on the table next to his iPad. The tension in the room was palpable. Mike fidgeted with the end of his tie, avoiding eye contact with everyone by focusing solely on his tablet screen.

It was Mike who started the meeting, with his presentation of the report findings. Dan settled in for death-by-PowerPoint, but Mike surprised him with the briefness of his hatchet job. He simply talked about the data they had gathered, and focused on the three themes of the evaluation. Dan listened to Mike's damning critique of his team 's work. It was filled with subtlety, nuance and veiled criticism.

"The evaluation data suggests that diverting much needed resources from the security services budget is unwise at this time. We can cite at least two examples where private contractors have been used by security services to deliver services that were once provided in house – see appendix two of the report. There has been no breach in security or fall in standards in either case. The elephant in the room here is that two deaths have been linked to Shady Fields in the last month, even though the service is being provided in house. We can only draw the conclusion that there is no benefit at all to the Shady Fields project, and that it should close with immediate effect."

Mike looked up from his iPad directly at Dan, but could not hold his gaze. The discomfort flowed off him in waves.

Celia looked at Dan. "I presume you have a response?"

Dan nodded.

"Ok then, let's hear it before we open up the report for questions."

Dan began. "Espionage and cybercrime are cited as two of the main threats to national security in the UK. We have residents in Shady Fields who, because of the knowledge they have from historic operations, are potential targets. In fact, one of them was the victim of an attack that ended his life. I mentioned him at our last meeting, he was the Trilby case study."

Mike began to smirk.

"The attack on Trilby had a number of interesting elements to it, which I'd like to outline here."

Celia began to shift in her seat.

"It does have a bearing on the evaluation, if you'll

indulge me?" Dan directed his statement at Celia, and she nodded for him to continue.

"The attack used a nerve agent called Tabun, probably of Russian manufacture. It was administered through the victim's medication.

"This was the second attempt on Trilby's life. The first resulted in the death of a senior member of my staff, Linda Bridges. She died from injuries sustained after being attacked and pushed down an escalator."

Mike's smirk widened, as Dan continued.

"The man responsible for Linda's death was pulled out of the Thames yesterday with a bullet through the back of his head; a clear indication that someone is cleaning house.

"We think the motive for killing Trilby is partly due to knowledge he gained in a previous operation, and partly due to a piece of software he developed which is still of value. We suspect the perpetrators feared that Trilby could damage them personally, professionally or commercially."

Mike couldn't help himself any more.

"How strange that they, whoever they are, were able to get past all of your security clearances and security systems to kill him right under your noses." Interjection over, the smirk returned firmly to its former place.

"That is indeed the point, Mr Shannon. Our investigations to date suggest that the only way it could have happened was if those responsible had help. Someone on the inside. All of our own staff are security cleared and vetted, but those who operate on a subcontractor basis are cleared to a different, lower level. We are investigating the possibility that Trilby 's killer was aided and abetted by someone working with us on a contract basis. Although they may not have been directly involved in his killing, they shared classified information that gave the killer opportunity or access."

Dan watched the smirk dissolve from Mike's face like butter on a hot crumpet.

"In light of these events, Celia, I am asking for the final decision to be delayed so that the identification of the killers is rightly given priority. We also need to ensure that full investigations take place of everyone who has attended, visited or worked at Shady Fields over the last six weeks."

Dan wondered what was going through Mike Shannon's mind as his words sank in. Judging by the colour that drained from his face he was certainly feeling something. Dan made a mental note that he would sit in on that interview when it took place.

Jean, who had remained impassive throughout the meeting, opened the folder that she had in front of her and looked at her papers.

"The decision to postpone is Celia's, but I would take this opportunity to ask Mike why the amendments to the financial projections that I sent to him last week are not included in the final report? Without them, I am concerned that the wrong conclusions regarding the project's viability may be drawn. The work Hilary

Geddes has done in that area is far more accurate than the 'best guess' figures that appear here. I think it is important that we are dealing with an honest representation of facts, don't you, Mike?"

She looked up and spoke directly to him as she said his name, and it amused Dan to see colour flood into his cheeks as quickly as it had left them moments before.

Celia addressed the group. "I agree. Dan, the report must take a back seat until this has been resolved. Indeed, this has sent shockwaves through the service. My own departure and recruitment for my replacement has been put on hold until the situation is resolved. I'd like to formally say how sorry I was to hear about Ms Bridges and William Wright, and if you need anything to help find the culprits, just ask."

"Thank you," said Dan, but he couldn't shake the feeling that Shady Fields may have just dodged a bullet.

Celia turned to address Mike. "I think you will find that there are two officers outside with a warrant to search your premises. They will need to question you and any of your staff who have visited Shady Fields."

Again his face drained of colour.

"Well, thanks everyone. Dan can I ask you to stay to give me an update in private, please?"

Jean and Mike left the room at the same time, but it could hardly be described as them leaving together.

The door closed, and Celia stared at Dan.

"What the hell is going on! A major nerve agent attack on home turf, two of our own murdered, the

CDC mobilised! The Home Secretary is having a meltdown! He wants someone's head on a plate for this and I have to give him daily briefings about our progress. Tell me we've got something, for God's sake!"

Dan gave her a rundown of events and everything they knew about the attack, including the poison eyedrops and how they were found, and the clean-up operation to date.

"So what leads are you working? You must have some ideas."

"Now we know about Dokka's involvement we are looking at all known associates, hits and operations he was involved in, and cross-referencing them to see if we get a match. Peter is helping us with that, and I'm waiting on bank statements to try to follow the money. There must be a trail, it was a hit after all.

"Oh, and Mitch has been working with us, too."

Celia raised an eyebrow.

"Is that wise?"

"I trust Mitch, and his involvement is only known to me, Hilary, Peter and now you. I decided to keep it like that because there have been a couple of coincidental connections to Bernard that have emerged, and we need to be able to discount them formally so he can be eliminated from enquiries."

"Bullshit!" said Celia, giving him a long hard stare. "I've been around the block a few times, Dan, and I know there's history between Bernard and William. I can't believe he would risk his career by being involved in something like this, but I am asking you to make sure you do a thorough job. Report directly and only to me. Do you understand?"

"Yes, of course," said Dan.

"Is there anything else I need to know?" Celia asked.

"Whilst going through William's things, Hilary found several recordings of meetings over the years between Bernard and William. These included a tape of William's disciplinary hearing, which clearly demonstrates the animosity that Bernard had for William. By today's standards, William could easily have put in a legal challenge which the department would have lost.

"The other recording was more recent. A meeting between the two of them just a week or so ago, just days before William was murdered. It doesn't give anything explicit, but it does raise questions about a couple of ops they worked on together. I need to know exactly what went on, so I need access to Bernard's operational files and his financials. That needs a different clearance level so that I don't trip alarm bells. I don't know how, but I do know he is linked to this somehow, Celia."

"Leave the security clearance to me; I'll organise it through Peter. Just tell him what you need, and please keep this close to your chest.

"We're both sailing close to the wind on this," she said, tersely. "Don't forget the daily briefings. And let's get to the bottom of this as quickly as possible."

Celia stood. Their meeting had ended.

Thames House had temporarily provided Dan with a hot desk – little more than a broom cupboard in the level two basement – while Shady Fields was in isolation.

The lift required him to swipe his ID badge to go down to the basement levels. It deposited him in a dull grey corridor, illuminated with strip lighting and lined with grey metal doors along both sides. It was uncarpeted, and the sound of footsteps echoing along the corridor added to the feeling of apprehension, particularly when you were working down here late at night. In addition, the chilled and recycled air had a harsh smell, like it had been scrubbed with metal polish. For a supposedly modern organisation, the service still had a traditional way of telling you your position in the food chain based on where your workplace was. He walked past several doors until he came to one marked 'Research', punched the code into the keypad his friend had given him, and entered without invitation.

"Well hello, stranger! You've aged since I last saw you." Peter gave him a grin.

"Thanks. You know just what to say to make a chap feel loved and wanted. I've just been in with Celia and she's given us the go ahead to check into Bernard. She is organising clearance as we speak."

Peter bought up his mail account, and in the time it had taken Dan to travel ten floors and walk along the corridor, she had already set up what Peter needed to practice his version of magic.

"So what am I looking for exactly?"

Dan consulted the notes he had made this morning before the meeting.

"We need his financials, looking for any significant withdrawals and deposits. We need sight of his service records from Tbilisi, Operation Greenday and the incident in Amman in particular. If we are to eliminate him from all of this we have to leave no stone unturned. I don't want something coming back to haunt us at a later date. He's no fool, and if there is a connection he'll have worked hard to conceal it.

"I'll be working here today, two doors along. Either call me to collect what you find, or drop it in to me in person. I'd rather there was no paper trail for this until we know what we are dealing with. Oh, and just for good measure, get me anything you have on Maguire's Consultancy's head of Public Service, Mike Shannon. That should keep you busy till lunchtime."

Dan made his way back to his temporary home and unlocked the door with the code they had given him at reception. The fact they were still using push button security keypads in one of the most modern buildings in London seemed laughable to him. It may be all biometrics above ground, but down here in the bowels of the building everything was manual. They wanted you to keep using your opposable thumbs.

He had a list of things he wanted Hilary to do, and a list of the things Mitch needed to be on the lookout for. He jotted a few more notes down, before picking up the phone and calling Hilary.

"Good morning Hilary. How are things today?"

"Fine, although I think people are still reeling from the shock. It's hit the residents hard; some worse than others.

"Charlie is still very cut up about it; his confusion seems worse than it has been for a while. And Rita is back in her Russian prima donna persona at the moment. Layla has been an absolute gem. I didn't realise she could speak Russian. Mitch is conducting interviews, and Layla or I taking turns sitting in with the residents, just to make sure they are ok.

"Layla sat with Charlie during his interview yesterday and was very good, according to Mitch. It wasn't an easy situation, but she showed real confidence. She actually stopped the interview and challenged Mitch because she was worried Charlie was about to incriminate himself. We still have no idea how the drops found their way into Charlie's possession, though."

Dan had been considering the conundrum, too.

"I'm in the dark about that as well. Why would they need to wipe the bottle if the drops were administered wearing gloves?

"Anyway, I do have some good news. I don't know what you said to Jean when she came down but it did the trick. At the meeting this morning she noticed that Mike had used his figures rather than yours. She suggested they needed to be changed as yours were, and I quote, 'more accurate' than his. Celia agreed. She also agreed to postpone the report findings and decision until this matter is resolved. So that 's one less pressure for us to deal with."

"Wow, that is good news! So we're out of the woods for the time being?"

"I wouldn't say that. There have been two murders on our watch. There must be an insider working against us. I've set a hare running to keep Maguire's out of the way for a while, but I need you to go through our staff records with a fine tooth comb. Use Peter to check out anything odd you find. Mitch will make the introductions.

"I'll call for an update tomorrow. From what he was saying it's going to be Thursday or Friday before they lift the quarantine, but if there's anything you need, or if you find anything of interest, call me.

"And Hilary, please take care. I'm not convinced that this is over yet."

Hilary was unsettled by Dan's call. She knew the decision to delay the enquiry didn't mean they were safe, but at least it meant that they could concentrate on the immediate crisis. Mitch was off somewhere in the building conducting more interviews, so that gave her time to get some essential work done, and she had to maintain a business as normal façade as much as possible. Their suppliers were finding it a little strange that their deliveries were being left at the main gate then ferried up to the house by staff, but the Norovirus notice seemed to be doing the trick for now.

There was a knock at the door and she let out an exasperated sigh. "Come in," she snapped.

The door opened and a woman's curly head appeared, much higher up the doorway than she had expected.

"Hi Marina Kinskey, CDC. Have you got a minute?"

Hilary stood and smiled. "Of course, come in. Sorry I was a bit snappy, but I just don't seem to be able to finish anything today. Would you like coffee?"

Marina loped across the room and Hilary caught herself staring. She was verging on immense, at least six feet tall, thin and angular, with a shock of shoulder-length hair that was the colour of a rusty bucket. She had vivid green eyes, magnified by the largest pair of tortoiseshell frames Hilary had ever seen. She had a wide smile, and spoke with a soft Scottish accent that was more Edinburgh than Glaswegian. Not what Hilary had imagined at all! Here was a woman who could never blend into the background wherever she went. She slumped into the chair opposite Hilary and sat waiting for her to speak.

"Thanks for coming to see me. I need an update so I can pull the major incident report together. What have you found so far?"

Marina slid a couple of typed sheets and a handwritten form towards Hilary.

"The form is the completed risk assessment. That's everything you need to complete the return for the

Care Quality Commission and the authorities. The other sheets are warning signs about what to look out for in the next two months, but really they're just precautionary. We're satisfied that this was a very targeted attack with a confined footprint and minimal risk to others. That was what was so interesting about the case, to be honest. Do you know how Tabun works?"

Hilary shook her head.

"Well, it's a nasty substance, but in certain forms it's very stable, as nerve agents go. By suspending it in eyedrops it was absorbed much more quickly, and required a lower concentration to be fatal. The drops interact with the tears in the victim's eyes from the moment they drop them in, and because tears drain through a small canal into the nose, the drug is absorbed into nasal mucosa, which is filled with blood vessels. When the drops were administered, they were essentially "pumped" into William's bloodstream, ensuring rapid absorption of the nerve agent. Doing that three times a day for a couple of days with Tabun would be enough to kill him. It was very quick."

Marina blinked again.

Hilary found her almost hypnotic; it was like watching the shutter action of an SLR camera. She spoke as if she had been discussing how to wire a plug.

"Would there be any risk to the person administering the eye drops?" she asked.

"If William had done it himself and spilled them, it would have been absorbed through his skin, so not as effective, but still toxic to his system. In a place like this your protocol would mean staff would have to wear protective gloves when giving medication so they would be protected from any spillage if they'd been the administrator. As I understand it you incinerate your clinical waste on the premises anyway, so any gloves, aprons, tissues etc. would be destroyed. That would reduce the risk of cross contamination even more. We are going through the clinical waste awaiting incineration, but I'm not optimistic. It was quite an elegant way to kill someone, actually."

Elegant was not the word Hilary would use.

34

Hilary was starting to feel the pressure. They were still under quarantine restrictions so she would be in charge here for the next few days at least. The knowledge that there was a murderer here with them hung heavy on her mind. If William was the only target, the threat may have disappeared. But no one could know that for sure.

She was reviewing the staff personnel files. The two staff members who were causing her some concern were Steve Johnson and Layla Strong. Steve had been with them almost twelve months now, and he had been one of their early appointments. He was ex-forces, medical corps, and bought with him experience of mental health nursing, in particular dealing with PTSD. He knew a little about dementia but was keen to learn more, and was particularly good with 'top floor' residents because of his physical stature. He had a good reference from an old commanding officer, his training and qualifications were excellent and his previous postings included Bosnia, Ireland and Iraq. His employment record had two gaps that were not accounted for in the file, though. They were probably nothing, but nevertheless, they were anomalies. There was no record of where he was posted between 2006 and 2008, and a similarly unexplained gap between his discharge in March 2016 and him joining the Royal Centre for Defence Medicine in Birmingham in October 2017. She scribbled a quick note to ask Peter to find out where he had been during those times.

Layla Strong's employment file contained no such gaps. Her references were excellent, and she was doing a first class job. She had received a promotion just before Hilary's arrival, which was entirely due to her commitment and the quality of her work. But the glaring anomaly in her details was that her birth name was different to the one she went by now. Her previous name was Vlasta. Alarm bells rang. This wasn't a coincidence. Hilary needed Peter to find proof that she was the daughter of Shura Vlasta. If her instinct was correct, a key part of William's history had been working here all along. She needed it confirmed so they could discover how it all fitted together.

She requested the information from Peter through a quick email. The telephone rang. She tutted under her breath, and picked up the receiver. It was Marina.

"Hilary, can you come to William's room at once, please? There's been a break in."

Hilary grabbed her mobile phone and card fob and was out through the office door before the line went dead, a sense of dread welling up inside her as she headed along the corridor towards William's apartment. She saw the now familiar flame-haired amazon figure waiting outside the door for her.

"I'm sorry to trouble you, but I thought you needed to see this immediately. This is how I found the door."

The door jamb had been forced and the door was standing open, but the yellow and black warning tape stuck across the frame was still in place. Hilary took photographs on her phone before they entered. Marina already had gloves on, and gave a pair to Hilary.

"I think we need to have a quick look around to see if anything has been disturbed. Mitch is on his way."

They walked around the small apartment but nothing seemed out of place. There was no evidence it had been searched, everywhere looked normal. They walked into William's bedroom where again nothing seemed out of place, except for the bed, which had been stripped. Marina opened the wardrobe door and called Hilary over. William's strongbox was open and empty.

"Do you know what he kept in here, Hilary?"

Mitch had entered the room silently, and was standing immediately behind them.

"I do," he said. "Amongst other things, it was where he kept his manuscript."

Bernard was angry. From the brief message he had listened to on his phone, it was clear that the evaluation review had not gone to plan. He'd taken a gamble that the panel would push through the consultant's recommendations without a challenge. They'd built a strong case for immediate closure, and with the two deaths, it seemed an obvious decision to make. He decided that if he was absent from the meeting he could distance himself from the final decision. It really shouldn't have been a difficult thing to achieve.

Dan must have asked for more time and got it. He shouldn't have left a mouse to do a man's work. He would deal with Mike Shannon later, but first he had another fire to put out.

William's death had solved one problem but created another by closing the building off. If the truth be told he hadn't expected William to die quite so quickly. He needed to retrieve the manuscript as quickly as possible, but he couldn't just saunter through the door now. He still had his inside contact, and it may be that if an opportunity presented itself the manuscript could be retrieved for him. He was also determined that the icon should be his once more. He hadn't gone to all that trouble to see it sold off with the old man's belongings. It was his by right, and he would have it back.

He could call Hilary and simply pull rank, but he had a feeling that she was not a pushover and that would lead her to ask questions he had no intention of answering. He decided he needed to go back to his original plan and get his contact to take the manuscript and the icon for him. Then he could bring closure to this whole sorry mess.

Steve Johnson was feeling anxious. He didn't know what he was going to tell Bernard. He could be a generous patron, but he was also very unforgiving. He had retrieved the eye-drop bottle from Charlie's overcoat pocket when he returned from his lunch with Bernard in London and used it as directed for three days up to William's death. After that, he'd put it back into Charlie's pocket, wiping it clean of any fingerprints, before returning the pure bottle to William's drug box.

He knew he was probably under suspicion, and being quarantined with everyone was worrying him. He wanted to make an excuse and leave, citing a family bereavement perhaps, but he was trapped.

Bernard had told him to keep his cool, but he was the one on the spot. And now Bernard had asked him to do one other job. He waited until the CDC people had left William's room, then jimmied the door open – his pass key would leave a digital trail.

He was too late. The strong box was already open, and the manuscript had disappeared, along with the photographs. He heard distant voices and, scared he would be discovered, he left the apartment. Whoever had taken them must have a pass key. Was it a member of staff, or one of the investigating team?

Bernard was paying him well for all of this, but that only mattered if he got away with it. He wanted out, so when he gave his report he would ask for help to get away. Bernard was powerful. If anyone could sort an escape plan, it would be him.

35

Shady Fields, 3rd April, Late Afternoon

Layla decided to drop in on Charlie after tea. She was concerned about him after the session with Mitch. He was in the garden room. There had been heavy rainfall that morning and there were standing pools of water on the pathways. They rippled as the droplets of rain continued to fall.

"Hi Charlie, how are you doing?" she said, seating herself in the chair opposite him.

"Oh Layla, I'm fine, thanks," he said glumly. "I had nothing to do with William's death, you know. He was getting more and more confused. He could've put that bottle in my coat pocket himself. His behaviour had been strange in the last few weeks, ask anyone."

"What do you mean, strange?" Layla asked, gently.

"Well, you know how forgetful he was? That was

definitely getting worse. He was misplacing things. He thought that stuff was going missing from his room, too. Although who he thought would want to take a bunch of old photos is anyone's guess."

Layla was paying very careful attention now.

"What about his photographs, Charlie? Were they of his family? I didn't think he had anyone."

"No, no," said Charlie shaking his head. "They were to do with his work, I think. You might not know it, but he was very clever with cameras. He designed and made them.

"He kept the pictures in an old document pouch. He was always misplacing it, but it turned up eventually. Sounds like the actions of a confused old man to me." Charlie shook his head slowly from side to side. "Comes to us all sooner or later."

Layla wanted to keep him chatting while he was relaxed like this.

"When was the last time you wore your overcoat, Charlie? Can you remember?"

"Yes, I wore it the day I went up to London, when we went for lunch at the club."

Layla pushed for more detail. "The day Linda had her accident?"

"No, no, it was after that. I went to the club in Mayfair and had a lovely roast with nice wine to boot. And he paid."

Layla was puzzled. "William paid? I didn't think you got to the club that day. Didn't the accident happen before you got to go for lunch?"

"No, not that day. It was the day I went for lunch with Bernard, at the Reform Club. He was showing off telling me about the history of the place, as if I'd never been. He probably didn't realise it, but it was a regular haunt of mine in the old days. I remember a very boozy lunch there back in the seventies with David Niven and that racing driver chap, er, what was his name…?"

He smiled conspiratorially, but Layla hadn't heard the name dropping. All she'd heard was Bernard's name. Somehow she thought it was significant, because nothing about that lunch had appeared in Charlie's daybook where everything he did was usually recorded. He had gone to London last week, but it was to see his solicitor, and Steve had accompanied him. She wondered if he was mis-remembering.

"Remind me, when was that lunch, Charlie?"

But Charlie was drifting, trying to recall something. "Graham Hill! that was the chap. Yes, think his son became a racer too you know. Sorry, what was that you were saying, Layla?"

She remained patient. "Your lunch at the Reform Club. Can you remember when it was?"

Charlie screwed up his face as if the act of remembering caused him pain. "It was last week. Wednesday? No, Thursday. Yes, that's right, it was Thursday. I think. He did it all very nice. Gave me the money for my train ticket. He even had his driver pick me up from the station. I put it down as an appointment with my solicitor. He said he didn't want to look as though he had favourites. Asked me to keep it to myself, so I did. Wouldn't be much of a diplomat if I couldn't keep a secret would I, eh?" He winked at her.

"And you wore your raincoat that day, Charlie?"

"Yes, it had forecast rain, but it held off so I didn't really need it."

Layla realised that she had to let Mitch know about this, because it might be important. She left Charlie reminiscing about the fact that David Niven, who had once played James Bond, had taken lunch with a real secret agent and knew nothing about it. It amused him greatly and left him chuckling as she made her way back up to the office.

She knocked on the door and heard Hilary call her in. She was sitting at her desk talking on the phone. When Layla caught her eye she motioned for her to sit.

"That's great, Peter. Really helpful. And you will get a hard copy to Dan? Great, thanks again, goodbye."

Hilary put the phone down and looked at Layla as she sat down. There was something different about her, but Layla couldn't say what.

"I was looking for Mitch. Is he around?"

"I saw him about twenty minutes ago, though I'm not sure where he is now. I'm glad you came up though; I wanted a word with you.

"We're going through all of our staff records making sure the information is up to date and accurate, and I have a question for you. On your personnel record you are listed as Layla Strong, but your immigration papers are different. Is that correct?"

"Yes. When we came to the UK my mother thought it would be a good idea. She thought that my Georgian name would be difficult for English people to pronounce, so she changed it by deed poll. My birth name is Sykhaara Vlasta."

Hilary looked at the information in front of her. "Your mother is Milena Vlasta and your father's name was Shura, is that correct?"

Layla nodded.

"Did you know that William knew your parents?"

Layla caught her breath. She wondered if she was in trouble. "Yes I did, although only in the last few years. I did not lie in my application though. I was honest about my name, but the form didn't request any other names. I just assumed when my security checks were done you would have found the information then. Am I in trouble?" Layla felt her face start to flush.

"No, not at all, but it is a strange coincidence that you have a link to William."

Layla felt her cheeks get hotter. It would be good to tell someone the truth at last.

"William Wright was our rescuer. He helped us come to England after my father was killed; I think they'd worked together. We were in danger when the civil war came, and William was very good to us.

"I knew nothing about my parents' link to him for years until my mother went back to Tbilisi. I'd qualified specialising in older people's care, so when William wrote to me saying that Shady Fields needed staff, I applied for the position. I love it here and it meant that

I could get to know him better. But it was William's idea that we shouldn't tell people who I really was. He said it might not be safe for me."

Hilary looked at her. "What do you think he meant by that?"

"I didn't really know. He did tell me that the person who worked with my father in Tbilisi was Mr Cummings, who comes here sometimes. He said he didn't want him to know I was here. He didn't say why."

Layla gave a sigh of relief. She felt as if a weight had been lifted off her shoulders.

There was a knock at the door, and Mitch came in.

"Hello. I thought I might find you in here. I've just got off the phone with Peter. He's complaining that he has a day job that we are keeping him from. Anything you need to tell me?"

"Yes," they both said in unison.

Mitch looked at Layla. "Has Charlie remembered something?"

Layla recounted her conversation with Charlie. "I did wonder if he had imagined it because there was a different explanation in his day book, but he was so certain I thought I'd better tell you."

Mitch smiled at her. "Layla, your instincts were right. The pieces are falling into place, and this is an important fact that we'd been missing. It makes absolute sense that he went to London on Thursday."

"Does it have anything to do with William's death?"

"Yes, I'm afraid it does, but there are still things we

need to know before we have the complete picture." He took an envelope from his jacket pocket and handed it to Layla.

"I found this when I was in William's room earlier. It has your name on it. It was underneath the icon on William's bureau."

Her name was written on it, in William's distinctive scrawl. She broke open the flap, took out the folded sheets and began to read.

Hilary told Mitch about Layla's name change, and he admitted he'd wondered about the connection. When Layla had finished reading the letter she looked up at Mitch. There were tears welling up in her eyes.

"Would you mind sharing the contents with us? I need to know if it has any bearing on his death," he asked.

The envelope had contained a handwritten letter and an old certificate. The papers trembled as she held them, and the tears began to flow down Layla's cheeks. Mitch handed her a tissue from the box on Hilary's desk.

"I know that it must be personal, and I'm sorry to ask, but we need to be sure."

Layla dabbed her eyes and took a deep breath.

"I think you know what's in this letter."

Mitch sat down next to her.

"Yes, I think I do. I think he tells you who really killed your father and why he felt he needed to protect you when you came here to work."

Layla dabbed her eyes again.

"Yes. He says it was all about money. William took something from Mr Cummings, but he took it in order to look after us. It was my father's by right, and he'd stolen it."

Layla felt a mix of emotions. Georgians were known for their passion and loyalty, but she could not remember feeling this sad in her life before.

"He couldn't save my father, so he decided to make things better for us instead. He says that the icon in his room is mine. He thinks it's quite valuable."

She handed the certificate to Mitch who scanned it quickly and let out a low whistle.

"This is a valuation from Christies for the Madonna and child icon; it was carried out in 2010.

"The valuation puts its worth at around two million pounds."

Layla's hands began to shake as she felt anger rise up inside her.

"You mean to say that this is why someone killed William, for the value of this painting?"

Mitch cleared his throat. "Layla, I know this is a lot to ask, but I don't want you to talk about this with anyone until we can bring William's killer to justice. Can you do that for me?"

She nodded, but she really wasn't sure that she could just stand by and do nothing. She folded the paper back into the envelope and handed it to Hilary.

"Please keep this safe for me until all of this is over."

"Of course," said Hilary, and took it across to the

wall safe. She quickly punched in the code, opened the thick steel door, and placed the letter and certificate inside.

Mitch watched Layla leave.

"The nicest smile holds the deepest secrets, the prettiest eyes have cried the most tears, and the kindest hearts have felt the most pain."

"I didn't have you pegged as a poet, Mitch," said Hilary, with some surprise.

"Ah. Deep waters, that's me."

"So, what information did Peter get for you, anyway?"

"Not much more that what he found originally in the files, but it was William's finances that were most revealing. Just after he came back from Tbilisi he had a lump sum of £350,000 paid into a bank account that he controlled, and from that account he sent a monthly transfer to Milena Vlasta in Georgia. Then three years later he transferred £139,000 to an English bank account, also in Milena's name, which Peter thinks was probably a payment for their house.

"There were other payments made around the same time. Those are likely to be for new identity papers and to get them both out of Georgia. William still had contacts there so it would have been fairly easy to arrange. He then paid the rest of the money in monthly instalments of about £1,200, until it ran out in 2006.

"He was trying to make up for the fact that Shura had died because of what William had encouraged him to do.

"I think the icon William left to Layla was one of a pair. He sold the first one, and kept the other for all these years. I think they were the items that Bernard smuggled out in the diplomatic pouch all those years ago.

"If all of this, chapter and verse, is in William's manuscript, it would clearly implicate Bernard. Only he would have had access to the money to buy the icons. And William also had photographs. Any enquiry would mean Bernard's career would be ended. I think Bernard hired Deni Dokka to kill William to keep it all quiet."

Hilary just looked at Mitch.

"It seems rather far-fetched to me. Someone as high up in the service as Bernard? Surely he would not have got this far if he was involved in murder, theft and smuggling?"

Mitch gave a wry smile. "Did you know that Kim Philby was tipped to take over as head of MI6 in the early 1950s? That was just before he was interrogated about being the third man in the Cambridge spy ring. At the height of his spying career, our country's worst soviet spy headed up the Soviet Counter Espionage desk for three years!

"Hilary, we've had some brilliant successes, but we've also had some spectacular failures too. I have a dreadful feeling that Bernard may turn out to be this century's howler."

"Did Peter find anything else out about Bernard?"

"Oh yes, we have a paper trail between a Russian diplomat stationed in Tbilisi who was selling Russian art on the black market to an unknown British diplomat at the time all of this was happening. Peter's confident he'll be able to prove that it was Bernard.

"He's also tracking recent transactions that were traced to a Geneva bank account. Peter thinks it was Dokka's. Bernard probably ordered the hit on Dokka to keep him quiet, too, but we may never be able to prove that. Once he has the proof he needs about the rest of it, Dan will take it to Celia. In the meantime, my guess is that Bernard's inside person here is Steve. We need to get him before he bolts."

Hilary was struggling to take this all in. Three months ago, the most dangerous thing in her life was eating dinner at her local sushi bar. She had been here a matter of weeks, had lost two people on her watch, and was possibly dealing with a murderer under her roof. She had wanted a challenge, but this had gone way beyond that. She couldn't allow anyone else to come to harm. They needed to flush Steve and Bernard into the open. The problem was that an animal backed into a corner is at its most dangerous, and she was very much a novice at this game.

36

Shady Fields, 4th April 2018, Morning

The coffee in the cup Steve was nursing was almost cold. He paced nervously around the staff room. His time was running out. He needed to make a move soon, but the lockdown meant that there was nowhere to go. He cursed Bernard for taking his time. All he had said was "Sit tight."

The door opened, and Mitch stood there flanked by Marina and Ben Faulkner.

"Hello, Steve," said Mitch. "We need to have a word."

Steve got up and headed towards the door. "I'm sorry, but I'm late for Rita 's medication. I need to go."

He tried to push past them, but Mitch remained in the doorway blocking his exit, staring fiercely at him.

"You need to sit down, Steve. Layla's covering the

morning meds round."

Steve returned to the table and sat. Mitch and Marina pulled up chairs either side of him, but he noted that Ben had stationed himself in front of the doorway, virtually filling it.

"I have to take a swab of your hands please," began Marina. "We're checking all staff and residents who came into contact with William in his last hours. We need to rule out contamination from the nerve agent." She took a small kit and a sample bag from her white coat pocket.

"I already had the test done yesterday, you didn't find anything," Steve insisted. "We wear gloves to administer drugs, anyway. I couldn't have come into contact with anything."

"Nevertheless, I have to do the test again."

She took the swab from the clear vial and asked Steve to present his hands. He had a distinct tremor. He flinched as she applied the swab to his skin, as if it were red hot. She concentrated on his wrists and forearms.

"Does it take three of you to do this then?" he asked, bravado creeping in.

"No," said Mitch, "but if there is contamination, you'll need to be moved to a decontamination facility. Just a precaution, you understand."

Marina put the swab back into the glass file, added a few drops of colourless liquid, and swirled it around. She held it up to the light and watched as it slowly changed to bright purple. Marina sucked the air in between her teeth. "I'm sorry, Steve, but that's a positive result. We need to isolate you straight away."

Steve looked panicky. "No that can't be right, I wore gloves when I put his drops in…"

Mitch stood up. "You will come with us now. There's a CDC vehicle waiting to take you to a decontamination facility. Special Branch will probably want to question you too."

Steve looked sick.

"I think I want a solicitor."

Charlie made the call to Bernard's private number from the card he'd been given at the Reform Club. Bernard answered straight away "Hello, who is this?"

"Hello Bernard, it's Charlie Bingham. You said it would be ok to call you on this number."

Bernard's tone changed immediately to oil-slick smooth.

"Charlie, how lovely to hear from you. I hope you enjoyed your lunch last week. Not the cheapest place to dine, but one of the more stylish venues, I think. What can I do for you?"

"Well, it's more what I can do for you, really. You obviously know about William…"

Charlie's voice tailed off.

"Yes, I heard. Terrible news."

"Before he died, he gave me his manuscript and I thought you might be interested in seeing it. He did tell me that you featured in it quite a lot."

Bernard's mind raced. He needed to get that

manuscript before anyone else could read it.

"Well it would certainly have to come into HQ for checking before being published. I could pick it up from you when I'm next down there." Bernard was trying his best to sound casual.

Charlie was fully prepared for him to feign nonchalance, so he turned up the pressure.

"Oh ok, well if there's no rush I'll ask Mitchell to drop it tomorrow when he comes into HQ. They're lifting the quarantine."

"No, don't do that," Bernard said, a little too quickly. "I'm coming over to see Dan tomorrow anyway, so I can collect it then. In fact, why don't you leave it in William's room? I can pick it up from there. I'll be there around 3.00 pm.

"And Charlie, there's no need to mention this, ok? People are upset enough about William as it is."

"Fully understood, Bernard," Charlie said, as he ended the call.

How strange that Charlie had succeeded where Steve had failed, Bernard thought. He was hoping that he also had the photographs, but he would cross that bridge when he came to it. He smiled at the unintentional pun.

Bernard wanted to get in and out of there quietly. He knew that Dan was scheduled to meet with Celia at 2.00pm, so if he drove himself, he could be there and back without anyone seeing him.

37

Bernard was well over the speed limit as he hammered the Morgan west along the M4. He would use all the power of his position if a wooden top pulled him over. National Emergency, serious incident, whatever. He would flash his ID and that would be that. He left the motorway at the Maidenhead junction and spent the remainder of the journey working out the best way to get in whilst avoiding detection.

The pass card that Steve had given him opened the outer security gate. He drove the quarter-mile to the house with a mounting feeling of tension. The CDC vehicles had gone, and there were fewer cars than normal in the car park. He pulled up away from the house, his car partially hidden by an overhanging willow tree. He used the pass again to open the front door, crossing the empty entrance hall to the staircase.

So far, so good, he thought, as he cautiously climbed the stairs. He paused outside the first floor fire door, opening it a little and checking the corridor. Good, there was no one about, his luck was holding. He walked quickly down the long corridor to William's room. The remnants of yellow hazard tape hung from the door frame. He pressed the pass card against the electronic sensor and heard the muted click as the door unlocked. Turning the door handle and entering the apartment, he closed the door behind him quickly and quietly.

The room was in semi-darkness, its curtains almost closed. He waited a few seconds for his eyes to adjust to the dim light.

He was expecting to see a package. What he didn't expect to see was the silhouette of someone seated on the small sofa.

A switch clicked, and a table lamp illuminated the room. The silhouette he'd seen was Rita.

Her eyes were fixed on Bernard. She was sitting erect, like a cat ready to pounce. Her garb today was a cream kaftan, heavily embroidered with gold thread around the neck and cuffs, and she wore the matching silk headscarf with tiny gold discs that framed her face. Her face was beautiful, with large smokey eyes and a ruby red pout. The package was next to her on the sofa.

"Hello, Rita, I wasn't expecting to see you. Where's Charlie? Is he here?"

His initial surprise at seeing her there had passed, and he had regained his composure. He quickly scanned the room. The bedroom door was closed, but there was no sign of anyone else.

She looked directly at him, her voice devoid of any accent.

"No he isn't, and he won't be coming. I asked him to call you. I knew you would be interested in this." She tapped the package with a scarlet talon.

"William gave it to me for safekeeping, but as he is sadly no longer with us it seems a shame for it to simply hang around. I thought it should go to someone who understands its real value. Wouldn't you agree?"

Bernard grasped what was happening, and quickly adjusted to his new fortune.

"I certainly do. But what makes you think I would be interested in it?"

He moved further into the room and stood next to a small sideboard. A tray held two glasses and a whisky decanter containing a couple of inches of amber liquid. He computed his next actions in a flash.

"Bernard, please don't insult my intelligence. I have read it, and I know exactly why you would be interested in it." Her long scarlet tipped fingers stroked the paper cover.

He decided to play along. "I'm flattered that William included me in his memoirs, but I fail to see why."

Rita smiled. "Well, I wouldn't say you were the starring role but you are a significant character.

Personally I think you make a good villain."

She stood, picking up the package and walking towards the fireplace, putting a little more distance between the two of them. The manuscript rested in the crook of her arm, close to her body. He knew she was taunting him.

"So what does it say about me, then?" Bernard wanted to know exactly what she knew.

"Well, Bernard, you feature in several chapters. You are introduced to the reader back in the eighties when you and William were both stationed in Tbilisi. You were a naughty boy back then. Black market trading no less. But you were a neat little spy, I'll give you that. You always cleaned up your own mess."

Bernard felt a sensation of discomfort rising in his gut.

"You make another appearance in Operation Greenday, back here in London. I would call that your 'Teflon' period. Nothing stuck to you then, did it? William captured your leadership style very well, I thought. 'Hard faced, duplicitous bastard with a hint of feigned concern!'"

She spat out the insult.

Bernard sneered. "The only ones who call me hard faced are the bleeding heart losers that can't cut it in the real world! I am not duplicitous, I'm successful!"

"If that's your definition of success, then I might add my own chapter about Jordan. What do you think?"

Bernard sat down in the armchair and looked at her

coldly.

"You mean the time when I saved you from being executed for killing a member of the Royal House? What good would that do you?"

Rita threw the manuscript onto the coffee table. It slid across the polished surface, stopping before it fell onto the floor.

"Did you know we've had a couple of new residents join us? Bill and Ben, the dynamite men? Well, they moved here last week. The circle of life is certainly at work here."

Bernard was unsure where this was going. Perhaps Rita was losing her train of thought. After all, wasn't that how this dementia thing worked? He felt he should play along.

"Yes I did hear they were coming. Although I can't say I remember them that well."

"Really?" said Rita "Strange, they remember you. You were the one that recommended them for the Amman job."

She inclined her head, quizzically. Bernard remained silent.

"The Saudis bought them in for the security contract. They checked for explosive devices at the official venue and at the hotels of attending dignitaries because of threats to disrupt the summit. Although I don't remember much about that time, they do. In fact, you'll laugh at the coincidence, but it was their plane that we came home on."

Bernard felt his blood run cold as she continued.

"Yes, they had spare seats. So when you needed to get me back home in a hurry, they were kind enough to accommodate us. Wasn't that nice of them? Of course, I was in a bit of a state. Do you remember? I had just seen the love of my life murdered right in front of me. I was distraught. But fortunately for me, you were there to help. You spirited me away from the garden and back to your hotel room. You cleaned me up, even gave me a change of clothes. Funny, that. Ben said how strange it was that you had a change of clothes ready for me in your room. At the time he said it was almost as if you were expecting me. I told him he was being ridiculous. You were just in the right place at the right time. You couldn't possibly have known I would be there."

She paused just long enough for dramatic effect.

"Unless you knew they were going to kill Saleem."

At that moment Rita signed her own death warrant, in Bernard's mind. He could not have her take over where William had left off. She would have to go.

"I had no idea they were going to kill him, Rita. I thought they would just rough him up a bit, but evidently that's not how the American mafia works. Saleem had cost them millions of dollars by giving the Russians insider information. They wouldn't let it go. They wanted their pound of flesh.

"Luckily, I was there to protect you. I made sure they left you alone. It was too late for Saleem, but I wasn't going to let them harm you. I saved your life!"

Rita threw her head back and laughed bitterly. "You

don't get it do you, you bastard? You didn't just kill Saleem, you killed me too. You destroyed our one chance at a future. He was my life. It would have been better if they had killed us both.

"I've lived a half-life since he was murdered. You triggered my self-destruct button. The drink, the drugs, the men. It was all orchestrated by you! I have lived a life of misery since that day and you are to blame!" She pointed her long index finger in his direction.

Bernard was angry that a work of a lifetime was being threatened by a bunch of has-beens with addled brains.

Rita continued. "I could finish William's memoirs with a final chapter of my own that shows your true character. It would be the final seal on your illustrious career.

"Let's be honest, you're the only one that has benefited from your treachery. I think your days of progression and reward in the service should be bought to a close. Don't you?"

Bernard desperately needed to buy a little time.

"I can see why you might think that, Rita, but it's all about perspective. Let's have a drink and let me put the record straight."

He stood at the tray with the whisky decanter, his back to Rita. He poured two measures into the glasses and added a small tablet to her glass. It fizzed for a second, before disappearing without trace. He turned and offered her the drink. She walked across the room and took it from him. Her hand shook slightly as she grasped the glass. She lifted it to her lips, and downed it in one. He felt relief flood his body. He downed his own too. His luck was about to turn.

Rita relaxed a little. She walked across the room and picked up the manuscript, before tossing it to Bernard.

"I was going to charge you for it, but I think you need to read it before we agree a price."

Bernard was relieved that he finally had the document in his possession. He tore open the wrapper and the photographs fell to the floor. He picked them up and could clearly see images of himself, his car and that fool Shura on the floor. William really had caught him in the act. He would never have been appointed as Celia's replacement if this had come to light!

Bernard wanted more time for the drug to take effect. He looked up from the photos towards Rita.

"Did you read about the artefact trading in here? Does he say what happened to the icons?"

Rita looked at him. Her cheeks had begun to flush.

"I didn't read it in there. William told me about it over one of our whist drives. We realised we had much in common. A life of service, and a shared hatred of you. He told me how you killed your Tbilisi agent because you were about to be discovered for black-marketeering. And about how he took the icons and sold one of them to look after the man 's family. Did you know that?"

Bernard sneered. "He always was over-emotional. That stopped him from being a decent agent. No room in this job for ethics, morals or feelings. That's why they call it collateral damage. William never had the stomach for it!"

Rita moved unsteadily towards the chair and flopped into it, Bernard walked towards her and sat down on the sofa opposite her. He wanted to watch this woman slip away. He had the time, after all.

"You know that he bought Shura's family here, don't you, and that his daughter works here at Shady Fields?" She looked at him with eyes that were struggling to focus.

"No. I didn't know that. My God, he really was a sentimental fool!

"Rule number one is never get emotionally involved with your assets. They betrayed their countries, so the likelihood is that at some time they'll betray you too if you let them.

"Who is the daughter, anyway?"

Bernard was intrigued. He'd never considered that possibility. But why would he? He hadn't cared what happened to the family after he'd left Georgia. They could have been killed as traitors by the Russians, for all he knew.

Rita dug her hands into the voluminous pockets of her kaftan.

"It's Layla Strong. She's Shura's daughter, and she knows the truth about her father. William has left the other icon to her in his will. He wanted to make sure you never got hold of it."

"Well, thanks for the heads-up. I'll pick it up before I leave. It was in his bedroom last time I was here. He stole it from me, and now I'll take it back. It'll be nice to have a windfall that I don't have to offer up as alimony payment."

He was starting to feel warm and relaxed himself. These places were always over heated.

Rita straightened up in her chair. "Why did you have to kill Linda? She was one of life's decent people. She looked out for everyone. She didn't deserve to get caught up in this."

"No, you are absolutely right, she didn't. The difficulty is, you can't always predict collateral damage. She was just in the wrong place at the wrong time. If it's any consolation the man responsible for that unfortunate blunder is now dead."

Bernard smiled at Rita. He watched as she stood and walked unsteadily around the back of the sofa so that she was behind him. She would have to sit down again soon. He could tell that the poison was starting to take effect.

As he turned his head slowly to watch her he suddenly felt a blade against his neck.

"Do you remember this, Bernard? It's the dagger Saleem gave me. The one you stole and passed to the Americans. The dagger they used to kill him.

"You were the only one that could have taken it. You knew where I was staying. You knew that they were going to kill him. You provided the weapon that would tie me to his murder. You needed to give me a reason to be grateful enough to carry out sordid little missions. A break-in here, a lock picked there. And now I've even got your precious manuscript for you."

She was flagging, she took a breath.

"But William has had the last laugh. The manuscript is worthless and always was. William told us what was in it, unfortunately for you…"

Bernard tried to move to take the dagger from Rita's hand, but he felt strangely sluggish. The blade bit into his skin, and he felt a tell-tale warm trickle run down his neck. He stiffened.

"Now, now. Be quiet, Bernard. You will no doubt be congratulating yourself on slipping something into my whisky. You always knew my weaknesses.

"But I have a much stronger constitution than you. My lifestyle has given me a high degree of resistance to substances, which is more that I can say for your sorry carcass! The whisky had already been doctored before you arrived. I have no doubt I am on my way out with whatever you gave me, but not before I have the chance to repay you for Saleem."

In a flash she grabbed his forehead, tipping his face up towards the ceiling, and drew the razor-sharp blade across the front of his throat. She let his head slump forward, while he grabbed at his neck. He tried to stand, but there was no strength in his legs. He could feel the blood pumping rhythmically out of the wound. It forced its way out between his fingers, making them sticky. He suddenly realised that this was how he was going to die. Unless someone came through the door right now he would bleed to death, and there was nothing he could do to change that.

Rita made her way back to the chair and sat again. She smiled at him.

"You've really helped me Bernard, thank you. I am leaving this life on my terms. I knew you would try something when you found me here with the manuscript. And now I can die happy, knowing that I have set the record straight and avenged Saleem, William and Linda. I've left my own record of events, which will soon be found. Everyone will know what you did in Amman and Tbilisi.

"But I have one last surprise for you. Before you die, you need to see what all of this has been about."

It took a monumental effort, but she rose to her feet and picked up the manuscript. She opened it, and held it up to his face so he could see the pages. The blood was freely pouring down his chest now, and pooling in his lap. He was seconds away from losing consciousness. He couldn't move and could no longer speak. She flicked the pages slowly enough for him to take in their contents. She watched him, as the puzzled look on his face turned to realisation, then to hatred.

His mouth opened and closed, but nothing came out. His eyes were staring at her in disbelief.

"Yes, Bernard, it's rubbish. Gobbledygook, meaningless drivel! As William's dementia got worse he lost the ability to write. His typing made less sense than if a troupe of monkeys had done it. You could have left him alone. He wasn't a threat to you. His dementia would have made his testimony unreliable. So these deaths are on your head.

"The best part of it is that you put yourself in this position. You gave me the opportunity to settle my score because you wanted to keep your secrets. Layla will be served by having her father's death avenged, and she will inherit the icon."

Rita's words were beginning to slur now.

"I hope you appreciate the delicious irony of me killing you with the very blade you used to betray me. That is the most satisfying aspect of this whole sorry affair. You will leave this world knowing that the things you coveted have been taken away from you. Those you betrayed have their revenge in the place you hate the most. You see, there is divine justice after all!"

That was the last thing that Bernard Cummings heard, before everything went black.

38

Shady Fields Aftermath

Dan found the bodies when he returned to Shady Fields. He'd guessed Bernard would try to recover the manuscript, but he had not expected Rita to be involved. She had left a message for him on his desk about the sequence of events and where they would take place.

She had known about Bernard all along. She recognised him on the numerous occasions he had visited but he had not recognised her until recently. He had manipulated her to work for him all those years ago, but as her addictions took hold she had become too unreliable for him. When he could no longer be sure of her discretion, he cut her loose and they'd lost touch.

She came to Shady Fields, and met up with William.

It was clear that William had decided to take his revenge against Bernard in an intellectual way, but her hatred went beyond that. And after Linda's death she knew she couldn't let Bernard's poison affect anyone else.

She had kept the secret of Saleem's murder quiet for so long it had become almost irrelevant, but the fact that she had kept the secret was not. It fuelled her hatred of Bernard, and her bitterness over what he had taken from her.

Rita saw the opportunity to take her revenge, but when William had been murdered, she knew she had to act quickly. She expected Bernard to try to kill her once he realised what was going on. She was prepared for that, it suited her purpose too. Ridding the world of Bernard was the last positive thing she could do.

Dan felt sure that the inquest into her death would find that she took her own life whilst the balance of her mind was disturbed.

He now understood why William had not let anyone read the manuscript. He knew that his dementia had deteriorated, and in his moments of clarity he could see that what he typed made no sense, but he refused to acknowledge it.

39

Thames House, 6th June 2018

Dan wanted to put the whole sorry episode behind everyone involved, but there was one last hurdle to clear before he could do that. This was the Civil Service, and the meeting to decide the final outcome about Shady Fields had to be held.

He was accompanied by Hilary today, and this visit felt very different to previous meetings. There were only three people on the panel: Celia, Jean Terry and Mitch. Celia looked suitably sombre as she began.

"We are here today to review the evaluation report and to make some decisions about the future of Shady Fields as part of our security services infrastructure. Do you have a statement you wish to make, Hilary?"

Hilary took a deep breath and began.

"Following the internal investigation at Maguire's, I

have worked closely with Mike Shannon's replacement, Sarbjit Ghiddar, to complete the report's findings. The report shows three clear outcomes. First, Shady Fields fulfils a vital service for the protection of national security, to maintain the integrity of the official secrets act on behalf of those who lose the mental capacity to do so for themselves. Second, the report shows that normal private care providers would not be able to offer a suitable, secure solution. Finally, the report shows that the outcomes delivered by Shady Fields exceed expectations and meet the tests put forward.

"Our recommendation is that Shady Fields becomes the preferred choice for retired agents, working as a sole contractor for the security services.

"To that end, we have enlisted a private financier to fund us to ensure we are financially viable. We will contract on a case by case basis with MI5 and MI6 to ensure we are not dependent on government funding."

Hilary breathed a sigh of relief, her message delivered. The rest was up to Celia and Mitch, now.

Celia gave a subtle glance of encouragement to Hilary.

"Does anyone have any questions?" There was silence. "OK, then. I accept the recommendations of the evaluation, and ask Mitchell Bennett, the newly appointed Head of MI5, to liaise with his MI6 counterpart accordingly. Hilary smiled, and mouthed her congratulations to Mitch.

Celia closed the report in front of her. The meeting

had ended. As everyone stood up to leave, she caught Dan's attention, signalling she wanted him to remain behind. Dan turned to Hilary.

"Can you wait for me downstairs. Celia wants to see me."

Celia reached into her desk drawer and pulled out two glasses along with a bottle of Dalwhinnie 'Winter's Frost'. Dan raised an eyebrow.

Celia smiled.

"What can I say? My kids know I am a mad 'Game of Thrones' fan."

She poured two healthy measures and handed one to Dan. They toasted William, Linda and Rita, and both took a sip of the golden liquid.

"And it's not a bad malt either."

He nodded his head in agreement.

"So, what do you want to talk to me about?"

"Well, congratulations are in order. I had confirmation from the Secretary of State this morning, the PM has approved your appointment as my successor. That only gives us six weeks handover, so you need to move up here permanently, as soon as possible. Will that be a problem?"

Dan smiled.

"No, not a problem. I know after everything that has happened that Hilary will make a great Chief Executive of Shady Fields. That was my plan when we appointed her in fact. I did think she would have a bit more time to get used to the lunacy around here, though. She's conducted herself exceptionally well since she joined us. She hasn't been fazed by the Bernard business at all. I've no doubt that she's ready to step up to the plate.

"Can I ask what the official line on Bernard 's death is going to be, by the way?"

She swirled the whisky around the glass again, and with closed eyes she inhaled the oily aroma. "All of the official documents are heavily redacted and marked Top Secret, Level 7 Clearance Only. His post mortem has also been sealed, so that won't see the light of day for the next seventy years. His wife and son will get his death in service benefit, so they won't be rocking the boat, and the PM is happy that there won't be the equivalent of a Kim Philby scandal on her watch. So everyone's happy."

Dan stretched his legs out in front of him and relaxed into the chair.

"And are we clear about the full extent of Bernard's activities?"

Celia nodded her head.

"Oh, yes. It turned out that he had not been as careful or as clever as he thought. His black-market dealings in antiquities started in Tbilisi, and continued right up until 2012 when his high profile meant he was too recognisable to continue. He added to his personal fortune and the money always came from his informer pot.

"We also know that he had links to American organised crime. They used him for intel on trade agreements and government contracts that were coming up for tender, for which he was paid handsomely. He gave up Saleem al Baadini and Rita for the same reason. He was fearful that they would come for him, so he shifted the blame and let the Americans take care of it. When he found out they intended to leave Rita alive to take the fall for Saleem's death he couldn't take the risk. So he bought her back here and made use of her training. But she became too unstable, so he fuelled her addictions and when she finally lost all credibility, he cut her loose."

Dan shook his head. "Rita carried that around with her for years What a complete and utter bastard! He must have been shocked when he visited Shady Fields and realised the two Jonah's that could threaten his career were in the same place."

Celia nodded in agreement. "There's no statute of limitations on revenge. It's funny, but I always thought it was you that he had a beef with. You know, something personal. I had no idea about William and Rita. The treasury request for the evaluation came just at the right time.

"We know he hired Deni Dokka to kill William. And although we can't prove it for definite, we think he had Dokka killed. It would have been simple to tip off his enemies to his whereabouts and let them do the job for him.

"Luckily for us, Steve was Bernard's insider, and when everything went pear shaped he was worried he would be next."

"Steve talked, then?"

Celia smiled. "I think the phrase is 'sang like a canary'. Marina Kinsky is a strange one, though. Do you know she's applied to join us?"

Dan shook his head. "I haven't met her yet, but Hilary was really impressed with her."

"She assisted in Steve's interrogation and got him so wound up about the possibility of having contaminated himself, he told them everything. About how Bernard had approached him and sorted his gambling debts out, and about how the breaks in his work history covered operations he was involved in for Bernard abroad. He used him to ferry artefacts, and more recently to drop information to his European and American contacts.

"Bernard got him to apply for the job at Shady Fields. He didn't realise he was slowly killing William. He got scared, and told us everything. He's been lucky – he'll get a deal. He'll probably spend time in an open prison somewhere, but only because the government doesn't want any of this to become public knowledge."

Dan downed the remains of his scotch.

"And what's next for you? You strike me as too young to retire, Celia. Why now?"

"I have very little choice, Dan. I have been diagnosed with early onset Alzheimer's, so I can't really continue, as much as I would like to."

Dan felt the jolt of shock, as if he had touched a live wire. "My god Celia, I had no idea. I am so sorry."

She waved his concern away airily.

"You now understand my passion and interest in

this project, Dan. My condition is in the family. My mother and grandmother were both affected. I'm only too aware of the ravages it can do. What you've done with Shady Fields has given me hope."

She smiled a rueful smile. "So when the time comes for me, and it will, I want to be treated kindly. Your project is not just for keeping secrets. It's for the people who have served their country to be treated with the same respect and dignity as they were when they were whole.

"Just out of interest, who is the investor that will fund the business?"

"Layla Strong. William left her his entire estate and, of course, the icon. All of it has been placed in Trust for Shady Fields. She says it's what he would have wanted, and it's what she wants, too."

Celia turned to look out of her office window. At the million pound view she purposefully deprived herself of through the deliberate layout of her office.

Dan put his glass down on the desk, and as he walked towards the door to leave her to her own thoughts he heard her speaking softly, almost to herself.

"Perhaps one day we will meet again, characters in a different story, and maybe we will share a lifetime then."

He closed the door behind him.

Printed in Great Britain
by Amazon